MW01124671

Castilian Knight

Book 1

in the

Reconquista Chronicles Series

By

Griff Hosker

Castilian Knight

Published by Sword Books Ltd 2019

SWORD
BOOKS

Copyright ©Griff Hosker First Edition

Contents

Dedication

To my readers, the
unsung heroes who
give me not only
inspiration but
constantly supply me
with interesting and
useful facts. Your
interaction with my
stories and characters
fills me with joy each
time I start to write.
This one is for you all!

Historical Characters

King Ferdinand of Castile, León and Aragon (1015-1065)

King García Sánchez III of Pamplona, King of Navarre, King Ferdinand's half-brother (1015-1054)

King Sancho Garces IV of Navarre (1054-1076)

Sancho, later King of Castile, son of King Ferdinand (1038-1072)

Alfonso, later King of Aragon and Castile, son of King Ferdinand (1040-1109)

Garcia, later King of Galicia, son of King Ferdinand (1041-1090)

King Ramiro of Aragon, King Ferdinand's half-brother (1007-1063)

Al-Muqtadir- Emir of Zaragoza

Al-Ma'mun – Emir of Toledo

Spain at the time the book is set

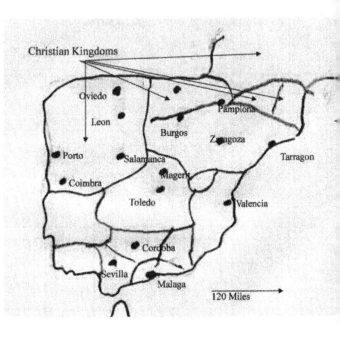

Prologue

The cattle raiders had struck Vivar in the depths of winter. Christian neighbour took from Christian neighbour and cattle raiding was a way of ensuring that a lord had enough food for his people in the long winter months. As Charles of Toulouse often said to his shield brother, Alfonso, Castile had nine months of winter and three months of summer so winter was a long time. It was a harsh and unforgiving land in which they lived, bordered by the sea to the north and west and by mountains and Muslims to the east and south. If their enemies pushed then there was nowhere to go.

Charles of Toulouse was a hired sword and he had fought against Moors, the French, the Aragonese as well as many other armies whose origins were somewhat obscure. He was thus named for he had been born in Toulouse when his father, a Norman warrior, had briefly served there. Charles was not French and he was not Spanish; he was a mercenary who was loyal to whoever paid him. Since he had married and sired a son, William, he had stopped wandering and ceased serving the highest paymaster. He now served Diego Lainez who had a good estate in Castillona de Bivar, also called Vivar, not far from Burgos. He took the lower pay for the security of a home; a family does that to a man. His new master was a member of the nobility, albeit a minor one, but he paid well enough and

Charles, who was Don Diego's armiger, his shield-bearer and leader of men, led the eight paid warriors who followed Don Diego.

As they followed the trail of the cattle thieves from Navarre, Charles rode behind his lord and his squire, Sancho. Charles did not have much faith in either of the men he followed for Don Diego was not a warrior and Sancho was a fat and lazy man who just waited for his spurs. The only men Charles could rely on were the men at arms he had trained and they were good. Another twenty retainers followed Alfonso, his shield brother and the reason they had chosen Vivar to settle, who rode at the rear of the professional soldiers. While Charles and the other men at arms had helmets, leather jerkins, long swords and round shields, the twenty retainers were the men who worked Don Diego's estates. There were millers and shepherds, cattle drovers and house servants. Armed with a multitude of weapons, some old swords and spears and some improvised farm implements, all had been ordered to mount horses and mules and follow Don Diego to the estate of Raoul of Bilbao whose men had stolen sixty head of his cattle. While Don Diego was a rich man, he could not afford to lose so many cattle. If nothing else, he had to show his neighbour that he was not to be trifled with. Don Diego's father, Lain Núñez, was a powerful landowner and was close to King Ferdinand the Great. Don Diego had a family name to protect and if he did not recover them then he would have to endure the wrath of his father.

Charles had been born to a Norman father and a French woman who had died giving birth to him in the southern Frankish city of Toulouse. He was from north of this land and within his veins coursed Norman blood but, like many of his people, his blood was liberally sprinkled with that of other nations. His Norman father had brought him up to be a warrior and Charles had become a good one. Since he had been twelve years of age, he had fought in one army or another and the weapons and armour he bore were a testimony to his skill. A mercenary had to be good for men who hired them were careless with their lives. You did not pay a dead man! He did not enjoy hunting cattle raiders but it would be easy money. There would be a bonus from Don Diego and that would please Maria, the woman who, since the death of his wife, had looked after his son.

He glanced at Don Diego who he knew was not a good warrior. Charles knew that if it was not for Don Diego's father, he would never ride to war for he was afraid of dying in battle. The Norman blood in Charles' veins told him that fearing death was a bad trait in any warrior. You rode to war knowing that you could die. If you were afraid then it was simple, you did not ride to war. Charles would have happily led the retainers to recover the cattle but Lord Lain Núñez had told his son that he ought to recover them himself and so the knight had mounted his horse and led his men north and east. It was a mistake and it would cost lives.

Charles knew how to scout. He had asked if he could lead but Don Diego wanted to be at the fore so that his enemies would know who led the retribution but Charles' eyes were more attuned to the ground than his master's. As they had been travelling eastwards, he had been looking at the sides of the trail they were following. He might no longer be involved in wars and battles but he would still do his job the best that he knew how. It was his Norman blood; his grandfather had been a Viking! He had become increasingly concerned as they had ridden along the clear trail of cattle and men for he had seen signs which disturbed him. Finally, he could remain silent no longer.

"My lord, we need to stop."

"Why, we are almost there? I can see the houses of his retainers. This interminable chase is almost over."

"Yes, my lord, and that is why I ask you to stop. See here, on the ground, there are hoofprints and they head up the slope to our left."

"And?"

"Why do horses ride away from the main trail? The cattle's hoofprints still head due east to the hall but ten horsemen went this way. And there are men on foot with them too."

Charles had his attention, "You think they plan to ambush us?"

The armiger nodded and sighed. If Don Diego had been a true warrior then he would not have required this explanation which merely wasted time, "They must have known we would follow and if they have their wits about them, they can ambush us and still keep their ill-gotten gains."

"What do you suggest?" Don Diego was a practical man. He knew how to fight with a sword and lance but he had no skill in battle and he did not enjoy war in any shape or form. It was a waste of his time and energy. He could be at home making the estate more productive and extracting more money from his businesses. Charles knew how to fight and defeat enemies and there lay the difference.

"Let the rest of the men follow the cattle and the ten of us can follow the hoofprints."

"But that puts the men who follow the cattle at risk."

Charles shrugged, "If we walk into an ambush then we are all at risk."

Don Diego saw the sense in that. He waved over his steward who led the retainers with the improvised weapons, "Luis, keep following the cattle. Charles thinks that there are men who lay an ambush."

"Yes, my lord." The portly grey-haired grandfather turned to the men who followed him, "Follow me!"

Charles took the opportunity to take the lead and he urged his horse up the slope. He did not wait for orders but drew his sword and he peered ahead to look for the place where the cattle thieves would strike. As soon as he reached the top of the gentle slope, he saw it ahead of him. There was a stand of trees that lay just half a mile from the hall. He could only see the roof and that meant there was dead ground between the trees and the hall. It would be a killing ground. The cattle would be led along it and when those following entered the dead ground then the ambush could be sprung. He hoped that Don Diego would not seek an explanation for his reasoning. Time was crucial.

"My lord, they will be waiting in those trees."

"You are sure?"

Charles sighed for time was being wasted while he explained, "There is dead ground beyond the woods. We should hurry, lord, for Luis and the others will soon be approaching the ambush!"

"Well done, Charles, you have earned your pay this day!" Turning in his saddle he said, "Draw your weapons! He spurred his horse and the courser he rode took off,

Charles cursed. His lordship had the best horse but he would have been better to wait for the rest. One man alone could do nothing but ten mounted men striking as one and riding boot to boot could sweep the cattle thieves from the field and give them a bloodless victory. Sancho, the aristocrat's squire. rode a palfrey and, already, was lagging behind Charles. Charles knew that Alfonso would be right behind, for they were shield brothers. Charles only rode a palfrey but he knew how to make a horse move and he dug his heels in and urged his horse to go to the aid of his lord.

At the front of the handful of charging men, Don Diego Lainez had something to prove. His father thought that he did not protect what was his and the loss of cattle would be seen as another failure. Although he had fought in some battles, he had not earned the glory that his father, Lain, had. Diego saw that as an opportunity to redeem himself in the eyes of the man who was close to the King. He and his father disagreed about many things but Don Diego knew that his father's connection to the King could only benefit his family.

The waiting mounted men heard the sound of the noisy retinue led by Luis and as soon as they appeared below them in the dead ground, they would fall upon them. Their leader, Ramon of Toledo, was like Charles of Toulouse, he was a sword for hire but unlike Charles he had ambitions. He was a Mozarab; these were Christian people who had lived under Muslim rule and intermarried. As such, they would find it difficult to have a position in the Christian lands without money. His master, Don Garcia, would reward him for his success in stealing the cattle but this ambush was an opportunity for Ramon to make a little extra for himself. The arms and horses of the men they killed and captured would be his. He had no wish to stay in this backwater any longer than was necessary. When he had enough treasure, he would take the men who followed his banner and they would hire themselves out perhaps to Robert Guiscard, the Norman knight who was carving out a kingdom in Italy. Guiscard did not care about the background of his men just so long as they could fight and had good weapons.

Even though there were only three of them who were close to the ambushers, Don Diego, Charles and Alfonso might have achieved surprise and routed Ramon and his men but Don Diego could not resist announcing himself and he shouted, "For Lain Núñez and Castillona de Vivar!"

The cry undoubtedly saved many of the men who followed Luis the Steward but they put the three men who charged into the mass of horsemen in great peril. Ramon of Toledo turned to face the threat and his men followed him as they countercharged. Don Diego was lucky in that his first slashing blow hacked through the arm of William Almarez, Ramon of Toledo's lieutenant, but that first success emboldened Don Diego who plunged into the heart of the ten waiting horsemen and six crossbowmen.

Now that Charles and Alfonso were committed to the attack, they showed that they knew war better than their master. Don Diego understood how to use a sword and the small buckler type shield but Alfonso and Charles knew how to kill. There would be no ransom if they had an enemy surrender to them and so they killed efficiently and quickly. As their two horses bowled through the horsemen, protecting the left side of their lord, they carved a path of death. Charles' sword was a Norman one gifted to him by his father and it smashed through the chest of the horseman whose small shield barely moved to block the blow. Alfonso's sword took the head of another man who had no mail coif about his neck. The two mercenaries were evening the odds.

Ramon of Toledo had been taken by surprise but he reacted quickly, especially when he saw his friend maimed. He shouted, "Crossbows!" His six crossbowmen were to have slain the leading horsemen but now, at a range of only thirty paces, the six bolts would clear six horses and Ramon would win!

Charles heard the shout and recognised the danger and he closed with Ramon of Toledo. The closer they were to the enemy the less chance they had of being hit. He shouted, "Alfonso, take out those crossbows!"

Alfonso hated to leave his shield brother but he obeyed orders. He galloped at the kneeling men, leaning low over his horse's head so that he was protected from bolts and could use his sword on the men who were vulnerable once their bolts had flown. Even as he charged, two of them sent their bolts towards Don Diego and Charles. The armiger flicked up his shield and managed to block one which hurtled towards Don Diego while digging his heels into his horse's flanks to position himself between the bolts and his master. The bolt hit with so much force that the tip protruded a finger's length inside the shield. The second bolt slammed into Charles' leg below the knee and above his boot, driving through the flesh and into the side of the horse which reared. The rearing horse drove back Ramon of Toledo who was about to bring his sword down on Don Diego's back. The aristocrat was surrounded by enemies who were keen to have the horseman's helmet, sword and horse. The rest of Charles' men, led by Iago and Ramon, divided to go to the aid of Alfonso and Charles. They were well trained. While Alfonso and Pedro ruthlessly despatched the crossbowmen, Charles ignored the pain and the blood gushing from the wounded leg and placed himself next to Don Diego's left side.

"My lord! Withdraw to the safety of our men! We are surrounded!"

Don Diego seemed to see the danger for the first time. Ramon of Toledo had recovered and was leading three men to end the lives of Don Diego and his armiger. Don Diego shouted, "Sancho, sound the horn!" There were twenty retainers who could come to their aid. Don Diego tried to back his horse from the fray but Ramon of Toledo and his two companions came at them determined to have the armour of the knight.

Charles had been a warrior for his whole life and he knew that what he was doing would cost him his life but he had no choice. His father had been a Norman and his grandfather a Viking; it was in his blood. He urged his horse forward and blocked one blow from a Navarrese blade with his shield while swinging his own sword beneath the man's shield and across his stomach. It left two men trying to get at Don Diego who was still backing his horse towards the rest of his men. Alfonso and Pedro had slain or dispersed the crossbows and raced to the aid of their shield brother. Even as Charles blocked a sword thrust from one warrior Ramon of

Toledo swept his sword across Charles' body. His padded undershirt helped slow the sword but it still tore a line across his middle and more blood flowed. Charles lunged with his sword and, even though he was mortally wounded, the point found Ramon of Toledo's nose and hacked off the tip. A sword heading for an eye makes any man back off and so did Ramon of Toledo. It allowed Alfonso and the rest of Don Diego's men to form a wall of swords around their master but it was too late for Charles of Toulouse. The warrior whose first blow had been blocked by the armiger now swung his sword at the head of the mortally wounded warrior. When it struck, Charles slid from the back of his horse but, even as he fell, his hand still gripped his sword.

Alfonso and the men chosen by Charles of Toulouse were angry and they hacked and chopped at the men who remained and Ramon of Toledo, his scarred face pouring blood, saw that all was lost and he fled from the battle. He had lost all. His men lay dead and he would have to find a new master sooner rather than later. As Luis and Don Diego's retainers charged towards the cattle which were protected by a handful of men, it was clear that Don Diego had won.

The aristocrat and Alfonso both dismounted and knelt next to the dying Charles of Toulouse. The blood was flowing from his many wounds as well as seeping from his head. He looked up as Alfonso tenderly took off his helmet. He gave his oldest friend a wry smile, "I came here for a quiet life, Alfonso, a mistake eh?"

Alfonso just nodded for he was a warrior and knew that a shield brother was badly hurt and there was so much he wanted to say but he would let Charles speak his last words.

Don Diego shook his head, "You saved my life! How can I repay you?"

Charles' voice was weak and told Alfonso that his friend was dying and that death would be soon. "My lord, I have a son, William, I ask you to provide for him. He comes from warrior stock and will be a good warrior. Alfonso can teach him to fight."

Alfonso nodded, "I will be as a foster father to him, old friend." Turning to Don Diego who should have answered instantly for he owed Charles of Toulouse his life, he said, "My lord, your armiger awaits an answer."

Don Diego had to reply in the affirmative even though he did not want to burden himself with the armiger's child. The eyes of his warriors were upon him and he nodded, "Of course. I swear by the sword I hold that William, son of Charles of Toulouse shall have a place in my house and that I shall do all that I can to make him a warrior." Don Diego was not a true warrior. A real warrior held oaths to be more valuable and important than anything. He said the words but they were empty as were his eyes.

Charles of Toulouse smiled, "Then I am content. Alfonso, give my father's sword to my son. Tell him that the blood on the hilt…" he got no further for he died. The grandson of the Viking warrior died with his sword in his hand and he was at peace. He could not know then,

nor could any, that his son's life would be
irrevocably bound with that of the man who
would save Spain, El Cid.

Chapter 1

*I am now near the end of my life and I have
done more than many men could even dream of.
I served El Cid, El Campeador, Rodrigo Diaz de
Vivar and I was proud to do so. I sit now, in this
west-facing tower in a Spain made more secure
because of the efforts of all the men with whom I
fought, and write of my life and the life of El Cid
before my memory develops more of the holes
and gaps I am greeted with each morning. Soon
I will forget my own name! Others may tell the
tale but none were by his side for his whole life
as I was. When he wandered after his exile, I
was one of the handful of warriors with him and
his wife. I was there at the end when the legend
of the man called El Cid took over from the
reality that was a most complex man but one, I
would have followed anywhere. I was true to my
oath and I never left his side. When he fought, I
was there! He is dead but the story of his life has
now become the stuff of legend. Troubadours
sing songs about the man they never met and the
truth of his life is disappearing. I must tell the
warriors of the future of the man who united
Spain, El Cid.*

My name is William son of the Armiger and
I was named after my father's father. It is a
Norman and French name and the people of the
manor in which I grew up found it hard to
pronounce. I usually answered to Will. I never
knew my mother for she died when I was born

and the woman who raised me, Maria, did not know her either. It meant I grew up imagining the woman born in Gascony, France. I made her into a beautiful lady; the daughter of a mighty lord and I had her fall in love with my father and run away with him. It was the sort of romantic nonsense troubadours sing of and it comforted me as I grew up with a foster mother and a foster father. In the absence of the truth, it was a comfortable story to help me to sleep on nights when I felt sorry for myself and tears came. I barely knew my father. I knew that he was the second son of a warrior who led a Norman warband and that he had been killed when I was barely six years old. All that I remembered of him was that he was an enormous man with hands that appeared to be as big as shovels but I also remember him as being kind and I vaguely recollected stories he told me. Fragments came to me when I slept, they still do. They were tales of warriors who sailed dragon ships and fought in shield walls. I learned more about my father from Alfonso who was now Don Diego's armiger or champion. Those who did not know us thought that he was my father because of the name but he was my foster father. He had sworn an oath to my dying father and he had kept it. He was the one whom I saw each day for he was training me to be a warrior. Don Diego had also sworn an oath that I would be looked after but he never even spoke to me and for a while, I wondered if oaths meant anything at all. It was as though he had sworn the oath and then forgotten it. That is not a good thing to do for the dead watch us and a broken oath never ends well! Being looked after by a servant and his armiger meant I slept in the hall which was surrounded by a high wall and a deep ditch. Maria was employed in the hall to work in the kitchens. She was always kind to me for she now had a position that was less parlous than being the nurse of the son of a sword for hire.

I worked from a young age but when I began to train as a warrior at the age of twelve, then my body changed and the first wisps of hair came upon my face making it obvious that I would have a red beard. The other men called me Will Redbeard and used it, at first, to mock me. I did not mind for I was the butt of many jokes. Then I just accepted it for Alfonso found it easier to call me William Redbeard, rather than William son of the Armiger. Fewer people mistook me for his real son. Alfonso wanted children and I know that he and Maria lay together and coupled but she never bore him a child. I knew not why but Alfonso was a kind man and a good teacher. A child and then a young man could ask for nothing more.

I began training as a warrior when I was twelve but I had been working with the warriors since I had been six. I fetched and carried and I learned to sharpen weapons. I mended shields and learned to sew leather. In short, I was so immersed in the world of the warrior that when I began to train it was as though I had been doing it my whole life. The life was hard but then so was that of everyone I knew except for Don Diego, his wife and his son, Rodrigo de Vivar.

Castile was a land surrounded by enemies from Muslim Moors in the south to the Christian Navarrese and Aragonese to the north and east. Despite the fact that my life was hard I enjoyed every day for I was with the best of men, those who would become my shield brothers. Alfonso was a hard taskmaster and I worked from dawn until dusk but I learned each day and I was improving. Alfonso commanded the ten men of the garrison. After my father had been killed, Don Diego had used the coin he had taken from the dead and from the lord who had stolen his cattle to strengthen the men who would protect him. I did all that they did and there was no allowance for the fact that I was still little more than a rather large child.

When I began my training proper, I had to work at the pel swinging the short sword from side to side, up and down to perfect the action which we would use in war. I would do this for hour upon hour with burning muscles until I stopped, exhausted. I learned to hate that wooden post and that, in turn, helped me to develop my skills for each blow was an attempt to kill the pel! The other men were kind to me but when we trained there were no allowances for the fact that I was little more than a youth. That helped me in later years but often, when I returned to my room at the end of the day, Maria would have to tend bruises and wounds. I grew up far quicker than others my age and my young body hardened and grew quickly to make me a potentially powerful warrior. I became bigger and stronger as well as more skilled. Each of the

retinue gave me some extra skill and that made
me a better warrior than I might have otherwise
been for I had a part of every shield brother in
me. Living in the hall meant I ate better than I
might otherwise. The table scraps were there for
a youth who was always hungry and the dogs
learned that my hands were quicker than their
jaws!

One evening as we finished for the day and
Alfonso and I made our weary way back to the
hall, I pointed to the son of the lord, Master
Rodrigo, "Why is it that he does not need to
practise for he is but a few years younger than I
am and I have done this since I was six summers
old?"

Alfonso had shrugged, "He should for one
day he will lead the men of the manor to war. He
should be at least as strong as they are but that is
nought to do with either of us. He is a lord and
we are common men. He has land and coin and
we have to earn it. Do not look above your
station. If you want to be a lord then when you
are trained you should seek a master who wishes
to carve out a land for himself. Your father and I
would have followed Robert Guiscard to Italy. If
we had then we would now be lords with great
estates."

I looked at him, "Then why did you not?"
He was silent and that was a sure sign that he
was hiding something from me. Alfonso was an
honest man but like all men he had secrets he
held from me while I was a child. The time was
coming when I would no longer be a child and
so I pursued him. "I pray you to answer me for I

am soon to be a man and will have hair upon my lip. I will ride to war when you go; I deserve an answer."

"You deserve only that which I choose to give you!" His stern voice relented and became softer. "It was your mother and it was you. We were heading for Normandy to join a conroi heading for Sicily when your father met your mother. He was smitten as soon as he met her and then your mother became pregnant with you. We never reached Rouen; instead, I heard of an opportunity to have a place here with Don Diego. I was born not far from here and we travelled to this place. It was the wrong time of year and the Pyrenees were treacherous. Your mother died and we buried her in a mountain pass. We found Maria who had just lost her child and she became your wet nurse. There you have the whole story now ask me no more."

"But why did you not go on your own? Why did you stay here?"

"Your father and I were shield brothers and we swore an oath. Such things are binding. Remember that, young Will." He looked over to Don Diego who was speaking with his franklin, "A man ignores an oath at his peril."

We had reached the water trough and were washing off the worst of the dirt. "And do you not wish to marry?"

He laughed, "I am too old and set in my ways. Maria does for me. When she lost her own child, she lost the ability to bear children. We lie together when we feel the need and I am content. I am a warrior and proud to be so."

"And what of me?"

"You will make of your life whatever you wish it to be. Don Diego promised to see you grow into a man and to train you as a warrior. When you achieve that then you make your own choices. You are not bound to Don Diego nor to this manor. You are not Castilian nor even Spanish. The world is yours and when you are a man, I will give you your father's sword. We have kept the money which Don Diego pays all of his men and you shall have enough to buy a horse and mail if you so choose, but first you must satisfy me that you are a warrior and that you can fight next to me as your father did. Only then will I give you the sword and your inheritance. Now I have spoken more than I like. Do not question me again!"

When I grew, I tried to have around me men like Alfonso but they were rare. Too many were shallow or self-serving and I never had more than a handful for I had high standards. That is why I stayed with the Cid for so long. He was the nearest I found to the man who raised me and to the warrior who sired me.

I am not certain how my life would have turned out had Don Diego's father, Lain Núñez, and Rodrigo's godfather, Peyre Pringos, not arrived with some horses as a present for Rodrigo upon his birthday. That it was unexpected was clearly obvious for, as the two noblemen and their retinues galloped towards the gates, servants were sent hither and thither to prepare rooms, food and to ensure that all was ready for one of the King's greatest friends. The two nobles were renowned warriors. Whilst Don Diego was known as a good manager of the land who made money he was not known as a warrior. The two men reined in but did not dismount. They were true warriors who were more than comfortable in the saddle. Don Diego on the back of his horse always looked like an untidy sack of wheat.

Lord Lain looked like a warrior and he had a commanding voice, "Fetch out my grandson, let me see if he is ready for a warhorse!"

I looked at the string of young mares and colts which were held by the men who accompanied Lain Núñez. All were young but they were either coursers or destriers, warhorses. The difficulty would be choosing the right one for all of them were less than a year old and you could not see what they would turn out like. I think that Rodrigo's grandfather wanted to see if his grandson had an eye for a horse. I could only look on enviously for I would be lucky to ride a sumpter and I had not even been taught to ride yet.

Rodrigo had been in the hall and his father must have ordered that he be presented as a warrior. He raced out with his small sword, short hauberk and helmet. I saw his grandfather nod and smile for he adored his grandson but Peyre Pringos shook his head and his face clearly displayed dissatisfaction.

"So, Rodrigo, how old are you now?"

"I have seen ten summers."

"Good and have you begun to train as a warrior? Have you begun to use the pel and the cinquain?"

Rodrigo wisely decided to tell the truth and he shook his head.

"Why has my godson not yet begun his training?" Peyre Pringos was a true warrior and it was obvious that he thought that Don Diego was failing in his duty. His voice was harsh and condemning.

Don Diego said, defensively but without conviction, "He has had a few lessons and he can hold a sword and a shield."

Rodrigo's grandfather shook his head, "Diego, you are the fruit of my loins but I swear that you exasperate me!" It was at that moment that his eyes lighted on me, "You boy, what is your name?"

"William the Redbeard."

"Ah yes, the son of the man who saved the life of my son. And what do you do, boy?"

"I am training to be a warrior and I serve Alfonso the Armiger."

"Do you use the pel?"

"Aye, my lord! I use it every day."

"Then show me and my grandson what it is that you do."

Every eye was upon me and I saw Alfonso fingering his sword hilt nervously. He was being examined every bit as much as I was. I forced myself to breathe easily. The breathing exercise had been an important and early lesson when I had begun to train and Alfonso had impressed upon me the need to control my body for when I fought, I would need a cool head. I took out the short sword which I used; it was the same size as Rodrigo's. I had two practise swings and then I went into my routine. I went high right, low left, high left, low right. I swung over my head and then repeated the first moves. I then began to swing at the middle. I grew in confidence and felt the sweat as my arms tired.

Rodrigo's grandfather shouted, "Stop!" I did so. "Are you tired?"

"A little, my lord, for we had a morning practice too but I can keep going if you wish."

I saw him grin. "Rodrigo, fetch your sword and buckler. Armiger, give your boy his shield. Let us have a bout. No blood, I just want to see how Rodrigo manages against a similar opponent."

Don Diego protested, "But he is not trained!"

Before his grandfather could answer Rodrigo said, quietly but firmly, "I am ready!"

As Alfonso came and strapped on my shield he whispered in my ear and counselled, "No showing off and for God's sake, no blood!"

I had fought others but they had all been the warriors of Don Diego's retinue who had been bigger than me and out of respect to my dead father had not taken it easy on me. Rodrigo approached me. He was wearing his helmet for if an accident happened then the son of the lord would be injured and not killed. I was not, I did not matter; it was to be expected. I saw, in his eyes, the hint of fear. I think it was the fear of failure rather than fear of injury and also the fact that although he had seen me on the estate, he did not know me. Was I a cruel youth who would enjoy inflicting pain? Certainly, as I came to know Rodrigo, I discovered that he was afraid of nothing save failure and dishonour.

He came at me in a rush. His blows were powerful for he had enthusiasm and some strength but they were not timed well and I either took them on my shield or avoided them. One came too close and I had to block it, hurriedly. The men I had fought hit harder and I blocked it and pushed him away easily with my shield. It was not a powerful push but he stumbled as his feet became tangled and then when he had recovered himself, he rushed at me, flushed and angry. I danced out of the way and when he swung wildly at me again, I used my sword to deflect him like a bullfighter. He fell flat on his face.

I saw Peyre Pringos roll his eyes but Rodrigo's grandfather dismounted, came over and helped his grandson to his feet. "You have courage but no skill. Your opponent here was more than kind." He reached into his purse and brought out a golden crown, "Here for you could have either hurt or humiliated my grandson but did neither. Armiger, you have a good one here."

I bowed, "Thank you, my lord." I sheathed my sword and seeing Alfonso's eyes, I hurried to stand next to him.

Peyre Pringos dismounted and said. "Let us see if you have a better sense of horseflesh. I have brought these horses. One is for you; you may have any of them. You choose it and it is yours. I hope you choose wisely!"

Rodrigo handed his shield and helmet to a servant, Pablo, who hurried over. He sheathed his sword and gave a slight bow to me. I wondered if retribution would follow the bout for then I did not know him. He walked down the line of horses. I confess that I knew little of horses. That part of my training had yet to come. I would not know which to choose and, in truth, it was a hard decision for all were young. How did a man know how a horse would turn out? He walked down the line and not only looked each horse in the eyes but also breathed into their noses and stroked their manes. He walked back down the line to examine them a second time. There was absolute silence for everyone knew that this was an important moment. As events turned out it was the most important of moments but how could we know that then?

He stood next to a grey. I would have called it white but I knew that horsemen called such horses grey. "I will have this one!"

His godfather waved an angry arm, "Babieca!" It meant barbarian for he had chosen the most ungainly of horses.

Rodrigo smiled, "Aye, godfather, and this is a good name for him and he shall be Babieca!"

Lain Núñez smiled, "Peyre, this is good. He has chosen and he has not done so blindly. You and I may not have chosen that one but Rodrigo will ride him to war and it is his choice. We both know that a bond between a horse and rider is special. He spoke to the horse and the horse spoke to him." Peyre shrugged. Lain turned to his son, Don Diego, "But you have not done that which you should! Rodrigo's training must begin now!" He pointed to me, "This half-trained peasant should be his trainer. They have a bond; I can see that. You will make this happen!"

Diego nodded, "Armiger, make it so."

I saw that Alfonso was less than happy but he had no choice and he nodded, "Aye, my lord!"

Peyre Pringos nodded, "And I appreciated, too, that you did not hurt my godson." He walked to the black colt which had stamped and snorted through the whole process and led him to me. "This is your reward; have this destrier and when my godson realises his mistake then you can swap." He gave me a hawk-like stare for he would have chosen this horse for his godson and he was telling me to prepare it to give to Rodrigo when he was ready. It was not a gift, it was a loan.

I nodded, "Of course, my lord, and I am honoured!"

He sniffed, "As you should be! Now, Diego, I hope that you are better at finding food than you are at training your offspring!"

Alfonso came over to me and was shaking his head, "What have you got yourself into? That is a stallion! He will hurt you; he is a killer!"

I shrugged, "As I could do nothing about the gift then I will have to leave it to God to decide if I should die riding this black beast!"

They all went indoors leaving just Rodrigo, myself, our horses and the retainers. I knew that Alfonso wished to chastise me but he could not. Rodrigo turned and said, "Armiger, let us take our horses to the stable."

Alfonso bowed. "As you wish, Master Rodrigo!"

As we walked the horses Rodrigo said, "My grandfather was right, you could have hurt me yet you did not."

Even in our first conversation, I knew that he wished me to elaborate. We seemed to understand each other without words. I nodded, "Your father has a good Armiger and his men at arms are well chosen. When I first started training, they could have been far harder with me and I just afforded you the same courtesy. I know what it is like when you have no idea what is expected."

He stopped and looked at me, "They were harder with you than you were with me." I nodded. "You are to be the one who trains me and I would not have you let up on me. I felt ashamed before my grandfather and godfather. I would not be so embarrassed again. I know that when I go to war my enemies will be far harder than me and I intend to be a good knight!"

"Then, my lord, I will do as you ask."

He laughed and shook his head, "I am no lord, yet, I am Rodrigo and you are Will. Let us leave it at that!"

"Aye... Rodrigo!" I looked at Babieca. "Why did you choose him? He looks a little clumsy and ungainly."

"He spoke to me." I nodded for that made sense. "You were given the one my godfather intended for me, what will you call him?"

I looked at the black stallion. I had not thought of a name but Alfonso's words came to me, "He looks powerful enough to eat me and I know less about horses than you do about fighting so I shall call him Killer for I fear that he will be the undoing of me!"

Rodrigo laughed, "I can see that we will get on well for you make me smile and I rarely do that in my own home."

After we had seen to our horses, I returned to the room I shared with Maria and, sometimes, Alfonso. Maria was at the table preparing food and Alfonso was sharpening his weapons, "I hope you know what you have got yourself into!"

I shrugged, "Did you not tell me that my grandfather believed in fate and that my father had said there were things a man could not control for they were the work of spirits?"

"Aye, and he could have been hanged or burned as a witch for such words."

"And what could I have done?"

"Let Rodrigo beat you!"

"Were you not watching, Alfonso? Only his father, Don Diego, would have been happy with that. This is good."

"No, it is not for I have to train you and Rodrigo!"

I shook my head, "You train me and I will be the one who works with Master Rodrigo. This is meant to be, Alfonso, surely you can see that!"

He sighed, "Aye, I do not like it but you are right!" Shaking his head, he laughed, "Normans and Vikings, they are best to be avoided!"

I laughed, "I have a fine destrier to show for it!"

"Which you cannot ride and you know not how to school."

I gave him a sly smile, "But you do, so all is well!"

He gave me a deserved clip about the head and it hurt. I smiled for I had earned the punishment.

As we ate, Alfonso told me the changes that would be necessitated by the new commands from Rodrigo's grandfather. I would still have to train in the morning with the rest of the garrison but I would also need to school Killer and be taught to ride. Alfonso agreed to rise an hour earlier with me for three days to show me what to do and then I would have to continue alone. I would have one hour less sleep each day! Rodrigo had much to occupy him in the mornings himself. He had his early prayers and then his lessons in reading, languages, law, as well as poetry and singing. I would have him from the afternoon until the bell sounded for the evening meal.

I was not worried about the weapon work; I had practised that for years but in terms of the riding and schooling of our horses I would be just three days ahead of Rodrigo. I was up with Alfonso the next morning and spent an hour being taught how to curb Killer's behaviour so that he obeyed me. Alfonso was a good teacher and rather than violence, which would not have worked with such a powerful horse, he taught me to become friends with the black beauty. On the second morning, we just spent half of the time schooling Killer and I was taught how to ride Sunflower, an old sumpter who was very gentle but would enable me to learn to stay in the saddle. The third morning Alfonso spent the whole time showing me the quintain and how to use it. Thankfully, the first part of the training was on foot and I could manage that. I could see that I would have to rise even earlier and lose more sleep if I was to master the spear used from the back of a horse! The swinging hoop looked like a small target to hit with a spear from the back of a lively horse such as Killer.

When I had first begun my training, Alfonso had used games to make the work more enjoyable and, when the training began, I did that with Rodrigo. We used the hoops and sticks which were almost like toys to quicken his reflexes and eye. He enjoyed the game but questioned its function. He did so out of curiosity for he was always one who wished to learn. "I enjoy this game, Will, but my grandfather wished me to learn to use a sword."

I nodded and, catching the small hoop with my stick, flicked it back at Rodrigo so that he had to move his hand quickly to the left to catch it. "And that is what you are doing. You are learning to make your hand and eye work together and to work quickly. Do not worry we will get on to the heavy work later, but you have to develop the strength in your arms and your back."

The last three hours of the day were planned to be spent at the pel and after half that time had elapsed, I saw that he could barely lift his arm. I knew that Alfonso was watching me with a critical eye but I was the one who had been charged with training the young noble. "Put down the sword. We will try something else for half an hour." I smiled, "This will help me with my training." He did so.

I was bigger and heavier than Rodrigo and what I planned would tire him but not only would it strengthen him it would improve my skills. We went to the quintain and I picked up the spear used for training. "I want you to take me on your shoulders and to be my horse so that I may try the quintain." His face questioned me but he nodded and lifted me up. I heard him strain as he did so. "Now run as fast as you can at the quintain." It was less of a run and more of a fast walk but it enabled me to lunge with my spear and hit the quintain. On the third pass, he stumbled and I tumbled from his back. It was a valuable lesson for me as I did not have far to fall but it taught me that I needed to learn to fall well.

"You have done well, Rodrigo, now take the spear and I will be your mount."

"Thank you, Will, for my back feels as though it is broken!"

All the training and exercise I had done, allied to my bigger frame meant that I could carry Rodrigo easily and I could actually run. In fact, it made my legs more powerful and Alfonso had told me that strong legs were necessary to be a good rider. After half an hour I had had enough of being a horse.

"Now we go back to the pel."

Rodrigo managed to hack at the pel for longer and it left us with an hour to groom and school our horses. I envied Rodrigo and his relationship with Babieca for while Killer often fought me, for no apparent reason, Babieca almost anticipated Rodrigo's moves. The last hour of each day was special for, while we schooled and groomed our horses we talked and we got to know each other. We learned that we had more in common than one might have expected. I did not know my father for he was dead but Rodrigo did not know his father because Don Diego was too busy for his son. I was surprised that when they ate their evening meal Don Diego rarely spoke to Rodrigo. He did not ask him how the training had gone and it was as though Rodrigo was invisible. That contrasted with the way Alfonso questioned me and commented upon what I had done. He was critical but, when I deserved it, complimentary. He had approved of my piggyback method of training but he thought I was not pushing Rodrigo hard enough. I had to balance the lack of training that Rodrigo had already done with the demands of becoming a knight.

When Rodrigo and I talked I learned of his ambitions. "My father is a man of business. He is more concerned with how many cattle we have and how much flour we produce. I would be a warrior. I envy you your father."

"But he is dead!"

"And yet when he lived all men respected him. I have heard Iago and Ramon talk of him. My father was lucky and did not appreciate him. When I am a knight, I will ensure that my men all know that I value them. That is how I would be; a warrior who has skill on the battlefield and is respected by friend and foe alike."

I had not yet fought in battle but Alfonso had told me that the battlefield was rarely a place of glory. Perhaps Rodrigo de Vivar might be able to attain such a reputation but when I fought, I would be lucky to live for I was an ordinary man with no coin and therefore worth no ransom.

"Alfonso has told me that the Moors whom we fight are cunning men!" Alfonso was a Spaniard and he knew of the skill of the Moorish horsemen and archers.

"But we have Christian enemies we need to defeat first. Navarre is a thorn in our side. It was the Navarrese who killed your father. My father fears that King Ferdinand will make war on them sooner rather than later."

"And that, then, is a good thing."

"For Castile, aye, but for my father, it is not for it means that he will have to go to war and his profits will suffer. It will bring arguments from my grandfather but like you, I think it is a good thing and I look forward to it. Perhaps by then, our horses will be ready to bear us!"

And so that first year passed. We both grew and, gradually, Rodrigo caught up with me. My training with Alfonso and the others made me as big as they were and I had skill. I passed that on to Rodrigo and we were more like friends than the son of a hired sword and the son of a noble. My exercises and regime broadened his back and strengthened his arms. Our horses improved as did my skills on horseback and I was able to ride Sunflower and use first the spear and later the lance to strike the quintain. Rodrigo was even more accomplished and improved so much that Alfonso thought I must have some special technique.

"No, armiger, he has natural ability. I give him the strength and an opponent who is bigger and a challenge; that is all!"

When his grandfather and godfather returned on his birthday, they brought mail and a helmet. Rodrigo had a shield already and they asked for us to have a bout. This time Rodrigo held his own. We knew each other well and cancelled each other out. I could have bested him for I was still bigger and stronger but I allowed an honourable draw which pleased everyone. Rodrigo's grandfather gave me another golden coin as a reward and called over Alfonso, "Armiger, your acolyte has done well. You should be proud."

"I am, my lord."

"Keep him sharp for within six months we go to war." He looked at his son, "All of us will go to war, although Rodrigo here will just have to watch." He ruffled Rodrigo's head, "But watch well, Rodrigo, for soon you will ride to war and follow the King's banner then all eyes will be upon you for you have the blood of a warrior in your veins!"

I saw Don Diego colour and knew that there was bad blood between him and his father. Would his failure to keep an oath make bad blood between him and his son?

Chapter 2

It was just six months later when the call came for us to go to war. The war was to be a punishment for the King's half-brother whose men had killed a popular Castilian Count, Bermundo. One of my shield brothers, Iago, explained to me the real reason, "King Ferdinand is looking for an excuse to go to war with Navarre. He either wants the country as a vassal or part of Castile and León." He seemed quite happy to go to war for there was always profit if you won. Alfonso had a good band of warriors despite the lassitude of Don Diego.

Killer was not ready yet and so I was given Sunflower to ride. Rodrigo would be going too but he would act as his father's second squire. That meant he would not be risked in the battle for he would act as a sort of servant. When we fought, he would guard the spare horses and the camp. Surprisingly, he viewed that task as a necessary one. As we rode towards Atapuerca he explained why, "You are older and stronger than I am, Will. As I have been training for just over a year, if I went to war I would, in all likelihood, die and that would be a waste of my life and your efforts. Better to watch and to learn. It is for you I fear, for you have not yet fought."

I nodded, "But it is in my blood. You are right in one respect, until I have slain a man then I will not know if I am truly of my father and grandfather's blood. Do not worry about me as I ride with good men whom I know that I can trust."

Although Rodrigo and I rode together, when we halted, before the battle, I went with Alfonso and the other mounted men who followed Don Diego to set up our camp and we discussed the reasons for this war. Alfonso put forward the public reason which Don Diego had told him. "King Garcia Sánchez and his men killed Count Bermundo; it was in battle but vengeance is needed."

Iago chuckled, "Armiger, that is not the truth of it. I have spoken already with Will; he is part of this band. He should know the truth!" I believed Iago's was the more plausible explanation.

Alfonso nodded, "You are right and, from now on, I shall treat you as a man. Officially that is the reason but the real purpose is for King Ferdinand to gain Navarre. It is an ulcer in the heart of his kingdom."

"We fight Christians?"

"There will be Moors as well as Christians arrayed against us." He saw the worried look on my face. "Trust to your shield brothers. You will not be in the front rank in any case. I will ride with Sancho and Raymond and flank Don Diego when we charge. You, Ramon, Pedro, Iago and Juan will be the second rank with the rest of our men and you will take the place of those who fall."

His words did not fill me with hope. If one of the men before me fell then the odds were that I would follow them far quicker.

We rose in the middle of the night and I prepared to go to war for the first time. Alfonso had given me my father's sword and when we returned to Vivar, if we returned to Vivar, then I would have my inheritance too. The sword was an old weapon of Norse design and had belonged to my grandfather. It was a long sword and it was broader than the Spanish and Moorish blades. Unlike the newer blades, there was no fuller. A fuller lightened a sword without taking away its strength. It meant my sword was heavier than it needed to be. It had a smaller guard at the hilt and was without decoration; it was a warrior's weapon. Heavier to lift than the sword I had used hitherto, I was grateful for the hours of practice I had put in. The helmet, mail coif and head protector I wore were also my father's. The helmet was conical with a nasal. I had worn all three before but not for long periods. Alfonso warned me that the weight would be more noticeable after a long day of fighting. The shield was not my father's. He had used the heavier round shield of the Norse. I had the smaller shield like the others and it was strapped to my arm. It enabled me to use my left hand for the reins of my horse. As Alfonso told me, my father's shield had a long strap and was harder to use than the smaller buckler type but he conceded the Norse shield afforded more protection for it was bigger. I had already donned my padded gambeson which Maria had made for me. It would merely soften any blows which were rained upon me. My leather hauberk, made of thick hide, would be my main

defence against swords, spears and arrows. I had
begun to attach small pieces of metal to it but it
would take many months to finish for all I could
use were the scraps of metal from the
blacksmith's workshop. As Alfonso said, even a
few of the metal pieces might make all the
difference between life and death. I was under
no illusions, a good blow from a sword could
slice through the hide, gambeson and into my
flesh. With a simple tunic over my leather
hauberk and a plain cloak about my shoulders,
we were ready for war. The knights wore similar
war gear except that more of them had mail
hauberks and their cloaks were brightly coloured
to mark them as nobles. They all sported spurs, a
sign of their nobility. With our spears in our
hands, we walked our horses to the gathering
place. We would mount at the last moment and
lessen the burden our mounts would have to
endure. Sunflower was slow and I would have to
continually urge her just to keep pace with the
others.

The two armies were arrayed before the
town. This was not like the encounter where my
father had been killed for this was an organized
and premeditated battle and there would be no
ambush. King Garcia knew we were coming and
was prepared. Alfonso told me that, in all
likelihood, the battle would have been arranged
by emissaries from both sides. Both sides had
men on foot including slingers and archers but it
would be decided by mounted men against
mounted men. The knights and men of Count
Bermundo had demanded from King Ferdinand

the right to lead the charge against King Garcia himself. King Ferdinand was a good general and knew the wisdom of allowing the Count's followers to lead the attack. We were allocated the right wing. Prince Sancho, King Ferdinand's eldest son, was with us although he did not lead the attack. Peyre Pringos had that honour.

This was my first battle and the formality of it surprised me. We lined up with the foot soldiers in the centre in three huge blocks and then the knights and cavalrymen lined up before the men on foot. We all dismounted. The priests and bishop came to bless us and to forgive us our sins. The King rode down the lines of mounted men so that we could all cheer him as he waved to us, calling out to men with whom he had fought before. Alfonso told me that was clever for those men would fight all the harder in battle and others would try to gain the King's eye so that he knew their name too. I saw that King Garcia did the same. The two rulers then joined their bodyguards, and when all was in place, horns sounded and battle commenced. I did not know what I expected but it was not this. The knights of Count Bermundo spurred their horses and charged recklessly and without much order at the standard of King Garcia as though they were desperate to be the first to die.

Peyre Pringos raised his sword and shouted, "For King Ferdinand the Great and Castile! May God be with us!" He spurred his horse but, compared with the reckless wild charge of the knights of Count Bermundo, our pace was almost sedate. Prince Sancho was just twenty paces from us as Don Diego had placed his retinue close to his father and Prince Sancho was under Lord Lain and Peyre Pringos' protection.

As we had waited for the order to mount, I had observed the heir to the throne. I took him to be about my age but there the similarities ended. Whilst my reddish-blond hair showed my ancestry, Prince Sancho had dark hair and olive skin for he was of the Spanish royal family. He was also slightly smaller than I was. That was not a surprise for I was the size of men and yet I had some growing left in me. The largest difference was in the war gear for Prince Sancho had a fine destrier and wore not only mail armour with mail mittens but when he pulled up his coif and donned his helmet, I saw he had a ventail about his face so that as he mounted, I could only see his eyes. The scabbard on his sword was also different from mine for it was richly decorated.

Sunflower was a steady horse and Pedro shouted to me as I began to fall back, "Will, dig in your heels. You cannot afford to be left behind."

"Sorry, Pedro!" I did as he commanded and the old palfrey responded so that I was boot to boot with him and Iago.

I could see through the gap that we were heading for a Moorish contingent. They had some warriors who were fully mailed but most were dressed as we were. Before them, they had men on foot who were half-dressed savages from Africa. They each held three javelins and they were running towards us almost as fast as the cavalrymen who followed them. They had real courage to charge mailed horsemen although as we had few bows and crossbows, they would be safe until Lord Lain ordered the charge.

To my left, I heard the crash and clash of arms as the knights of Count Bermundo struck the bodyguards of the King of Navarre. It was a terrifying noise for horses screamed and whinnied in panic and the death cries as knights and guards were lanced, speared and butchered filled the air. This was my first battle and I realised then that no matter how big the battlefield, a warrior had but one battle and that was in the small area before him. I did not take my eyes from the scene to my fore. The Africans were fearless. They were less than thirty paces from us when they hurled not one but two javelins in quick succession before turning to run back towards their own advancing horsemen. I idly wondered why they did not use the famous mounted horsemen who could use bows. I saw that at least twenty of the Africans were unlucky and were either speared or trampled by our men. However, they had had success. Some of Lord Lain's men had been unhorsed and Don Diego's squire, Sancho, had dropped his spear for he had been wounded.

Peyre Pringos' squire sounded the charge and we dug our heels in to gallop. Rodrigo's godfather had shown his experience for he had waited until we were on the downslope of the valley and it was an easy move to make. The Moors, in contrast, were charging uphill. I heard

cries as more Africans were trampled and then I
saw Alfonso pull back his spear. We were about
to strike the enemy line and so I moved my
spear back slightly and rested the head across
Sunflower's neck. Already I was sweating and I
wondered if I would have the grip to thrust with
the spear. Thoughts and fears filled my head: I
had never struck a man. I knew how to thread a
spear into a quintain or to strike through a
swinging hoop. I had even rammed it into a
dummy stuffed with straw but I knew that a man
would be a different prospect. Would I be able
to do it? Suddenly my shield seemed too small
and inadequate, hanging on my arm. My father
had had the right idea for his shield had
protected half of his body including his leg and
shoulder! No wonder the Normans were so
successful. All of these thoughts passed so
quickly that I barely registered them.

Then we struck although we did not do so at
the same time. Some men had ridden ahead of
their peers while some of the enemy had done
the same. Thanks to Alfonso the Armiger, we
were tighter together and the spears and lances
all lunged as one. The Moors struck too and I
saw spears and lances shattered and splintered.
Jorge, who was next to Alfonso, must have
suffered a wound for he dropped his shattered
spear and held his hand to his face. Although he
hung onto the reins his horse charged obliquely
across the front of Prince Sancho and his men. I
dug my heels in and Sunflower bravely filled the
gap. She had been a horse used for war but she
had passed her better days and this was unfair. I

should be riding Killer but he was not ready and so I joined Alfonso and Raymond in the front rank.

The Moorish frontline had also been disrupted and I was relieved to see that there was no opponent for me to spear. Then, as Raymond thrust his spear into the side of a Moor fighting one of Prince Sancho's men, a Moor with a blue cloak and painted face appeared from nowhere and lunged at me. I had not even seen him approach and that was a lesson to be learned for I had become mesmerized by the scene before me and it almost cost me my life. One moment there had been no one before me and in the heartbeat it took for me to glance at Raymond, he had appeared. I managed to do two things at once: I flicked my shield up and rammed my spear towards him. It was when my spearhead ground against metal that I knew he had mail beneath his cloak. His wooden lance shattered but mine was a steel headed spear that had been sharpened. Alfonso had chosen it for me as it had a tapered point and the point was able to penetrate and break a mail link. As it did so it broke the link and the ones next to it too, allowing the head to enter his cotton quill undergarment. The speed of his horse drove him up the slope and forced the spearhead deeper within his body. I am strong; I knew that already and I punched with all of my might even though the pressure of his body was forcing my arm back. I could not see the Moor's face for he had a mail mask covering it but I saw his eyes widen as he neared me. I twisted the spear and I must have struck something vital for, clutching my spear shaft he fell from his horse. I remembered my lessons and released my grip on the spear.

The battle was no longer mobile and fluid for the two armies had hit each other. Some of our men were deep in the enemies' lines and some Moors were in ours. Men and horses had fallen and when horses milled around it stopped the momentum of a charge. Horses had halted and Christian and Moor exchanged blows from the backs of horses. I began to see that a man could not practise for this. The uneven nature of a battlefield littered, already, with the detritus of war, meant that you could not predict when a horse would move and you needed quick reactions and reflexes. The infantry had now joined the battle and their axes and pikes could do terrible damage to horses and riders alike. This was the most dangerous phase of the battle. I drew my sword, my father's sword, and I looked around for an opponent. Alfonso was fighting two men and I just kicked Sunflower in the ribs to make her lurch towards the nearest of the two. The Moor's back was to me and there was no honour in the blow I struck but Alfonso had already told me that such honour was for nobles and not for swords for hire. Standing in my saddle I brought down my blade to split the helmet and head of the Moor in twain. My height and strength meant that the blow was a mortal one and blood and brains spewed forth. Until I had struck the blow, I had not known I could do it but Alfonso's life was in danger and I had no time to think.

49

Before I could take in that I had killed a man with a sword, Alfonso shouted as he fenced with the second Moor, "Prince Sancho is in danger! Get to him!"

I saw that the King's eldest had either outrun his guards or they had been slain. He was twenty paces ahead of me and he was whirling his horse and sword to keep the Moorish horsemen from him. His armour and helmet marked him as someone of importance and the Moors were trying to take him. Sunflower was tired but Prince Sancho was down the slope and I urged Sunflower to go to the Prince's aid. I held my sword behind me and swept it across the back of the nearest Moor I encountered. He, too, wore mail but my sword was not only sharp it was heavy. It bit through cloth, mail, cotton, flesh and, finally, his spine. His body arched as he fell to the ground and Sunflower took his place. Prince Sancho's sword came swinging towards me and I barely managed to block the blow with my shield.

"Prince Sancho, I am on your side!" The Prince managed to block a spear thrust at him as he turned to see me. I reared Sunflower to smash his hooves into the head of a Moorish foot soldier who thought to spear the Prince from below.

"Back your horse up the slope, Prince Sancho, we are isolated here!" Even as he nodded and backed his horse towards the safety of Alfonso and the rest of our men another Moor stabbed at the Prince's right side with his spear. Standing in my stirrups, I brought down my sword to smash the spear in two and then, turning the blade on its side, I back slashed across his chest. This time I did not manage to penetrate mail but the force of his movement and my blow made him tumble across the back of his horse and we had a gap. The men on foot surged forward when they saw us falling back but Alfonso brought Don Diego and the rest of our men racing to our side and, with some of Lord Lain's men, we managed to retire away from danger.

We formed a line that ebbed and flowed, surged and retreated as men fell or an advantage was gained. I found myself between the Prince and Iago. I killed no more for Iago and Alfonso were unbeatable that day. I had no idea how long we had fought but I felt exhausted for blocking blows and striking back was even harder than working the pel, for you had a horse to control and enemies came at you from all sides. Suddenly a voice, far to my left cried, "King Garcia is dead! The standard has fallen!"

The news must have reached King Garcia's Moorish allies for a horn sounded and they began to flee. I waited for the order to chase them but Peyre Pringos' squire sounded the recall. Our battle was over. Alfonso grinned at me, "I should have bet Pedro that you would survive. I would have made money."

I was not surprised that the others would bet upon me. It was their way. I nodded, unable to speak. Prince Sancho had lowered his ventail and he said, "And I am happy that you did survive, for I could have been in danger." I saw

Alfonso roll his eyes. He knew that if I had not reached him then Prince Sancho would have been a prisoner or worse. "What is your name?"

"I am William the Redbeard and I serve Don Diego de Vivar."

"Ah, the one who trains Rodrigo de Vivar." He held out his hand and I clasped his forearm, "I will send a reward to you when we are back in camp and now, I must find my father and see if he and my brothers have survived. Who knows, I may be King and not know it!" He sounded quite cheerful about the prospect.

As he rode off, I saw that Don Diego and his wounded squire had left to return to the camp. Some other knights were pursuing the Moors and men of Navarre. This was the time when a man could have an easy victory. Attacking a fleeing man meant it was unlikely he could fight you and victory was almost assured. Alfonso and the others had dismounted. He had taken off his helmet and he said, "And now a lesson we cannot learn at the manor. Find those you slew. What they had is yours."

I dismounted and took off my helmet and then my shield. I hung them from my cantle and let Sunflower's reins drop. She would not move for she was exhausted; this would be her last battle. I saw that the horse of the last man I had slain had not moved and I took its reins. Poor Sunflower would not have to endure another battle and I tied the reins of the gelding to Sunflower's saddle. I took the sword from the dead Moor. It had a thinner blade than mine and I did not think I would use it but it was treasure.

He had an intricately decorated dagger and sheath. I took both as well as his purse.

I was about to leave him when Iago said, "He has a mail hauberk and it is a good one, take it." The Moors wore shorter hauberks but it would be better than my hide one.

I saw that the man had been killed when his neck had been broken and I was pleased. I was young and did not relish taking mail from a bloody and broken body. It took longer to strip the body of the hauberk than I expected. I hung it on my new horse which I named Berber for the man I had killed had been a Berber. By the time it was dark I had collected weapons and treasure from the men I had slain although two of them had had their mail already taken by others. I did not mind for I could only wear one hauberk at a time.

Ramon was incensed that others should have taken my booty. He glared angrily at the other men at arms who were equally laden with booty, "Are we barbarians that we do not respect the rules of our profession? You did well, Will the Redbeard, and better than others who were slower down the slope and yet reap the reward of your labours." His wild eyes dared any to challenge him but they knew his reputation and they backed off.

I smiled, "I am just happy to have survived my first battle and, in all honesty, I did not expect the booty we have taken." I felt like a rich man. I had coins from Lord Lain and now that I was a man Alfonso had promised me the back pay which he had saved for me when we returned to Vivar. To cap it all I had a purse full of coins and rings taken from the dead. War was profitable! We walked our weary animals back to our camp.

After we had seen to our horses and gathered around our fires for food, we discovered that King Garcia was not just slain, he had been butchered by the men of Count Bermundo. The King of Navarre's son, Garcia, was young and his mother, the Queen, would be regent until he was of an age. Until then he would be housed in León and King Ferdinand had, to all intents and purposes, enlarged his Kingdom. Officially, the Kingdom of Navarre was now a vassal of Castile as its ruler was a virtual prisoner of King Ferdinand. Of course, there would still be Navarrese we needed to scour from the land but all had been won in one battle. King Garcia had thrown the dice and he had lost.

Rodrigo came to ask me about the battle rather than his father and I took that as a sign that we were closer than he and his father. It was made easier by the fact that his father had left our camp to speak with other knights. When I had told him how it had gone then he questioned me closely about each blow I had struck and my thoughts as I had done so. I had recovered my spear and he examined the spearhead. "I would have used a lance but I can see the benefits of a spear."

"A well-struck lance can kill quickly but if it strikes a shield or good mail then it will shatter." I smiled, "I confess that I did not know this until I fought. I think I learned more in that battle than in the years I have been training with Alfonso."

He asked me how it felt to split open a head and I told him the truth, that I had not even thought about it; I had just reacted. He seemed satisfied with the answer.

"Jorge will lose an eye and Sancho, my father's squire, is with the healers but we won."

I nodded. "And I learned the value of a good horse. Sunflower is old and she handled herself well yet had the battle gone on much longer, then I would have lost. The sooner our horses are schooled and we can ride them to war the better."

"I fear it will be some time for me for I have much to learn and you are older. I envy you. You fought at the Battle of Atapuerca and all I did was to spectate and admire the courage of our men!"

"Do not worry, you will fight one day and we still have much to learn. I learned today in this battle and I can pass that on to you when I train you. I doubt that there will be many more battles now. King Ferdinand just has to rid Navarre of those who oppose him and then we shall have peace."

Rodrigo shook his head, "We need to come to some arrangement with the Moors before that can happen. We have made great strides but there are vast numbers of them to the south of our land. We must learn to accommodate them. I watched them fight and saw that they are fierce and fanatical warriors. The men of Navarre fled before the Moors did."

I was older than Rodrigo but he had the ability to think and he was able to see further than I could. It was another reason that, as we grew older, I was happy to follow him but I get ahead of myself; the tale I tell is barely begun. I had just fought my first battle and Rodrigo de Vivar had barely begun to train as a knight.

One of Prince Sancho's knights came to our camp later that night with a fine silk robe. "The Prince wishes you to have this, William son of the Armiger, to remember the great service you did him and Castile this day."

"I thank the Prince but I am not worthy." I was not sure that I knew what to do with it. I was used to rough and ready clothes made for me by Maria. When would I get to wear this expensive garment?

When he left, Rodrigo told me that the gift was an expensive one. I deduced that he had taken it from one of the Navarrese Moors who had surrendered. It was far too big for the Prince. I did not mind that it was a cast-off. I was honoured to be noticed by the heir to the throne and it showed how far I had travelled. I put it in my war bag where I hoped it would not be ruined. Now that I had Berber, I could use Sunflower as a baggage horse. I had less likelihood of being robbed that way!

I think Don Diego hoped that we would go home but King Ferdinand and his three sons had different ideas. Our victory was so complete that, even as Don Diego prepared to travel home, the King summoned his senior leaders to a meeting. Don Diego would be sorely disappointed. Lord Lain represented the knights who lived close to Burgos. I was happy to still be on campaign for I had a horse to become acquainted with and new weapons to sell. There were many warriors, mainly foot soldiers, who had not been engaged and when they had had the opportunity to pillage the battlefield, found that the best had been taken. As Iago told me, we had taken the risk and therefore should have the greatest reward. While the King held his council of war, we held an impromptu market close to our camp where we sold our surplus to those who had not taken any. I found it worthy of note that Rodrigo chose not to spend time with his father but with Alfonso, me and our men. He got on well with us and loved to talk of war. He interrogated Alfonso about the time he and my father had spent as mercenaries. When Alfonso asked politely but forcefully that he be given the chance to go with the other men to drink in the town, I was left with Rodrigo. I was slightly resentful too for I wanted the chance to drink with my shield brothers.

Rodrigo seemed happy just to sit and talk, "You know you should read some of the works by writers of military history. The Romans have much to teach us."

I nodded but shifted a little uncomfortably, "The problem is, Master Rodrigo, that I cannot read."

He was appalled, "Then I shall teach you! A man must be able to read and then he can learn from the past and not repeat their mistakes! We will start on the morrow. The light is too poor in the camp!"

Just then his father's servant, Stephen, came for him. "Master Rodrigo, the Council of war is over and your grandfather is with your father. You are sent for."

With head hung, he turned to go, "I will see you on the morrow, Will, and you did better than well this day; you saved the life of a prince and I envy you!"

My life had changed in a short time and now I was envied by the son of a noble. I wondered what my father would have made of that!

When Alfonso returned with the other men, somewhat the worse for the drink they had consumed, they brought news that we were to head into the southern part of Navarre, in the words of King Ferdinand, "*we are to give over the time which remains to campaigning against the barbarians and strengthening the churches of Christ.*" The peace we had enjoyed against the Muslims now looked as though it was ended.

When I saw Rodrigo, the next day, he told me that this foray was inevitable as Jerusalem had fallen to the Muslims and the whole of Christendom had now rallied to fight the sea of Islam which threatened to engulf our Christian world. It meant that my lessons in reading would be delayed for Lord Lain, Rodrigo's grandfather, was with the vanguard as was Prince Sancho. His father, King Ferdinand, had rewarded his courage with the command of one-third of the army. Lord Lain Núñez was the second in command to ensure that the King's eldest did not make any dramatically disastrous mistakes. That meant that Don Diego and his men were also at the fore. While Rodrigo was delighted, his father was less than happy. With a wounded squire and one of our men returned to the manor he feared for his life.

For me, this was the beginning of my new life. Until I had thrust my spear into the Moor I had not known if I was a warrior. Now I knew and I embraced it for it was in my veins. I was meant for war!

Chapter 3

A campaigning army is neither neat nor orderly and we spread out on the roads which wound south towards Toledo. There the Taifa who held power were the Dhū al-Nūnids and their Emir was al-Ma'mun. Alfonso had told me that Toledo would be hard to take and, as Rodrigo was riding with us, he listened and absorbed that information. It was how he accumulated such a vast knowledge of Spain and the Moors that some thought he was an academic rather than a warrior. While Rodrigo loved to read and did so voraciously, he was also a good listener. While he listened and I drifted in and out of the conversation, I was learning about my new horse. Berber was a slightly smaller horse than Sunflower but he had been bred for war. He had powerful shoulders and responded well to every touch of the reins. I was still new to riding but the more I rode Berber the better I became and it would help me when I came to ride Killer. I was taking a risk for I did not know him well yet but the road south was a good proving ground for we were the vanguard. If the enemy were waiting for us then we would be the first to find them and I would learn more about Berber.

I heard Alfonso talk of the city that was Toledo, "It is perched atop a hill and that means that you would need siege engines and war machines to break down their walls. All the while your horses would need food and the grazing would soon be gone. Fetching cartloads of fodder for horses takes forever. I do not think that King Ferdinand will risk a siege. He will attack and take smaller places which do not require siege engines."

"So, Alfonso the Armiger, why does the King do this?"

Alfonso was patient; I knew that better than any because I had often tried and tested his patience. He smiled, "You know when you spar with Will here?" He nodded. "You sometimes try to make a winning blow but often you probe for a weakness or a gap you can exploit. So does the King. He will try to take smaller places. Some he will take and we will all be richer for that. Others he will not and he will store that information. All the time he weakens our enemies and our men live off the Taifa of Toledo, we eat their food and our horses graze on their grass. His ultimate aim would be to make it a vassal for then it would pay tribute to Castile."

"Thank you, Armiger, that is most useful and I wish that my father had explained it to me. It seems that I cannot impress him, no matter how much I try."

When Alfonso did not try to justify Don Diego, I knew that he thought the same as Rodrigo. The conversations between father and son were cursory at best.

When we had marched to the battle, we had been close to home but now we were in the lands ruled by the Dhū al-Nūnids and, as such, we took more precautions against ambush. The horsemen formed two columns on either side of the foot soldiers. This time the archers and crossbows were present for we were going to attack and threaten the lands around the capital of the Taifa, Toledo. You cannot force a fortress with a horse!

Prince Sancho was young but the times in which we lived meant that the young learned quickly to be men or they died. I had been just six years old when I had followed Alfonso to chase down Moorish raiders. All I had to do was to hold the horses and, to be honest, the small knife I had was more likely to injure me than to wound a Moor. Although they were much older than I had been when I first went to war it would be the same with Prince Sancho and Rodrigo except, they would not be horse holders. I could see, as we rode, that Rodrigo was desperate to be closer to his grandfather and the Prince. He wanted to learn from them. He had an appetite for knowledge. I was no leader and I would follow orders my whole life. Lord Lain was the mentor of the Prince and the heir to the throne would be like a sponge soaking up knowledge. Rodrigo had to make do with Alfonso and his men.

After two days of travelling south, the front of the column stopped on a high piece of ground overlooking a small valley with a trickle of a river running along the bottom, hidden from the town by trees. We had reached a Moorish settlement although I knew not where we were; it was just a small and nameless town but it had

a wall around it and was defended. I daresay
Alfonso knew it for he had campaigned with my
father before they had joined Don Diego. As I
said, I was no leader and all I was concerned
about was food, drink and a bed. It soon became
obvious that they would not be forthcoming for
Alfonso was sent for by Don Diego who,
himself, had been summoned to the head of the
column by his father and the Prince. Rodrigo
came with us. The Prince and his advisers were
sheltered by the handful of trees while the rest
baked in the hot sun. The warriors in the town
would know that there were mailed men at the
top of the hill but they would have no idea of
numbers. The vast snake that was our army was
stretched out for over two miles and lay in the
dead ground below the top of the ridge.

Don Diego waved Alfonso forward but we
were all close enough to hear the words.
"Armiger, I want you to ride to their walls and
ascertain their numbers."

Alfonso gave nothing away to Don Diego
but I knew that the Armiger was annoyed for he
had a habit of clenching his fists and then
unclenching them when something displeased
him. I think it was a device to calm himself. I
recognised it as did the rest of the men but I was
sure that Don Diego would not for Alfonso's
face remained neutral.

"Yes lord." His eyes flicked to Lord Lain,
"Is that all, my lord?"

Rodrigo's grandfather chuckled, "Not quite,
Armiger; if you could annoy them enough to
make some chase you that would be useful for a

prisoner is needed. While you draw their attention, we will be surrounding their town." He nodded to his son.

Don Diego said, "Take my banner from Sancho here."

Alfonso took it and gave it to me. I felt proud for I would be carrying a banner and that was only done by the bravest of the brave. "Thank you, my lord!"

Alfonso turned in his saddle. "Iago, you and Ramon, flank William. Raymond, next to me and the rest of you behind the standard." He kicked his horse in the flanks and we made our way down the road. It was a Roman one and was cobbled. When we were out of earshot he said, "Be ready to turn and run and, Will, you are in the greatest of danger. Are you wearing the new mail hauberk you took from the Moor?"

My heart sank and, shaking my head, I said, "It is on Sunflower."

He said, shortly, "From now on wear it until we reach the safety of Vivar!"

I suddenly felt less confident and somewhat naked. I looked at the others. They had all benefitted from the battle and all wore mail; all except for me. I was lucky that I did not need to worry about my shield, it was strapped to my arm and I could still hold the standard. If I was a better horseman then I could use it as a second weapon but I was too inexperienced. It took me all my time to control Berber!

Iago said, quietly, "If they send arrows, as I expect them to, then pull the shield and standard before your face. Protect yourself and we will watch out for you."

Ramon said, "Aye, he should have sent Sancho."

"But he was wounded!" I know not why I defended Sancho. He was not a pleasant man and took pleasure in demeaning me.

Ramon shook his head, "It was a scratch. Sancho does not like to go to war."

"But he is Don Diego's squire!" In those days I thought a squire was someone of importance and it was only later I learned that they were little more than glorified servants.

"And he just waits for the day he is knighted and is given a parcel of land. Then he will go to war no more!"

Alfonso shouted, "Ladies! Shut up!"

Iago and Ramon chuckled and Iago said, quietly, "And the Armiger is less than happy too." He patted Berber's head. "We may get to see if this Moorish horse has a fast turn of speed today!"

As soon as we began to descend the hill the gates had been slammed shut. I guessed that Prince Sancho had already sent men to race around the town and seal it off but I could not see them and if I could not then neither could the defenders. The walls did not look high but they were made of stone or perhaps mud. I could not differentiate yet for we were too far away. That it was Moorish was soon obvious for they had one tower which dominated the wall and the gates looked very solid. I saw men on the walls. Moors were known to be good with bows and

javelins and they had boy slingers and a
slingshot could fell a man easily. I wore a coif
on my head and my arming cap, as well as my
father's helmet, but the Moors were accurate
enough to aim for my face, my hands or my
legs! My hide jerkin and metal plates might
protect my body but I could still be permanently
hurt. I felt my stomach begin to knot. I was
afraid. I had not been afraid when I had charged
for I had been in the second rank and then the
battle had been in my blood, besides I had filled
my head with questions. This was different as
this would be a slow and steady approach and
we would not be expecting to fight, besides
which we had no weapons to hurt those on the
walls.

Alfonso rode as slowly as we dared for the
town was in the process of being surrounded and
he wanted the attention of the town on our
pathetically small number of men. I was
estimating the closing distance as we
approached. I was desperate to know the range
of the Moorish arrows sent from the fighting
platform of the wall which went around town. I
could not bring myself to ask. The arrow which
was sent in our direction not only answered my
unspoken question, it did so directly, for it came
at me. Iago's earlier words saved me. As I saw
the missile leave the bow, I held the shield
before me, trusting that my helmet would protect
the top of my head and that my shield would
stop an arrow from hitting my face, neck or
chest. I braced myself for the slam of the steel
barb and the pain which would follow. There

was a crack for the arrow hit my shield and it penetrated through the boards. Had it been aimed in the middle then I would have had an arrow stuck in my left arm.

"Halt!"

I was aware that Ramon and Iago nudged their horses so that we became one enormous target but their shields were ready to protect me. I felt somewhat safer although if they had sent a shower of arrows then there would have been little that any of us could have done about it.

Alfonso did not turn but he said, "Are you hurt, Will?"

"No, but there is a hole in my shield!"

"Better your shield than your body. That was a warning arrow. I will speak to them and buy more time for the Prince."

I knew that Alfonso spoke some Arabic and he jabbered off words that I did not understand. There was no reply and so he shouted a second time. This time there was an answer and Alfonso said, "Turn quickly and let us race back to Don Diego. They have given us to the count of twenty and then we are fair game!"

I needed no urging and I turned Berber and dug in my heels. He was a lively horse and Iago warned, "Just canter. If you gallop it looks like we fear them."

"And we do not?"

He laughed, "Not in this lifetime and in the next one I shall be in heaven where there will be no heathen Muslims!"

The arrows never came for we moved out of range too quickly although not quickly enough for me! When we reached the Prince and Lord Lain, they ignored us and waited for Alfonso to give his report, "I hope I bought you enough time, Prince Sancho, but I could not risk these men and I did not manage to annoy them enough to send men after us."

The Prince nodded, "You did well and that should be enough time. You asked for their surrender?"

"I did. I told them that King Ferdinand was on his way and now was the time to seek terms."

Prince Sancho looked impressed, "Don Diego, you have a good Armiger. Thank you." He looked at me, "And thank you, too, Redbeard! I can see there is more to you than meets the eye."

I handed the standard to Sancho. After what I had been told about him, I viewed him in a different light. He said neither thank you nor commented on what we had done. He looked through me as though I was invisible. I saw now that there were warriors and those who played at warrior. I hoped that Rodrigo was not like his father and his father's squire. I did not think he would turn out like that but I was young.

We took our position again and Rodrigo said, "Were you frightened, Will?"

"I was wetting myself but I dared not move. I have learned a valuable lesson. If you have mail then wear it!"

He nodded but I could see that he was not thinking about me. "The Prince and my grandfather were clever. They used the smallest number of men to fix the enemy's attention and

now this town is ours! This might be a lesson
well learned for the future."

I shook my head, "We have surrounded it,
that is all."

"And we have done so with a huge army.
They will have no stores laid in and are not
ready for a siege. This will end in negotiations."
He waved a hand at the fields around the town.
"There is grazing for our horses and crops which
they can eat. The Moors will not be happy that
we eat their food. They fight or surrender. It is
that simple.

Remarkably he was right. We pitched camp
in a huge circle around the town and, as we were
the vanguard, we had the best position, which
was close to Prince Sancho and his camp. King
Ferdinand joined his son and Lord Lain and we
were privy to their conversation as our tents
were just behind theirs. We had lit our fires and
begun to cook a couple of sheep we had
managed to take while the camp was being set
up. No one complained that we had plundered
before the command was given. I was desperate
to see the damage to my shield but as the
youngest member of the retinue, I had to work
the hardest. Rodrigo actually helped me
although, as he later told me, that was because
he wished to be close enough to the King's fire
to hear their words; he was cunning. I was given
the task of gutting and skinning the two sheep. I
had done the job many times before and I had an
excellent skinning knife. I had not bought it;
when we had captured some cattle thieves, I had

taken it from the body of one killed by Alfonso. Rodrigo watched me as I completed my task.

"Your life is more interesting than mine, William, although I suspect that if I swapped, I would find I had lost more than I would have gained."

I laughed, "And there you would have it. It is I who have to dig the latrines and then fill them. I am given the task of watering and feeding the horses. That will change as I move up the retinue but until I am Armiger, my life will be one of uphill struggles."

"When I am lord, I will have you as Armiger."

"And Alfonso, you do not wish him?"

"He is my father's Armiger. I will choose my own man. I will choose all of the men who will fight for me. I want men who are loyal to me. I would have Alfonso but he has served my father for too long and his loyalties lie there. Besides I want younger men with me when I ride this land and free it from the King's enemies." I admired his confidence.

Once I had skinned and gutted the animals, I began to butcher them. I had lived with my shield brothers long enough to know how they liked their meat and when I handed the carcasses to Iago, he nodded his approval. "If you ever give up soldiering then become a butcher for you have the knack of it! Now you can see to your shield!"

Rodrigo had already taken the place on the log which was closest to the King's fire and he was listening intently without appearing to do so. I took the shield and, after breaking off the head and the shaft, took out the arrow. The narrow head had entered close to the joints of two boards and the shaft had filled the hole. The shaft and flight I threw into the fire for I had no use for them but the head was metal and I kept it. There was just one small piece of arrow shaft remaining in the shield and I was going to punch it out when I realised that it fitted perfectly. I took out the knife I used to take stones from horse's hooves. It had a blunt tip but the edge was sharp and I sawed the two ends smooth. As I looked at the shield, I realised that when we found a weaponsmith I could borrow his anvil and beat the arrowhead flat. I would be able to use it to cover the break in the shield. Satisfied I laid down the shield.

Ramon brought over a skin of wine and two beakers. He frowned when he saw Rodrigo. It was unusual for a noble to sit with common men and I knew he worried that one of us would have to go short. I smiled, "I will share my wine with Rodrigo, Ramon."

Rodrigo realised his mistake and began to rise, "I am sorry, I…"

Ramon shook his head, "You stay here, young sir, I dare say that Juan can always steal another one!" He handed me the two beakers and the skin. "Keep a place for me; this is a good spot."

I poured the wine and Rodrigo said, "My father has good men."

I nodded and drank the wine. I could not tell a good wine from a bad one. This one tasted fine, "They are the best."

He drank and when he wrinkled his nose, I then knew that this wine was not the best! He lowered his voice, "But they are not appreciated, I can see that." He shook his head, "I have some years before I can be knighted and begin to be the warrior of my dreams!"

"You dream of being a warrior?"

He nodded and began to tell me how he saw his future. I could tell that he read a great deal for he spoke of famous warriors and heroes from the past. I had only heard of one or two of them. He was single-minded and knew what he had to do to become one. "That is why I am pleased that you will train me. We are close enough in age that we can be friends and yet you have a strength and a skill which I admire. My first goal is to become Will Redbeard in body and skill."

I was flattered, "Then that just needs hard work and I know that you are not afraid of hard work."

I was too hungry and engrossed in the stew to listen to the words from the fire behind, but Rodrigo both ate and listened. When he left us to return to his father's tent, he looked pleased. He spoke to me before he left to tell me what he had heard, "King Ferdinand will not waste men attacking this town. He will demand tribute. That is clever for a man only chooses to fight when he knows that he can win!"

For a youth who had never yet drawn his
sword in anger, Rodrigo de Vivar had a great
deal of confidence.

The King knew his business and the town
paid tribute and fed us. They also promised not
to send men to fight Castile for a year. We
repeated the feat four more times before we
returned to our homes as autumn approached
and the campaigning season was over. It had
been a highly successful summer campaign. As
an army, we had lost but a handful of men and
we had received large quantities of tribute, not to
mention the loot we had found for ourselves.
Rodrigo was appalled when none of our retinue
received the rewards he thought we were due.
The tribute went to the King, the princes, the
senior lords and even lesser lords like Don
Diego, his father. As his father did not share the
coin with us it caused an argument between
father and son and that resulted in a beating for
Rodrigo. He bore it like a man but that day saw
a change in him. He obeyed his father in all
things and he did all that was asked of him but
he spent an increasing amount of time with me
and with the retinue. The gap which had existed
between father and son became a gulf as wide as
an ocean. More than that he began to train every
hour of the day that he was not engaged in his
studies and would have trained long into the
night.

The situation continued for a year like that
until one of his father's relatives was sent to us.
Álvar Fáñez was a little younger than Rodrigo.
His father had been a poorer relative of Don

Diego. Like me, his mother had died when he was young and his father had died during the winter as a result of a fever. Don Diego was forced to take him in by Lord Lain. The fact that his father resented the imposition made Rodrigo warm to his cousin even more and they became firm friends. Rodrigo took to calling him, Minaya, little brother. Of course, for me, it meant even more work for I had two of them to train and Minaya was even less skilled than Rodrigo had been. I was lucky that Alfonso was sympathetic to me and I had less training to do with the rest of the men.

While Rodrigo had his studies then I worked with Minaya. I had learned from some of the mistakes I had made with Rodrigo and it was, I confess, much easier. As he was not the lord's son, I also used him for my own purposes. He got on with Killer as well as Babieca and he was able to help school them. It meant that six months after Minaya had arrived, Rodrigo and I were able to try out our horses wearing mail and helmets. As it was Rodrigo's birthday, we decided to hold a mounted bout. We had never done so before. I do not think his father would have even bothered watching us had not Lord Lain, Peyre Pringos and Prince Sancho arrived unexpectedly.

Once again, I had an audience when I did not want one. Alfonso and the rest of the men were also watching. I saw money exchanging hands and knew that they were gambling. I knew that some would bet on the outcome while others would bet that I would fall from my

horse. Having watched both horses train I knew
that Babieca was cleverer than Killer; Rodrigo
had chosen well, but Killer was stronger. We
were using practice swords as we did not wish
for an injury. I had worn the mail many times
now and I felt comfortable in it. Rodrigo's was a
present from his mother and he was unused to it.
I knew that the Prince and the others had come
for a show and so I determined to give them one.

We rode at each other with blunted lances.
Rodrigo's missed my head while I went for the
easier blow to the shield. My lance shattered and
Rodrigo almost fell from the saddle but he was a
good rider and when he retained his saddle there
was applause and cheers for him from his
godfather and grandfather. We drew swords.
Rodrigo was stronger but I had the ability to
fight for longer as some days I had spent six
hours at the pel. I let Rodrigo waste his energy
on my shield. I knew how to deflect a blow. I
had shown Rodrigo but he was not yet as skilled.
When he began to tire, I then used Killer's
power to force back the tiring Babieca and
rained blows on Rodrigo's shield. I was actually
relieved when Lord Lain rode into the arena to
halt the battle.

"Enough, you two have shown me that the
future of León is in good hands with warriors
like you. Diego, you should be proud of your
son and your man at arms!"

"I am." Don Diego's paucity of words was
riddled with insincerity; he sounded bored.

Everyone noticed. I saw Prince Sancho
frown and then he spurred his horse and rode to

speak with us. He smiled and spoke to Rodrigo's grandfather, "With your permission, Lord Lain, I would take these two youths to my home and help them train for I see potential here. In time, young Rodrigo may be ready to be knighted. What say you?"

Lord Lain nodded, "I am happy but what do you think, Rodrigo?" It was interesting that they assiduously ignored Don Diego.

Rodrigo nodded, "I would say I was happy for William Redbeard had made me what I am but I could not go without my cousin, Álvar Fáñez."

Prince Sancho shrugged and Lord Lain said, "That might prove to be for the best. His estate is managed by my son but that coin might help to keep the three of them, eh, Prince Sancho?"

"Perfect!"

He might have thought it perfect but Don Diego did not and darkness spread across his face.

For myself, I wondered at the change. I would no longer be the youngest of the retinue and I would not have to train with the men and then train Minaya and Rodrigo. On the other hand, I would be leaving my home, my foster mother and my foster father. I was leaving my world and going to a royal palace. Would I cope?

Chapter 4

"Of course, you will cope for you are your father's son, in addition to which Maria and I have brought you up as though you were our own son and we have taught you well." Alfonso's words belied the obvious sadness in his eyes and Maria was weeping and stroking my hand. "And we shall have more room now that you are gone!"

Maria shook her head and began to sob, "I care not! I have nursed this one since his mother died and he is the only child I shall ever have and now he is taken from us!"

Alfonso and Maria had grown closer over the last few years as Alfonso's grey hairs had begun to proliferate. He said, quietly, "He was never yours to keep; we have had him for a short time and we should be grateful for that."

"You are right." She nodded and stood on her tiptoes to kiss my cheek, "I will go and pack his war bag."

When she had gone Alfonso said, "I will see you again for Don Diego will be called upon to serve with Prince Sancho and his father." I knew he was right but did not expect it to happen for Don Diego would seek any excuse he could not to go to war. "Of course, I may well have to find a replacement for you." It was then I saw something in his eyes I had not seen before and when he spoke, I heard the same pride. "Will, you are a good warrior! Had you stayed then you

would have been Armiger above all of the others
for you have something no one else does, you
have the blood of the Northman and fighting is
in your veins. I have seen you shed blood but a
couple of times and yet you did so very easily. I
was older than you when I slew my first Moor
and he did not die as swiftly as yours. You have
a skill and you should use it."

"Thank you, but whatever natural skill I
have had you have honed and I am grateful. I
shall miss you, Maria, and all the rest of my
shield brothers."

"We are your past and you should think of
your own future. When the two youths are
knighted look to yourself. You already have
money and you have the opportunity to earn
more with Rodrigo and his cousin. You can do
something I could never do, you could buy some
land and become a hidalgo!"

"A lord?" I shook my head, "I doubt that!"

"Your father dreamed of such a thing. He
spoke of how his people had wandered the seas
looking for land and when they found
Normandy, they each became a lord. His family
would have stayed there, you know, but your
grandfather fell out with the Duke. You could
fulfil your father's dream."

Until that moment I had never really
thought about the reason my father had left the
north to become a sword for hire. Perhaps
Alfonso was right; as much as I enjoyed the
company of the two cousins, I would become
redundant someday and I had to think of myself.

I found it hard to say goodbye to Iago and the others and they to me. I suppose I was like a younger brother to them all and I knew that I had never complained nor objected to any of the labours they had set me which had endeared me to them, for all men like a trier. Of course, they bantered and mocked me, that was their way and they did it as much with each other, yet I knew that any of us would have laid down our lives for our shield brothers. I would miss that. I was going to a different place and a different world where I would be a virtual servant to Rodrigo. I would sleep with servants and not with warriors. I suppose that was what I feared the most.

Iago handed me a dagger in a beautifully made scabbard, "We took this at Atapuerca and we wish you to have it. The weapon is a boot dagger and the scabbard fits inside the top of your buskins. It is a handy weapon to have." I clasped his forearm and the tightness of the grip was a measure of the mutual affection. "I know not how they will cope with having a peasant like you living in the palace! Just remember to piss in the pot in the corner and not in the bed!" They all laughed and we resumed the banter.

"Aye, and when I see you remember to doff your forelocks!"

Ramon growled, "That will be the day!" He clasped my arm, "Take care, little brother!"

Alfonso said, "You had better come for Rodrigo and Minaya are already in the courtyard."

Juan said, "I will fetch your horses. Go and say goodbye to Maria. She will find this hard to bear."

Maria was in my quarters. The leather bags which contained all that I owned was packed. Maria's face still coursed with tears. Alfonso said, quietly, "I will take these to your horses."

When he had gone I held the nearest person to a mother I had ever known, "Thank you, mother, for you have raised me well and know that I will love you and pray to God to keep you safe until the end of my days."

That brought forth a succession of sobs and I just held her until they subsided. She still had her head buried in my chest and her words seemed to speak directly to my heart, "My own child died and I buried him in a field for he was not baptised. I have tried, with you, to make you the best that I could and I believe I have done so. You have something he would never have had, you have the chance for advancement and I will watch, from afar, as you climb."

I knew that she could not read and I could barely write, despite all the best efforts of Rodrigo so written communication would not happen. "I dare say that Master Rodrigo will send news home to his family and I will try to do so for you."

"Will!"

Alfonso's commanding voice was not to be ignored. I reached into my leather purse which hung on my belt and took out one of the gold coins Lord Lain had given to me. "Here, this is for you!"

Her eyes widened, "I could not…"

Folding her hand about the coin I said, "But you must for to refuse would break my heart. Buy yourself something Maria; make it frivolous and for you. Then, when you look at it, you will think of me."

"I need nothing to make me think of you, Will, for you are ever in my heart."

"Will!"

Kissing her on the top of the head I said, "I must go."

When I emerged, I saw that they had packed my war gear on Berber's back. Rodrigo and Minaya were already mounted while Rodrigo's mother, Donna Isabella, was weeping and was being comforted by her ladies but of Don Diego, there was no sign. Alfonso and the other men were joking with Rodrigo for all were fond of him. He had not behaved as a normal lord would have done, he had spoken kindly and respectfully to them and showed a genuine interest in them. As I stepped into the light, they all cheered, jeered and catcalled me. Had Don Diego been present then they would have remained silent. I saw the estate priest, Brother Pedro, blessing the two young nobles. We were leaving to live in Navarre for Prince Sancho had been charged with ridding the land of all those who opposed his father. Such a task would put our lives at risk and Lady Isabella was ensuring that her only son was blessed.

I mounted Killer and as usual, he bridled, snorted and stamped. Iago and the others laughed. Iago said, "I tell you what, Armiger, I believe I will still win that bet. Master Rodrigo, I beg you to let me know when this black beast kills Red Will here and then I will make coin."

Rodrigo laughed, "Aye, I will do but I have to tell you, Iago, that William here is getting better each day. By the time we reach Pamplona, he will have mastered his mount!" He waved to the four servants who were bringing the horses with the belongings of the two nobles and they mounted their sumpters. "And now we had best go for we have many miles to travel before we reach our first bed for the night! Farewell mother, know that I will write!" That brought floods of tears and, waving, we left the only place I had ever known as home. I did not know that we were embarking on a journey that would take us as far to the south as Algeciras and as far west as Valencia. That day, as we left, I thought that the journey to Pamplona would be as far as I would go!

The first part of our journey was towards the valley of the Ebro and we would still be in the land of Castile. As such we would be safe and Rodrigo's position meant that we would be able to have lodgings in religious houses. The first one was at the Ermita del Santo Christo del Barrio. We were guaranteed a good welcome as Lady Isabella's father had endowed it with a bequest in his will. We still had thirty miles to travel and this would be the longest that Rodrigo and I would have ridden our war horses.

It was unusual to use war horses to travel for they were normally reserved for war but it was part of their schooling. The thirty miles would bend them both to our will, or so I hoped. I planned on making Killer my packhorse on the next leg of the journey. I had decided to show this fierce beast that I was his master. While we rode, Rodrigo showed that he, too, had been thinking about our horses. "We need to buy palfreys. This journey will be good for the schooling of our war horses but we should not do it too often for we need them hungry for war and not weary of walking."

As the newest member of our trio and the only one without a warhorse, Minaya had also thought about it. "Having horses is one thing but will we be able to stable them in the royal stables? It is we who are invited to Prince Sancho's palace and not our horses."

"You forget, cousin, that one reason why my father did not come to say farewell is that he is still angry at losing your income. Until you are of an age Prince Sancho is paid to house and feed us. I assume that means our horses. You look at everything as half empty! This jug is more than half full! Let us enjoy life! You will have money enough to buy a warhorse."

As we rode, I glanced behind us at the four servants we had brought with us. One of them, Pablo, would be staying on as Rodrigo's body servant. He was the most reliable of the four. I knew the others a little for our rooms had been close to the servant's quarters and I had eaten with them. Two of them I neither liked nor trusted. I had no doubt that they would do their job until they reached Pamplona but I doubted that all three would return to Viva! This was the frontier. Closer to León there was safety, law and order, but closer to the Taifa of Zaragoza, and the Kingdoms of Catalonia and Aragon, there was a great deal of unrest and brigandry. The mountains were a haven for bandit chiefs who could rule a fiefdom and exploit the conflict between Christian and Moor. I would not rest easy until we reached Pamplona, Rodrigo might think that the jug was half full but I was of the same mind as Minaya.

The Ermita was a haven. The cells we were given were small and the servants had to sleep with the horses but we would be safe, dry and we were fed although it was plainer fare than Rodrigo and his cousin were accustomed to. I did not mind it. In the servants' quarters, the best food we ate was that which had been left over from the master's table and whatever Alfonso had hunted and given to Maria to cook. When I told Rodrigo, he was appalled. Minaya laughed, "Cousin, you are so well-read and yet you are so naïve! Do you think your father would waste coins feeding servants when they will be quite happy with bean stew and rye bread?"

Rodrigo's education had begun when I had started to train him, it began to accelerate when Minaya confirmed my words.

As we left the Ermita the Canon warned us of the dangers we might face for we were due to pass through the wild mountains and, until we reached Miranda del Ebro, we would be at risk from bandits and brigands. It was a journey of little more than fifteen miles yet it would take all day for us to reach it and when we did, we would almost be in Navarre. With that warning ringing in our ears, we rode, but we travelled prepared for war.

Once again Rodrigo showed his naivety for he wondered why the local lords did not rid themselves of the danger posed by these bandits. They both looked to me for answers as I was older than they were. My father and Alfonso worked in the borderlands for many years and Alfonso had told me of the problem. I gave them my version of what I had learned, "Some men are not good enough as warriors and cannot endure the life on a manor and so they are either dismissed or they leave. They gravitate to those places where they have little work to do and can prey on the weak and on travellers. These men understand the ways of the lords they have left and know how to avoid their traps and ambushes. Eventually, the lords give up hunting them as they, personally, are not harmed by the bandits. Lords, kings and princes are immune from such attacks. Three youths and their servants, with mail, weapons and two warhorses are perfect fodder for them. We will need to keep a weather eye open for ambush and enemies."

The road climbed and twisted through the foothills. There might be the odd shepherd but other than that the only people we would meet would be fellow travellers. We met one such group at the top of the col. It was an Aragonese lord, Fernandez del Esplus, on his way to León to seek a favour from the King. He had with him a retinue of fourteen mailed and armed men. The col was a natural place to rest for it came at the top of a long and steady climb in both directions. He did not know us but the red cloaks worn by Rodrigo and Álvar told him that they were the sons of nobles and he took me to be their bodyguard. As such he ignored me.

"You two are a little young to be travelling with just one guard in this land."

"Yes, my lord, we are on our way to join the household of Prince Sancho in Pamplona."

"Ah, now I understand; then I would make good time on this next section for there are forests and woods in which bandits lurk and make shelter well before dark. Had I more men I would send some to escort you but I fear that these hills are safe for no one." He mounted his horse, "May God be with you."

It had been many months since the battle of Atapuerca. In that time Rodrigo and Álvar had improved dramatically but I was still uncertain if they could handle themselves in a fight with cutthroats and bandits. Our warhorses alone would draw them like flies. We mounted and I turned in the saddle. Pablo was reliable and I spoke to him, "We may be attacked, Pablo. Ensure that you have weapons and protect the bags, horses and our war gear."

He glanced at the two unreliable ones, Juan and Raoul, "Aye Will, and you will protect the young master?"

"You know that I shall do so." Stephen was the quiet one and I was unsure how he would react if we were attacked. I nudged my horse next to Rodrigo and Álvar, "You two, don your coifs and helmets. Fasten your shields on your arms."

"That will make us look foolish!"

"Better foolish than dead, Álvar. I have been hit by an arrow and but for my shield, I would still be carrying the wound. Humour me!" I fastened my own shield on my arm. Now it had the arrow, beaten thinly and cut up into four pieces attached to the front. I had not finished armouring my shield yet but I had to find more metal and then work it. The four pieces I had attached already had been the work of four nights!

Rodrigo asked as we headed down the road towards the now threatening stand of trees, "You think that we might be attacked?"

"Let us say that if we prepare to be attacked and know what we should do if we are then we have a greater chance of survival. I am hoping that the bandits will not notice that we have mail beneath our cloaks and surcoats. It will give us a chance. The other advantage we have is that while we will be mounted, they will be on foot. If we are attacked then listen for my command, obey it and follow me."

"Your command?"

Rodrigo said, grimly, "Aye, Minaya, for he is our captain until we win our spurs. I have seen him fight and I trust his judgement."

Álvar had not asked the question to be awkward, that was not his way, he just liked order and to know where he stood. Rodrigo's answer satisfied him.

I left my helmet on my cantle as I wanted to use my eyes and ears. If danger came it was the work of a moment to don it. I also relied on Killer. He was an unpredictable animal in many ways but he did not like strangers. When Lord Fernandez had been speaking to us, he was stamping the ground and snorting angrily until they left. If he smelled someone new, he would react, I knew not how for it had not happened yet when I had been riding him. The road twisted down and through the trees but I saw that it was a thin stand and if anyone was hiding there then they would be easily seen. Killer just trotted down the road seemingly unconcerned and I took that as a good sign. Behind me, I could almost smell the tension as Rodrigo and Álvar peered into the trees. I had dismissed the thin stand and was peering into the distance where, further ahead, I saw a forest proper. Close to the edge of the forest the trees looked to be growing closer together and there was undergrowth but I knew that further back there would be less growth and men could move around more easily. For some reason, my eye was drawn to the right-hand side of the road. It was instinct that made me do so and when I involuntarily pulled Killer's head to the right, he responded by whinnying and snorting. He had sensed something. I could see nothing but I took action in any case.

"Draw your weapons! Pablo, watch the horses!"

"Aye, Will!"

I hoped that if there were ambushers ahead then the sight of the three of us drawing our weapons might deter them. When Killer became agitated then I knew there were bandits ahead and I had just dug my heels into his sides when I saw the arrow fly from the forest. I had not obeyed my own orders and my helmet hung upon my cantle. With my sword in one hand and shield in the other, I could not don it. I flicked the shield around to block the arrow but it soared over my right shoulder. I could not see the bowman but I knew the approximate position and when three more arrows were sent in my direction, I was able to hold my shield before me and two hit it while another missed. I learned, that day, that a moving man is a harder target to hit. My instinctive move had put the archer off.

"Charge!"

All of Alfonso's training came rushing back to me. I lowered my head to make a smaller target and held my sword behind me. I used my knees to guide Killer and, as I peered over the edge of my small shield, I was rewarded by the sight of the bandits, or four of them at least, hiding in the eaves of the forest. Three held bows and one a wood axe. I had not looked around since the first arrow but I could hear hooves behind me and I assumed that Rodrigo and Álvar were close behind and obeying orders. That I was the target of the bows pleased me for the two nobles would be safer. As I drew to within twenty paces of the four men two arrows hit my shield which now resembled a hedgehog and one slammed into my shoulder. The

Moorish mail was good and, aided by my cloak and surcoat, prevented the arrow from penetrating into my flesh but it still hurt and I felt as though someone had smacked a piece of wood into my shoulder!

There might have been other bandits but Alfonso had taught me to fight those before me and so I had four enemies to deal with. My sudden charge had put them off and one bowman fled. The other two were each attempting to nock an arrow and so the most dangerous enemy was the man with the wood axe. I leaned from the saddle to the right while pushing Killer's head to safety as the axe was swung wildly at my horse. My movement upset the axeman's aim and my sword ripped across his middle while his axe missed my coifed head by less than a handspan. I felt the air as the blade scythed over me. Pulling myself up made Killer veer to the right and I was able to bring my sword down and split open the head of the bowman whose arrow was nocked but not yet released. I reined in Killer for the other two bowmen had fled and then I whirled around my horse. I saw that Rodrigo and Álvar were chasing through the woods after, I presumed, the other bandits and I shouted, "Fall back! That is a command!"

I saw that Pablo had dismounted and was tending to the leg of Stephen who had been hit by an arrow. I saw that Pablo's saddle also had two arrows sticking in it which told me he had been lucky. Juan and Raoul were cowering behind their horses. They had shown their true worth. There was a dying archer lying in the eaves of the forest. I dismounted and led a skittish Killer towards him. Killer did not like the smell of blood. The bowman had been slashed by a sword and it had sliced open his face from his cheek to his jaw. That would not have killed him but it would have disfigured him for life. The wound which would kill him was the sword thrust to his middle. The contents of his stomach lay before him.

Just then Rodrigo and Álvar returned. I saw that Álvar was holding his right arm and his sword was sheathed. Rodrigo's sword was bloodied and this told me that Rodrigo had used his weapon on the dying man. I looked down at the wounded man. "You are a dead man." He nodded for he had no mouth with which to answer. "Would you have the warrior's death?" He nodded. I took my sword and held it in two hands. I placed the tip on his Adam's apple and he closed his eyes, "May God forgive you your sins!" I drove the blade down and he juddered before dying.

Álvar looked away but Rodrigo never took his eyes from the dead bowman.

Sheathing my sword, I turned, "How is Stephen?"

Pablo smiled with relief, "It missed the bone, William Redbeard, and he can continue but he will need to see a healer. I used wine to clean it."

"And the animals?"

"They are well."

91

"Good, Juan and Raoul, you are piss poor guards. Let us see if you can collect weapons. Search the three dead men and bring their purses and weapons to me and I want their full purses, too. If you try to cheat me then you will pay a heavy price!"

Juan was the more unpleasant of the two and the more aggressive. He was shorter and broader than I was. They emerged from behind their horses and Juan said, belligerently, "We obey Don Diego and not a Norman wretch! Search them yourself if you want their purses. We will not do your dirty work for you."

The look on his face told me that he thought I would back off but I had been trained by Alfonso and in two strides I reached him and hit him with my fist so hard that I broke his nose and dislodged teeth. He fell to the ground and did not move. I grabbed Raoul by the tunic and pulled his face towards me, "Do you wish to argue?"

He was shaking so much that he could barely speak. "No, Will Redbeard, I will do this! We are all friends here!"

He hurried off and I reached down and took the dagger from Juan's belt. He would not face me but he might try to stab me in the back. "Rodrigo, watch Raoul and make sure that he does not run and that he brings back the full purses."

He was grinning, "Aye, Will!"

I turned to Álvar, "And you, come and show me the wrist you hurt."

His mouth dropped open, "How…?"

"You tried to stab the bowman and you were riding hard. When the sword was ripped upwards it hurt your wrist. Is it broken?"

"I know not."

"Waggle the fingers." He did so. "Then it is sprained. Pablo, bind Master Álvar's wrist."

Pablo and Stephen were happy for they had survived and they had agreed with my treatment of Juan and Raoul as they did not like the bullies either. "Aye, Will Redbeard."

Raoul came back. He had the axe and three daggers. I took the daggers and put them and Juan's in my saddlebags. I saw Juan beginning to stir. Taking the purses from Raoul, I said, "Put the axe on the sumpter and then wake your friend. He has a decision to make."

While he went off, I looked at the sky. If we hurried then we could make Miranda del Ebro by dark. I went to Álvar and while Pablo tended him, I drew his sword. "What the…"

"I borrow it only." Raoul went to Juan and pulled him to his feet. I strode towards them with the sword in my hand. I saw both of them recoil; they were cowards. I flicked the sword in the air and held it by the blade. I proffered it. "Take it!" Juan did so and I smiled when I saw that it was heavier than he had thought. "You have two choices; fight me here and now or kiss the hilt and swear by Almighty God that you will obey every command I give from now on." I drew my sword and he dropped to his knees. There was no way that he was going to fight me.

"I swear, by Almighty God, that I will obey every order you give, William Redbeard!" His voice was breaking with fear. He was a bully and a coward.

I took the sword from him and returning to a grinning Álvar, sheathed it for him. "Now we have wasted enough time, we ride. Pablo you and the others lead. We will follow in case the bandits return." I did not think for one moment that they would but I was taking no chances.

They say that when men are born they are a piece of clay and they are shaped by their parents, their friends and the events around them. In El Cid's case, I do not think that his parents had that much effect upon him but the incident with the bandits on the road to Miranda del Ebro did. He took in everything that had happened and he learned from it. The three of us rode at the rear of our small column. "Did you expect Juan to refuse to obey your order?"

"Let me answer your question with a question. The four servants your father sent with us, what is your opinion of them?"

"Juan and Raoul are the worst servants on the estate and my mother will not have them in the hall. Stephen is pleasant enough but he cannot be entrusted with complex tasks. Pablo is the best of them."

"And you asked for him to come, did you not?" He nodded. "Then, like me, you mistrusted them. I expected them to run sometime between here and Pamplona. I still do. I was looking for an opportunity to show them what would happen if they did. Have the courage of your convictions, both of you, and believe in yourselves." He continued with questions about the decisions I had made and how we had defeated the bandits. It was all part of his education for a warrior could learn much from such small skirmishes.

We made the town before dark and we went to the Hidalgo to report the attack. He was concerned for we were going to serve with Prince Sancho and this might reflect badly upon him. "Did you bury them?"

I shook my head, "I have two young charges to escort to Prince Sancho and they are my priority." Taking out the purses I said, "Here are the bandits' purses. I thought that they could be given to the poor of your town."

He gave me a strange look, "You are not a noble."

I shook my head, "I am a man at arms and I train these two warriors."

"Then I will take them for the poor and offer you the hospitality of my home. Your servants can sleep in the stable. The one who is wounded will be tended by my priest."

And so that night I dined at a lord's table although it was to Rodrigo and Álvar that he spoke. Lord Philippe was no fool. If the three of us were to be housed with Prince Sancho then it could do him no harm to be pleasant to us. I learned much by simply listening. I learned that Catalonia had ambitions to take over the Taifa of Zaragoza and that King Ramiro of Aragon harboured similar ambitions. It explained why Prince Sancho had come to Navarre for he was an astute man and his presence would warn the two kings of the consequences of such an action.

I also learned that the Emir of Zaragoza, al-Muqtadir, was considered a weak leader and that Taifa was ready to be taken over.

We left the next morning and this time we were advised the roads to take and the places we should stay. Two days later we arrived at Pamplona and became part of the court of Prince Sancho. It was a world in which we would live for the next sixteen years. Indeed, I thought that I would end my days in that court as did Rodrigo and Álvar. That was not meant to be but then courts were the most treacherous places in the world and it should have come as no surprise to us that murder could stalk its halls!

Chapter 5

As I expected I was relegated to the warrior hall when I arrived. Rodrigo and Álvar were the sons of nobles and, as such, were to be accommodated close to the Prince. There were other young warriors, too, but none as young as Rodrigo and his cousin. The Prince had made the same offer to others whose fathers were nobles and this was the beginning of the cadre of young nobles who would follow Prince Sancho and latterly, Rodrigo! When we arrived, Rodrigo took charge and he sent back Juan and Raoul to Vivar for Stephen was not yet fit to travel. He sent a letter with them. The fact that they never arrived came as no surprise to me but was a lesson in human nature for Rodrigo. He thought to give them a chance but a leopard does not change its spots. It worked out well for Stephen and Pablo were both able to serve the two young nobles and their lives were easier than they would have been with Don Diego. Mine, on the other hand, was not. I was new and, in the eyes of the men who followed the Prince and the Navarrese in the castle, I was a country bumpkin. It was worse than being the youngest man in the retinue of Don Diego.

The one-armed Gascon warrior, Roger of Bordeaux, who was in command of the warrior hall, was a pleasant man and I had no issue with him. Nor did I with the men who served Prince Sancho for, in the main, they ignored me. It was a handful of men who followed a lord who was a friend of Prince Alfonso, Don Gonzalo Ordóñez, who held lands in Aragon that caused dissension. When we were introduced to the man he looked down his nose at us and I could see that he liked neither me nor the two lordlings I followed. It may have been that Prince Sancho liked us and, for whatever reason, he wished to be closer to the Prince than any; I never found out the true reason. I found it strange that he was close to Prince Alfonso who was still at his father's court.

The cause of their dislike of me was immaterial for from the moment the six of them swaggered into the barracks, I was a marked man. That they had no honour was marked by the fact that they first asked Roger of Bordeaux whom I served before they began to abuse me. Once they learned that I was a servant of the son of a minor noble with neither money nor power and, worse, that Rodrigo appeared to be close to the Prince, they began their attempt to intimidate me.

"What is that smell?"

"I know not, let me sniff the air. Ah yes, someone has come from Vivar."

"They say that all of those who come from Vivar are sired by the same father. It makes them simple and docile. Perhaps this is one such."

"Or perhaps some pig has wandered in from the field. It is hard to tell the difference."

I looked up at them for this would result in violence and I was weighing up the best one to take down. None were as big as me despite the fact that they were, largely, older. One, however, had a long stiletto dagger in the top of his boot. He would be the most treacherous. One was broad and looked to be the strongest of the six but looked slow while the others had nothing about them that was remarkable. I returned to the unpacking of my war gear which I did carefully and meticulously.

One, the broad, slow one, poked me in the back, "Hey you, peasant, we are talking to you."

I stood and turned. As soon as I stood, the fact that I was taller than they were, came as a complete surprise to them and I saw hands go to weapons. I kept my hands on my hips with my feet balanced.

Roger of Bordeaux shouted, "Keep your hands from your weapons!" He was telling me that although I was on my own, he would not allow them to gang up on me and use their arms and weapons.

I smiled when I spoke and used a calm tone. It was the voice I used to calm Killer but this time I was lulling them. "I am sorry for I thought you were addressing another, you see I was not born in Vivar. But, if the insults are meant for me, then I say that you," I poked him in the chest, "are a liar," I poked him again, "and a fool and I do not enjoy being poked in the back so do not do so again." I did not turn away for I saw the broad, slow one take in what I had said and then his eyes told me that he intended to rush me. I used my left hand to deflect his flailing fist and then hit him so hard on the side of the head with my right hand that he collapsed in a heap at my feet. Iago had taught me the blow. There was a possibility that the man could die although I guessed he had a thick skull and a small brain and so he might survive. I turned him over with my foot and I smiled, "Are there any more insults? For, if not, I would take a walk into town and enjoy the cleaner, fresher air, there."

I pointedly put my sword onto my belt. They wore swords but mine was broader and longer than theirs. I tucked a dagger into the back of my belt and said to Roger of Bordeaux, "Is my war gear safe here? Or should I ask Prince Sancho if he has a safe chest I can use?"

Roger laughed, "Aye, it is safe here as are you, my friend." As I passed him, he said, quietly, "But, on the street, I am not so certain."

I asked, equally quietly, "And when does the town watch begin their duties?"

"An hour before sunset." He looked at the sky through the open door and smiled for he knew the reason for my question, "Soon."

"And that is all that I ask." Most towns, especially a large one like this, had a town watch. Although not professional, they were men of the town who were given a duty to protect their streets during the hours of darkness, they would be led by one of the members of the garrison. He would probably be an older soldier, someone like Roger of Bordeaux. As I headed out of the castle gates, I spied the surcoats and shields of the town watch. They were dark green with a crown atop a shield with a white lion. It was a distinctive livery. They were assembling before they began their patrol of the town and its walls and I walked boldly up to them, "Excuse me, I am new to the town and you look like honest men, where is the best place to get some decent food and pay a fair price for a good beaker of wine?"

As I expected that began a debate amongst the watch for each man would have his favourite drinking place. Their sergeant, a greybeard, silenced them by saying, "Listen, my friend, go to the Leg of Lamb and say that Ramon sent you. It is just the other side of the main square. Who knows, I may call in and see if my advice was correct."

"Well if it is, sir, then I will buy you a beaker too," I spoke politely and deferentially. I was a stranger in a strange town and I needed to make friends quickly.

I nodded and strolled slowly away for I was not in danger, yet! It was still light and if I was any judge then the ones who wished to do me harm would wait until night fell. I was not worried that they would kill me. Roger of Bordeaux would report that I had been threatened but they might wish to hurt me and small injuries and wounds could put me in danger on the battlefield. I had my leather jerkin studded with metal as well as my sword and dagger. I hoped that I could handle them but I missed my shield brothers. Iago, Ramon, Juan and the others would have backed me up!

Maria and Alfonso had brought me up well and I knew that politeness and a ready smile won people over quickly. So it was that when I mentioned the town watch to the landlord and asked what he recommended then I was treated like an honoured guest. When I added that I was in Pamplona to train young warriors for the Prince then I was doubly welcome. The food was good and I liked the wine. More, I learned a great deal about the politics of Navarre. I discovered that the King had not been popular and his son was a different proposition. The fact that he was with King Ferdinand seemed to meet with the approval of the Navarrese. I learned about Aragon and its ambitious King Ramiro. After I had heard the words of the men in the inn, I saw him as a greater threat than any dissenting Navarrese nobles. I had just finished my food and was contemplating asking for the bill when four of my tormentors entered. That told me that the remaining two would be waiting in ambush. The landlord frowned for the four did not simply enter, they almost burst in.

Rather than the effusive welcome I had received the landlord said, "What is this? What is this? I pray you act like gentlemen or I shall be forced to call the watch. This is a good inn and we do not suffer rowdiness."

It was then that I saw the sly one with the knife was the leader and he smiled the false smile which comes from the mouth and not the eyes, "Sorry, landlord, we were just eager to sample your food."

They sat at a table where they could watch me and the door. If I attempted to leave, they could quickly follow me. I was in no hurry. The talks I had had with Rodrigo had taught me much about strategy and I knew that keeping an enemy off guard and not doing what they expected could often reap a good harvest. I waited until they had ordered their food and it had arrived before I said, "Landlord the bill." It was reasonable and I gave him a healthy tip; it brought a beaming smile. As I stood to leave, I saw the dilemma I had created. They could not leave yet for they had neither eaten the food nor paid the bill and they glowered and glared at me. I kept my hand on my sword as I left the inn.

There was no one waiting outside the door and I peered into the dark. They would be waiting on the far side in the shadows of the street which led to the castle. It meant that I had the empty square to cross. During the day there were stalls under the covered precinct but now it was frequented with doxies and whores plying their trade before the watch moved them on. The fact that I could hear them as they called out prices told me that the watch had not yet come to the square. I walked across the middle of the large open area and when I sensed a movement to my right I knew where the watchers lay in wait; it was close to the street I would have to take to get to the castle. I calculated, as I walked, that they would attempt to attack me when I left the square and headed up the narrow street leading to my potential sanctuary. I had measured it when I had walked down to the inn and it was not long, just a hundred paces, but they would have clubs and other weapons to beat me senseless. One of the men had to be the broad, slow one and the other would be the young man who was almost the same height as me but he was slender of frame. He would use a blade while broad and slow would use a cudgel or a club. The broad and slow one would have vengeance on his mind for I had both hurt and humiliated him in front of his friends. I heard a commotion behind me and knew that the other four had either paid their bill or fled. I ran quickly, for it would be easier to defeat two and then try to face the other four rather than all six at the same time. As I left the square, I realised I had caught them by surprise. Skulking in the shadows they had barely turned to come at me and I balled my fist as I neared them. The taller of the two came at me and I swung my fist at him. He expected it to hit his head as I had done with broad and slow and his hands came up protectively. When I hit his middle, I knocked all the wind from him and he fell to the floor trying to suck in air, unsuccessfully.

Broad and slow was wary for I had smacked him hard once before. He held his hands before him and came at me slowly. Hearing noises from the square I ran at him and, as I pulled back my right fist to strike him, I also aimed my running, right leg. I hit him between his legs with my right boot for he was watching my fist and he fell as though poleaxed when I connected with his groin. Although I ran and only had the last few paces to reach the castle, the time it had

104

taken to defeat two of them had allowed the other four to close with me and I heard swords being drawn from scabbards. I turned and drew my sword and dagger. I backed myself against a wall. There were four of them but they would find it harder to get at me if they could not get around me.

"Sneaky little bastard, aren't you?" The sly one with a knife held a short sword and his knife. The others had short swords too.

"So, it takes four of you to defeat one man from Vivar! How sad, I had expected better!"

"It matters not for when we finish with you, we will have your manhood and you will never work again!" That told me what they intended and it would involve taking my fingers or my hand. Although he was talking, I was watching his eyes and I saw him lunge at me while he spoke, with the short sword held in his left hand. It was a feint for his knife was in his right and he was a knife man. I shifted my shoulder and, keeping my sword ready to parry the others I lunged with my own dagger. He thought I was like his friend, big and slow. I was not and my hand darted out so quickly that it was a blur. He contributed to his own downfall for he brought his own knife across and all he succeeded in doing was deflecting my dagger to tear into his cheek. He almost lost an eye. He screamed in rage and that was the signal for the others to attack. I swung my sword at head height while I used my dagger to stop the sly one from gutting me. I felt a short sword slide across my left thigh and blood began to drip. While I still had the strength, I used the last of the power in my left leg and, lifting it, stamped on the knee of the advancing man. The knee bent the way it was not supposed to and he fell screaming.

Even though I had had the best of it until then things might have gone awry had not Ramon, the leader of the Town Watch appeared. "Put up your weapons or die!"

I was more than happy to sheathe mine but, as I did so, sly one rammed his knife at my middle. I would have died had I not been wearing my leather jerkin for the knife slid along the side of the metal studs. As it was that one blow cost him his life for Ramon rammed his sword through him and it came out near his shoulder, "Treacherous dog!" He whirled and held his sword at the throat of the next man. "Move, I beg you, for then I will slay you and the other killers!" Their weapons clattered to the cobbles and he said, to me, "Friend, are you alright?"

I nodded. "Aye but I have a wound for my troubles."

The landlord ran across the square and pointed accusingly at the five men who survived, "Four of these came in to do this man harm and followed him when he left. Six to one! They should be hanged!"

A crowd had gathered and, like all crowds, joined in with the murderous murmurings. Ramon held up his hand, "We will have justice. I will take these to the Hidalgo for his judgement." He held out his arm, "Come friend and lean on me. There must be a healer in the castle!"

What began with a hearing before the Castellan ended with the Prince and Don Gonzalo Ordóñez as well as other senior knights passing judgement. I said little for Ramon, the landlord and Roger of Bordeaux did all the talking for me. When he had heard all Prince Sancho said, "You have been wronged and I give you the opportunity to pass judgement. For their attempted murder they could be hanged. Is that your wish?"

I shook my head, "I wish no man to be hanged, so long as they swear not to seek revenge then I am content."

The Prince glared at Don Gonzalo Ordóñez, "And that was as well-spoken as you and your men could expect. You will pay a fine of forty silver pieces for the trouble you have caused the watch and give William Redbeard five gold pieces as compensation. More, you will leave Navarre and return home. That is my decree. Do you wish to challenge it?"

Although he was fuming, I am not sure if it was with me, the Prince or his own men, the knight nodded and bowed. He left the next day. I thought that it was over but it was not and it was like the throwing of a stone into a pond. The ripples went on and on, seemingly forever. When we met again, I was a man grown and Rodrigo was El Campeador but, again, I am ahead of myself in the telling of this tale.

I had not planned on telling Rodrigo of the fight but that was a forlorn hope. The word of the fight and the death had spread like wildfire in the Great Hall. Don Gonzalo Ordóñez's early departure prompted the gossip and it was fuelled by the servants who had been privy to it. I suspect it would have been hard to hide the fact that I had a long cut down my thigh. It had required stitches and I was glad that the healer knew his business. The wound was the first which had required a healer and, in my life ahead, there would be many more.

I was ready in the outer bailey with the weapons we would use to train when Rodrigo came directly over to me and concern was written large all over his face. "You were wounded?"

"It was a scratch!"

Álvar stepped back to look at me, "You took on six of them and yet you have but one wound!"

"Come, it is in the past and we forget it. We have work to do here first."

Rodrigo shook his head, "I need to understand everything for we are bound, Will Redbeard, and what hurts you affects me."

I could see that we would get nowhere until I told them and so I did. When I had finished Rodrigo rubbed his chin, "Odds mean nothing then."

"I do not understand."

He smiled at me, "I am comparing your fight with six men to a battle. I can see now that the same principle could be applied to a battle. You were outnumbered and yet you eliminated the threat of a third of your enemy and then went after the most powerful of the rest. That is a strategy I could emulate."

I shook my head, "You forget the intervention of the town watch."

"I forget nothing, Will. Your words tell me that a man should never fight alone. He should have around him men whom he can trust. He should know that when his back is to the wall there will be others who will watch it for him. I want you two with me in each battle that I fight."

Álvar laughed, "Cousin, you are not even a knight!"

"But one day I will be and then I will lead my own retinue but you two will ever be at the heart of it."

I handed them the training swords, "That may be your view now, Rodrigo, but when you are a great lord then Old Redbeard will be relegated to holding your palfrey while you and Álvar, here, charge off to glory." I was thinking of Roger of Bordeaux and Ramon of the Town Watch. Neither were nobles and their positions were a projection of my future.

His face became serious, "My body may change and I may attain a higher position but what will never change, I swear, is the heart and mind in this body. I will never leave either of you behind. Where I go so do you."

As El Cid, he was true to his word and was the only man I ever knew who kept his word no matter what.

This was not the time of campaigning and winter was soon upon us. If I thought the winters in Castile were severe the ones in Navarre were worse. We trained each day but some days it was so cold and the snow flew so thickly that it was hard to see. I would have cancelled the training as did every other warrior in the castle but Rodrigo insisted that we continue. One particularly cold and wet day saw us finish almost blue from the cold and the wet. Our weapons, helmets and mail would need much work and Álvar questioned his cousin. "I cannot see what we have gained, Rodrigo. We will now spend hours cleaning our weapons. Pablo and Stephen will be up all night scouring our mail and helmets and for what?"

He was shaking with the cold and had suffered as much if not more than we but he said, firmly, "We now know that no matter how bad the weather then we can fight. When it is cold and wet enough to chill a man's bones to death, others will think of retiring or fleeing but we will know that we can endure. It is as simple as that."

That was Rodrigo who was the complete warrior. He had dedicated himself to being the best knight that he could and every waking moment was spent on preparing himself to be that warrior.

We had been in Pamplona for two months when a letter came from Vivar. It was from Rodrigo's mother. The missive inquired after his health and asked why the servants had not returned. I had learned to read but did not do it well and Rodrigo read the letter aloud. When he reached that part he looked up, "You said that

Juan and Raoul would not return. How did you know that and I did not?"

I shrugged, "I know men. It is how I knew that the men of Don Gonzalo Ordóñez would try to hurt me. You see good in men, Rodrigo, but I see into their hearts and I know who has the bad seed."

"Then I will ask you to do that when we go to war."

When he had finished reading the letter I asked, "You said, go to war; is there one planned?"

He and Álvar nodded, "The purpose of the Prince's presence here in Pamplona is now clear, Will. When spring comes, he will head south to Zaragoza where he intends to make al-Muqtadir a vassal of his father. He has said we can come with him. We are not to fight but to help guard the royal standard of Castile. It is a great honour."

"Then we have much to do for so far we have worked on fighting whilst our feet are firmly on the ground. I can tell you that fighting from the back of a horse is a different prospect altogether."

By the time February arrived, we had used our time well. Álvar had bought a good horse although it was not a warhorse like Babieca or Killer but it was a horse bred and trained for war; he used his inheritance wisely. Álvar could read well and Rodrigo had encouraged him to read the histories from the Greek and Roman writers. He called his horse, Ajax. Both of them tried to have me give Killer a nobler name. I laughed and shook my head, "The beast now responds to his name. He may not like it but he knows it. I would not begin to teach him a new one. I gave him the name and I will have to live with it."

Life in Pamplona was different for me compared with Rodrigo and Álvar. Occasionally they would not train as they would be hunting or hawking with the Prince. When the days became short, they would enjoy feasts and entertainments in the Great Hall. My enemies had gone but that did not mean that I was in the midst of friends. There were few Castilians other than the lords and knights. I was still resented but left alone and that isolation would have been hard to bear but for the one-armed warrior, Roger. We had some things in common, not least the fact that neither of us was a Spaniard. He had heard of my father for my father had great skill on the battlefield and while such deeds often go unnoticed by the high and the mighty, princes and kings, warriors for the working day and swords for hire appreciate them. We soon had a bond and rapport and, after Roger taught me to play chess, we would spend hours at the board. Chess is a game of the mind with long silences while moves are planned. Sometimes those silences would be broken as Roger or I would reveal, sometimes inadvertently, facts about ourselves.

He learned no secrets from me for I had none, as yet, to reveal, I was as an open book with little written on the pages. He did, however, deduce things from my words. "I can see that you will not be like your father, Will."

"What do you mean?"

"I can see that you have great skill; probably as much as your father and you could make a better living serving a lord who wishes to have a good swordsman leading his warriors, but you will not choose that road. You will follow this Rodrigo de Vivar."

My fingers hovered above the knight I was about to move, "I am still young and there is a whole future unlived before me. You cannot know."

He smiled, "I know. You have been here for some months and I have observed you. Your whole life revolves around Rodrigo. If he allowed you to be his chamberlain then you would never leave his side. You play chess with an old one-armed warrior because there is little else to do and your mind needs occupation." I flushed for he was right and he laughed, "I hit the mark. Now do you pick up the knight or is there another move you wish to make?"

For my part, I learned that Roger had never married and he had followed his lord his whole life. When he had lost his left arm at a battle with the Moors his lord had deserted him. Giving him ten silver pieces and a horse, he had abandoned the man who had followed him for twenty years. I knew, when Roger told me that tale, it was not for sympathy, that was not his way, it was as a warning that Rodrigo could abandon me in the future. Roger had been lucky. An old comrade who had become a knight for services on the battlefield had secured Roger a place as a gatekeeper in his master's castle. From there he had carved out a niche for himself which culminated in this last post in Pamplona. He knew he would end his days there.

"I have become wiser, Will, I used to piss away the money I earned on ale and whores. Losing my arm made me plan for the future. When I am thrown away again, as I know I shall be, I have coin and I will buy myself a little inn here in Pamplona and end my days playing chess with my customers and serving only those that I like!"

It seemed to me a wise plan and I wondered if I should do something similar. Thanks to Alfonso, I had a chest of coins which had been the wages I had been paid before Atapuerca. Added to the coins I had been given I was not poor. I would not waste my money and I would let it grow for the lean years which might lie ahead.

Chapter 6

We went to war in March when the weather had barely improved and there was dampness in the air. My leg had healed but the wet weather made it ache. Once I had known we would go to war, I had ensured that the three of us could fight as one from the backs of horses. We would be heading south to the Taifa of Zaragoza where Prince Sancho would begin to make life so hard for the Emir of Zaragoza, al-Muqtadir, that he would sue for peace and accept the overlordship of Castile. I learned this partly from Rodrigo but also from Roger. He was the one who explained how it would be done as we spoke the night before we left the castle of Pamplona.

"The Prince will take a relatively small army. His horsemen and knights are Castilian and they will be the sword he uses to defeat the enemy. The men of Navarre will be on foot. They will be the spears, bows, slings and crossbows. Navarre will be the shield he uses against the Muslim attacks. Your Prince Sancho is a clever man for he knows that al-Muqtadir is no warrior. He likes poetry and a rich life added to that he has just fought a war with Toledo and his army is weaker than it was. Castile is in the ascendancy and Prince Sancho will garner accolades from all when he succeeds in subjugating a Moorish Taifa." Roger was a clever man and when we left Navarre, I missed him and his conversations. For a brief time, he had replaced Alfonso. Both represented the father I had barely known and so desperately wished to emulate.

Pablo and Stephen had to come to war too and they would be with the baggage train where they would watch our spare horses and our war gear. All five of us would share a tent. This was in direct contrast to most of those born of noble blood who had tents while their men made crude hovels. In the chill March air of the Castilian mountains that was not a pleasant experience. As the bulk of our army moved on foot then our pace was slow and we rarely made more than fifteen miles a day and we faced an eighty-mile trek along the Ebro Valley. Of course, speed was not important as Prince Sancho intended to take each town along the way for that way we would be fed at the enemy's expense and we could take what little treasure the towns held. Although our army was relatively small, less than eight thousand, we would outnumber the garrisons of each of the towns. As I had discovered on my first siege, the mere presence of a large force frequently encouraged a town to surrender. Roger of Bordeaux, who had participated in a number of sieges, told me that a protracted siege cost the attackers men and when the town was taken then retribution was bloody.

We travelled just fifty miles in ten days but we had taken many towns without a sword being removed from its scabbard. Each time we took one, messengers from the captured town were sent to Zaragoza to urge the Emir to talk. That he wished to was apparent very soon, for we always received a reply which was not belligerent, but there was a faction which wished to fight us and that became obvious as we travelled down the valley. The closer we came to Zaragoza the more resistance we met.

There was no battle, as such, but there were attempts at a skirmish or an ambush. The line of march was thus; a body of mercenary horse archers led the way. They were Berbers and, as such, were expendable. Then came the household knights of Prince Sancho. There were twenty of them. The Prince and young nobles like Rodrigo and Álvar followed. Behind the Prince came another body of knights and then the foot soldiers followed by the baggage train and finally the last conroi of knights. Light horsemen rode along the flanks of the Prince and the standard as an extra layer of protection. The Prince allowed a different youth, each day, to carry his banner. Prince Sancho was a good general and a wise one. Rodrigo learned more from him than any man, save perhaps myself, and I am modest enough to know that he learned more from books and from innate ability, but Prince Sancho gave him a model for a leader and he emulated that model. The young nobles were honoured and thrilled to carry the banner of Castile. It also meant that the young nobles who rode with the Prince were regularly rotated and he came to know them. That was a vital skill to learn and Rodrigo learned it well. Prince Sancho knew the character, strengths and weaknesses of each and every one of the young knights who would become the core of his successful army.

It just so happened that it was Álvar's turn
to carry the standard so that Rodrigo and I
flanked him as he rode behind the Prince and his
two squires. The ambush we encountered was a
clever one. We were descending into the valley
of the Aragón River where a narrow bridge
afforded us a crossing. The bridge naturally
narrowed our column so that the outriders who
had flanked both us and the Prince were no
longer there. They had ridden ahead to secure
the southern bank. In addition, the Berber scouts
had not done as they ought and they had not
checked beneath the bridge. When the Prince
and his standard were in the very centre of the
bridge a triple attack took place. Horse archers
emerged and sent arrow after arrow into our
Berber mercenaries at the head of the column
who broke and fled. As soon as they did so then
their attackers fled too. The vanguard of knights
recklessly pursued them and exposed the sons of
the nobles who rode before the Prince. At
exactly the same time more Moorish horsemen
attacked the baggage train and the horn was
sounded summoning help. The knights who
followed us were not yet on the bridge and they
turned to ride to the aid of the baggage train. It
left the Prince isolated and protected only by
young untried warriors who were yet to be
knighted. Apart from his squires, the most
experienced warrior was me.

I knew that the Prince and the standard were
not equally important, the Prince was more
valuable, but the standard was guarded by my
charges and when the Moorish warriors

swarmed up the side of the bridge, the third of the attacks, my initial thought was for Álvar and Rodrigo. I had drawn my sword when our Berbers were attacked so that as the first black head appeared next to me, I swung almost without thinking and my broadsword hacked into his head making him fall and knock the next Moor into the river. It seemed I was the only one with his wits about him for even the Prince seemed stunned by the unfortunate turn of events. I shouted, "Protect the Prince and the standard!"

It was only then that swords were drawn and the Prince shouted, "Sound the recall!"

The horn was sounded by the Prince's squire. Rodrigo blocked the blow from the curved sword of the Moor who clambered up his side of the bridge with his shield and swept his sword around to hack into the Moor's neck. With luck, Álvar would have nothing to do for the two of us could protect him. My early reaction to the threat meant I was able to slice at fingers, arms and unprotected heads as they tried to gain the parapet. The young warrior next to Prince Sancho's squire had been slow to draw his sword and he paid the price as a javelin was rammed under his armpit to emerge through his collar bone on the other side. Raymond, the squire on my side, found himself fighting two men.

I said, "Álvar, ware right!" and urged Killer forward into the space vacated by the dead warrior. Killer's hooves did half of my job for me and clattered into the skull of one of the

119

many Moors. Raymond slew a second and I brought my sword over to hack through the arm of another climbing Moor. I could see, across the river, the first of the Prince's household knights as they raced back to help their prince. The Moors at the southern end of the bridge were already hacking and stabbing their way through the young warriors and their horses.

As I glanced to my left I saw, for the first time, the potential that was Rodrigo. I had not seen him in combat for when we had fought the bandits, I had had my own battle to fight. Now, as Raymond and I cleared our side of the bridge I saw the sheer power in Rodrigo's arm. All those hours at the pel had paid off. He was fighting just half-trained Moors but these were the fanatical ones and I saw one whose left arm Rodrigo had taken and he was still trying to fight. Rodrigo had to split the Moor's head asunder to stop him. Even though he was doing well, he was tiring and I wondered how long we would have to hold. In my case, I was not particularly tired but hacking through bone and metal helmets had taken its toll and my blade was becoming blunted. I smashed my sword across the face of one Moor and barely broke the skin with the edge. My powerful arm, however, broke his jaw and cracked his skull. He plunged to his death in the bloody, body filled river.

And then it was over for the household knights had ploughed into the back of the Moors trying to get at the Prince and we had eliminated all those who had hidden beneath the bridge. The bridge was clear and an angry Prince

Sancho shouted, "Get across this damned bridge and reform!"

As we rode across the bridge, I saw the flower of Castile lying dead, maimed or wounded. The ones at the fore had borne the brunt of the attack. They had been training to be warriors but were, obviously, not as ready as Rodrigo and Álvar. They might have been older but they had not been as well trained and that had made all the difference. The bridge had been a long one for it spanned two arms of the river and an island. Once on the other side, we halted and Prince Sancho looked at the dead Berber warriors. He shook his head and said, to no one in particular, "I have learned a lesson this day, no, I have learned many lessons, but one is that my scouts will now be my men and not mercenaries."

I thought that was a little unfair for most of the Berbers had died. I said nothing. I was not even a noble, I could not comment.

He turned to Rodrigo and Álvar, "You two did well and kept the banner safe! Well done!" I was ignored, as I had expected for I was not a noble and paid swords were expected to fight well.

Raymond, the squire, turned to me and said, quietly, "And even if the Prince does not recognise what you did know that I do, William Redbeard. You have a mighty arm and I am glad that you are on our side."

We buried our dead and flung the enemy into the river. We had managed to secure a pair of prisoners and they were fetched before the

Prince. Prince Sancho was angry and I wondered what he would do. He showed a cruel and ruthless side. He had the right hands of both of them chopped off and the stump sealed with fire and then sent them to Zaragoza with a message for the Emir. "If I lose one more warrior on my journey south then I will put the men of his city to the sword. The women and children will be sold into slavery and I will tear down every mosque that I find!" It was draconian, to say the least, but Prince Sancho was angry. He had lost twenty potential knights as well as many household knights. They were like Rodrigo and Álvar, young, callow and untried but he had hoped to build them into a cadre of men who would follow his banner.

I said that he had not noticed me but I was wrong for as we headed towards Zaragoza, he waved me forward to speak with him. "I understand that you did me great service again at the skirmish on the bridge, William Redbeard."

"I am here to serve, Prince Sancho."

"Nonetheless, you deserve a reward. However, that is not why I called you here to speak with me. Young Rodrigo and his cousin acquitted themselves well, better than most, and that, I believe, is down to your training. When we return to León I would have you train my other young warriors. I would have you as my Campi Doctor and I will pay you five silver pieces a week. What say you?" He must have sensed hesitation for he smiled and said, "You will still be Rodrigo's man!"

"Then I accept." The Prince and I were the same age. Both of us had been given responsibilities normally reserved for men who were older than we were. It was a sobering thought. I would have the raw clay of young warriors to mould and yet it was only a year or so ago that I was as they were. I had to thank Alfonso for all that I had learned. He had been a good teacher and, perhaps, I had been a quick learner. I had heard the term Campi Doctor when Rodrigo had read aloud sections from the books he studied. It was from the time of the Romans and was the man who trained soldiers and then offered advice on how they should be used in battle. Whilst I was happy to train, I knew that I had little experience, yet, of battlefields. It soon became obvious that Prince Sancho saw me as a trainer and not as an adviser. I was happy with that position.

The money I was to receive would be useful and, as we approached Zaragoza, I thought of the fortuitous circumstance of meeting Roger of Bordeaux. He had shown me a future I had not considered. What would I do when I was no longer a warrior? I was so engrossed in my thoughts that I did not speak for many miles. Álvar questioned Rodrigo about his bloody sword. None had come near Álvar and he had yet to slay an enemy. I knew that he was envious of his cousin. "Were you not afraid, cuz?"

"No, Minaya, and yet I thought I should have been for these were wild warriors and not bandits fleeing for their lives, but I saw you with the standard and the Prince before me and knew that I had to kill or the standard might have fallen."

"How did it feel when you sank the blade into flesh? Was it like when we gutted the deer?"

I stopped my musing and looked at Rodrigo. He shook his head, "I had not time to think for I knew that I had to strike and strike to kill. It was what Will taught us. Heed his lessons, Minaya, they will keep us alive."

The gates of the fabulous city of Zaragoza lay open as we approached. The Emir was no fool and the maimed men had told the Emir of the anger of the Prince of Castile. Most of the army camped outside but the knights and the young warriors I would train were allowed in and were quartered in the fantastic palace. Zaragoza was not a fortress although it could be easily defended. It was a white wonderland of beautiful buildings, fountains, churches and mosques. It felt as different from Pamplona and Burgos as Rome and a primitive hill village in the Pyrenees. Now that I had been elevated a little, I was part of the Prince's entourage. His steward, horse master, squires, priest, quartermaster and servants were all housed close to the Prince. His dozen or so closest household knights, since the bridge his bodyguards, were closer but it felt strange not to have the poorest quarters. Rodrigo and Álvar were housed with the survivors of the fight on the bridge. There were just eighteen of them and although we did not know it then, they would become the foundation of the knights who would eventually follow Rodrigo de Vivar. Their heroics on the bridge made them someone the others could aspire to be. That, of course, was in the future for Rodrigo was not even close to being a knight.

Al-Muqtadir was a gentle man and he was courteous. That he spoke Spanish told me much and showed me he was a diplomat. He was at pains to apologise to the Prince for the actions of those he called headstrong rebels who had acted without his knowledge. The Prince did not accept that, "Emir, a leader is responsible for the actions of those he leads. Once he abdicates that responsibility then he should also abdicate his throne!"

As a reward for their action on the bridge, Rodrigo and Álvar were present and they carried the standard of Castile once more. I saw Rodrigo looking on in admiration for the Prince who, although young, was showing a command of diplomacy that was impressive. It took just a morning for the negotiations to be concluded. Zaragoza would pay tribute to Castile and in return not only would Castile not attack Zaragoza, but the Kingdom would also fight to aid her new ally. It was Rodrigo who explained how clever that was.

"The only Christian states which might threaten them are Aragon and Catalonia. King Ferdinand would dearly love them to try for then he could make war on them and enlarge his hold on Christian Spain. It is more likely that another of the Taifa states will attempt to do so and that would also give Castile the chance to become a larger state. I am pleased that I was taken from Vivar. I had learned more in half a year than in all the time I lived at home."

I, too, was learning but then I knew little anyway and so I had much to learn.

We stayed a month although the army we had brought from Navarre was sent back to Pamplona. They cost money to keep in the field and there was no need for them. King Sancho Garcés and his mother, who was now regent, could return to Navarre once we reached King Ferdinand's court for Prince Sancho had scoured Navarre and Pamplona, in particular, of all those who were a threat to King Ferdinand. We had a longer wait in Zaragoza than we expected for although it was a rich place it took time for the Emir to collect the first of the tribute he would pay to Castile. I used the time well, for I would not begin my duties until we returned west, and I spent some of the coin I had accrued on some clothes which were more fitting for the life I was about to lead. The rough and ready clothes made by Maria were serviceable but if I was to dine, albeit occasionally, with Prince Sancho then I needed to dress appropriately. I also bought some good quality boots for they had fine bootmakers in Zaragoza. Rodrigo and Álvar did the same for the merchants of the town who were keen to stay on the good side of a potentially vengeful Christian army and the prices we paid were low.

Then we began the long and tortuous journey back to León. It was made harder for we had left Navarre in March and after the

campaign and the wait for the tribute almost two
months had passed. It was getting close to hot
summer and even though we were all mounted it
was a slow journey. The only consolation was
that we were housed and bedded on our journey
north and west. I was housed with the young
warriors I was to train and I began to get to
know them. The fact that I was an uncultured
peasant from the country might have been a
problem had not Rodrigo and Álvar been there
and the other young men seemed almost in awe
of the two of them. Even then Rodrigo had the
ability to draw good men to him. Of course, my
size and skills with weapons also intimidated the
young men. We had no chance to train as we
headed across Spain but I began to give some
order to their lives.

Hitherto, Rodrigo and Álvar apart, they had
had much freedom. They retired when they
wished as well as drinking as much as they
wanted. While on the road they had no order and
rode as though on an outing to visit a relative.
All of that changed once I took charge. I used
exactly the same methods which Alfonso had
used with me and I set a time when they would
retire and sleep. I had them do so once they had
prayed. After sleep, they rose, not when they
wished but half an hour before the rest of the
Prince's entourage so that they were dressed and
ready for the day before anyone else. Rodrigo
and Álvar were already used to it and the young
men soon adapted. They all had servants but I
had the young men saddle and groom their own
horses each morning before we rode. At first,

there was resentment until Rodrigo explained why. He told them that they needed to become as one with their mount and he told them of our journey through bandit country where our skills with horses had helped us. I also assigned places on our line of march and I rewarded good behaviour and the like by promoting them up through the column. The ones at the back, close to the servants, did not like the demotion and it was a way of encouraging good habits. The closer we came to León the more disciplined they became and even Prince Sancho noticed the change. As the towers and walls of his father's capital appeared in the distance and we stopped for our last halt before reaching home he spoke with me, "I can see that you are a good appointment, William. Already my future lions of León are taking shape. It is early days but we have peace, at least for a while, and you will have time." He pointed to the east of León. "I have an estate over there, outside of the city and that is where we will be based. I have, perforce, to spend much time at my father's court." He shook his head, "I would that I did not but I have two brothers and two sisters." He laughed, "You have brothers and sisters?"

"No, my lord."

"Then you are lucky. My father is hale and hearty yet already my siblings salivate over the division of his kingdom. I know that you will do so, but I would have you use every moment of daylight to hone my young cubs, so that when the time is right and they are lions I will have knights who fight the way that you and Rodrigo do. Then we shall see a single Kingdom of Spain."

Over the next years, I reflected upon those words. Prince Sancho and I were close in age, closer than he was to either his brothers or Rodrigo. That I was of low birth meant that I, alone, out of all those he knew, could have no aspirations to take what was his. I think he used me as a way to speak aloud his thoughts. I had not sworn an oath to him but it was in my blood to honour the unspoken bond between a lord and his most loyal of men, the men my grandfather would have called, hearth weru.

Chapter 7

Lion's Den, Prince Sancho's home, was some miles from the city and had a strong wall around it. The estate was a rambling sort of place which reflected its owner for Prince Sancho had his own ideas about what he wanted. Prince Sancho had not yet married for he liked the company of warriors and surrounded himself with the bravest and the best. I always thought that he would marry once he had established himself but he never did and his home reflected the philosophy of the world of war. The hall was functional and it was sparsely decorated and furnished. The only adornments were simple tapestries and wall hangings that depicted the scenes of great battles. He had already begun work, before he had left for Pamplona, on a hall for his, as he called them, cubs. It was barely finished by the time we arrived and that suited me for I was given command of it and its completion. His closest knights were housed with him in the hall. A separate building housed the servants and there was another building which was for the men who guarded the walls. They were the equivalent of Don Diego's men, the ones with whom I had served and learned my trade. I made a point of getting to know them for I was but one step away from them and my association with them helped me to keep my feet firmly on the ground. There were also plenty of stables as well as all the other buildings which a mighty lord might need.

However, what marked the estate as different from any other that I had ever seen was something Rodrigo told me was called a gyrus. He explained that it was something the Romans had used to train their horsemen. It was an area enclosed by a low fence and there was only one gate in and out. It was next to the other fenced off area where men could practise fighting on foot. The gyrus was, however, where we did the real work. It was where I trained the cubs to fight together and I confess that much of what we did came from the Romans but it came through Rodrigo. He was still a voracious reader and while my lessons had continued and I could read, I could not read Latin. He read and told me what the Romans did. I copied their ideas for they seemed to me a sound foundation and any Empire which lasted as long as that one had must have had much to commend it. Alfonso had taught me the basics of riding and I knew how to fight on the back of a horse but the Romans had training methods that were new to me. I had the young warriors learn to ride boot to boot. At Atapuerca I had seen the advantage of presenting a solid, mailed front for in that lay self-protection and it was also a formation which, when training was complete, could move around a battlefield together. Had I tried this with Alfonso and the men with whom I had trained then it would have been doomed to failure for they were older and this was a newer idea. The young warriors I trained thought it was normal and took to it easily. It made my task easier.

Each day had a similar routine: the first hours of the day, before they had even breakfasted, were spent in prayer and then lessons from the estate's priest, Father Bartholomew, on all that they would need to become a knight and a lord. I used those hours to prepare the gyrus and to devise the exercises for the day as well as to continue to work with Killer and make us of one mind, mine. Once we had eaten then we began by spending the morning at the pel. Once their shoulders burned and they tired then they would use the quintain. After a short break for food, the afternoon was spent in making them work as a unit. They learned to interchange their lines so that weary men at the fore could be replaced by fresher men from the second rank without disrupting the combat. Once they managed to do that then I could see the potential begin to be realised. They learned to obey the sound of the horn instantly. I had seen, at Atapuerca and on the bridge, the dangers of men losing their heads. The horn controlled them.

Rodrigo and I grew closer; physically he was becoming a man and that helped but I was changing too. I was almost full-grown but my mind was expanding as I learned more from him. Each evening, after the meal and while the servants cleaned up, most of the young warriors would play chess and other such games. One or two diced while others practised a musical instrument, for playing and singing were seen as ways to woo a fair maid and were part of the training to be a knight. Even Álvar joined the others but Rodrigo and I would sit and talk war.

One night, a few months after we had arrived, I heard raucous laughter from the table. When Rodrigo frowned at the noise, I realised that I was not doing my job for he saw the laughter of his peers as a distraction and it was not, it was an opportunity not to be missed. I stood, "Rodrigo, as much as I enjoy these talks and games of chess with you, for they give me the education I never had, it is not fair on you. You are a young man and you should enjoy the company of your peers. Besides, these are the men you will lead into battle and you should know them, inside and out."

"Me, lead them?"

I laughed, "It is as plain as the nose on your face, Rodrigo. They all look to you, even Álvar and they know that you are the best of them."

He was always a modest man and he shook his head, "The best?"

"I am the campi doctor and I see each of you work out each day. You are never beaten even though sometimes you are easy on your opponents for you do not wish to humiliate them. It will not be long before you can best me, too, although that may take a year or so more for you have growing to do. While you get to know them better, I will visit with the men of the garrison and I will speak to them. You can get to know your warriors and their minds."

And so, I had less time with Rodrigo and that was sad but we still found moments to talk of war. More importantly, he and the other cubs became as one. Instead of instructing me, each night, he instructed them. The very nature of the group meant that he also laughed more and engaged in horseplay and that, too, was a good thing.

The time I spent in the garrison hall was not wasted. They were all good men but none could compare with Iago and the others I had left in Vivar. However, I got on with them and they had heard of my reputation. Warriors, true warriors, like to be around those who they think are better than they are and they try to emulate them. I learned much from the garrison as they had all served with King Ferdinand at his palace in León and understood, better than I, the politics of the court. Once they knew I was discreet then they revealed all about the politics and intrigues of the royal family. Sancho was the best of the King's children. Perhaps that was because he was the eldest boy, I know not. Prince Alfonso and Princess Urraca, his elder sister, were very close and they did not like Prince Sancho. His other brother and sister, Prince Garcia and Princess Elvira were younger and had, as yet, not formed their alliances. From what I was told it was a nest of vipers and there was little love lost between any of the children.

The oldest of the garrison was Pedro and he had served King Ferdinand when he had been just a Count. "The King had problems with his brothers and half-brothers. He has dealt with most of them but one still remains: Ramiro of Aragon is his half-brother. If Prince Sancho has his wits about him, he would have his brothers killed now and then he will inherit all of his father's kingdom instead of a division which will undo the King's work!"

I was still naïve and I did not think that such a thing could even be contemplated. I would learn! However, it explained Prince Sancho's frequent visits to his father's court. That he did not enjoy it was obvious when he returned but he had to go to see who was plotting against whom. It was a world of intrigue and treachery and the princesses appeared as bad as the princes.

The next year or so passed without us going to war and that enabled me to increase the skill of the young warriors. Prince Sancho sought out others to replace the ones who had died on the bridge and the task I had thought was a short one proved to go on longer than I had expected. I did not mind for as Rodrigo's skill increased so did his ability to help me to train the younger warriors.

I learned more about Rodrigo in that time. He rarely had letters from home and when they did come, they were from his mother. It was as though his father resented him. I was the only one who appeared to notice this but then I knew him better than any, including Álvar. Each time a missive came from his mother and there was no message from his father he threw himself into his training and, while normally unbeatable, he would be so good that his opponents lasted but a few strokes. It would have been inspiring to watch if I did not know the cause. After one such bout when he almost hammered Alphonso, son of Diego, into the ground, I took him to one side.

"Rodrigo, that was a fearsome fight." He nodded. "And you came close to breaking Alphonso's arm."

He looked at me in horror. He had been so involved in the fight that he had not noticed, "I did not, did I?"

"Aye, you did. And I know the reason: it was the lack of a letter from your father." He was suddenly vulnerable and looked at me in terror as though I had entered his soul. I spoke quietly, "I understand it but you cannot allow those feelings to affect the way you fight. You need to be detached."

He looked terrified as realisation set in, "You must tell me when I am like that for I did not see it myself!"

I shook my head, "If you are to be the warrior I think hides within you, then you must win this battle with yourself and emerge victorious. Control yourself."

"You are right and I am in great danger of becoming that which I do not wish to be. I will pray to God that he heals my troubled mind for a man should be close to his father."

I said nothing because he was right and yet he would never have that degree of attachment to his father. He began to search for someone who could take the place of his father. At first, he tried to make it me but when I realised what he was doing I stopped him. I was flattered but it was not healthy. He was still searching and it came as no surprise when he transferred that affection towards Prince Sancho. This time I did nothing to dissuade him from such a course of action and I wonder, now, in the twilight of my years, if that was the right decision. It was inevitable that it should happen for the Prince spent an increasing amount of time with his cubs, although as they were now well trained and had grown into men, he often referred to them as his lions, the lions of León.

King Ferdinand held a tournament once a year. Now that I had trained the young warriors they attended. They could not participate in the tournament, that was reserved for knights but Prince Sancho wished to show them off. He had used some of the tribute from Zaragoza to have tunics made for all of us. They were red and bore the symbol of Castile, a castle, on the front. It made for a dramatic show and when we rode towards the tournament grounds every eye was turned to us. This was the first time that I saw Prince Sancho's siblings. They had not accompanied their father when he had fought at Atapuerca but now they were present.

I am not sure how I would have viewed Alfonso, the Prince who would follow Prince Sancho and become King of León had I not seen, at his side, Don Gonzalo Ordóñez. I know that it coloured my judgment. Whatever the reason I did not like Prince Alfonso from the moment I saw him. I saw that he and his sister Urraca were close. They were already in the stands erected to watch the combats and their heads were closeted together, almost like lovers.

The other reason I had such an opinion of the brother and sister was their reaction when Prince Sancho was greeted by his father.

King Ferdinand held out his arms and boomed, "Ah, the hero who brought me Zaragoza now brings me his young lions! Come, my son, embrace me that all may see how I feel about you!"

The affection was both mutual and obvious. The looks of hatred upon the faces of Urraca and Alfonso were clear to me but, then again, I was looking directly at them while everyone else was watching the King and his son.

As the two took their places in the centre of the viewing platform, I led the young warriors to stand together where we would watch our knights perform. On the short ride from our home, the young men had chattered like magpies. Soon they hoped to take part in the tournament, for all of them hoped to be knights. Knighthood was not something that came as a right; it had to be earned. The King or Prince Sancho would tell a young warrior when he was to be knighted. If a warrior excelled in a battle then the warrior might be invested there and then. On the other hand, it could be decided that they had all of the skills needed to be a knight and be knighted at Lion's Den. Rodrigo and Álvar often asked me why I was not a knight for I had done enough in battle to warrant it.

My answer, that I was not noble-born, both shocked and disappointed Rodrigo. "That is not right! What does the parentage of the warrior mean?" I knew that he was thinking of his own father. "Your grandfather was a Norman and there the Duke awards a knighthood for all those who are worthy. If you returned to Normandy then you could be a knight!"

He was right, of course, and the thought had crossed my mind but I had set sail on a course which would keep me in Spain. I had begun a journey and it was bound up with both Rodrigo and Álvar. I could no more abandon them than I could cut off my right arm.

As we watched the tournament begin, I looked at the knights who fought with detached professionalism. They each wore the livery of their lord, King Ferdinand, as well as his sons. I had seen some of the knights before because they had been with us at Atapuerca and in Zaragoza. I knew none of those who wore the colours of the princes Alfonso and Garcia. Tournaments were not war but men could die and could be wounded. The combats on foot rarely resulted in death but limbs could be broken by overzealous blows. On horseback, however, it was a different matter for riders could fall and hitting the ground from the back of a galloping horse could be fatal. A fallen man could be prey to the clattering crash of a death-dealing hoof. All in all, it was a dangerous business and I did not understand the need for it. When I had mentioned my doubts to Prince Sancho, he had told me that it was to help mould men into a cohesive fighting unit. That did nothing to persuade me for I had achieved the same end in the gyrus. I knew that I was young and knew less than Prince Sancho and so I remained silent.

I saw the attraction in the spectacle as King Alfonso's armiger began the tournament with a combat against Prince Sancho's armiger, Don Raoul. Don Raoul was a good warrior and I had been asked to spar with him more than once. The fact that I had been asked to do so several times was a compliment for the knight found it hard to beat me. He was gracious after each combat and I was happy to help for I learned much fighting such a wily old warrior. I think the reason I held my own against one of the greatest knights in the land was the fact that I was strong and my whole life was the sword and spear. Knights had other matters to occupy them.

The combat was on horseback and the two knights thundered towards each other with blunted weapons. As they both used the smaller, round shield of Iberia, this was a risky way to fight for a slightly mistimed blow could result in a splintered lance and although both knights wore mail, wooden splinters could take an eye very easily. Both knights were good and their lances struck the shields and shattered. The crack sounded like thunder and the ladies who were watching squealed with shock at the sound. The two men drew their swords and began to exchange blows. They were equally matched and shields blocked swords while each sought an opening. I saw Rodrigo watching the two men not to see the outcome but to observe their technique. The whirling horses were the key to the combat. No matter how well a knight fought, if his horse made a mistake then the battle would be over. Raoul's horse made that mistake and the sword which was pressed at his throat marked the end of the bout. All applauded for it had been a good beginning.

There were combats on foot as well as more single combats. Then there was the mêlée where the four teams of the King and his son would fight together and the winner was the last team standing. It was a measure of the leadership of the team and the way that they had been trained. As campi doctor to the cubs, I had been consulted by Don Raoul and the Prince. I had been both flattered and nervous but I had given them my advice. The result was that when the mêlée began, Prince Sancho's team fought together. Prince Garcia's men were the first driven from the field followed very quickly by Prince Alfonso's men. When Don Gonzalo Ordóñez was unhorsed by Raoul I took particular pleasure in the fall. With just two teams left it was hard to see which would win but the superior cohesion of Prince Sancho's meant that they won and the King's team were defeated. Prince Sancho looked ecstatic but he had the good grace to turn to me and nod. He appreciated the work I had done.

The two sets of knights gathered to congratulate each other and the King and his children descended from the stands to greet them. This was the end of the tournament and while the knights and the royal family would return to the palace for a victory feast, the rest of us would go home. It just so happened that

Rodrigo, Álvar and I were close enough to the royal party to overhear their words.

"Sancho, my son, your men are truly well trained. This bodes well for the future. I can see how you managed to subjugate Zaragoza so quickly."

"My knights work hard, my lord, and I have higher hopes for my cubs for they are almost lions grown."

The King saw Rodrigo, "And here is one in whom I know you have great faith. Are you still aspiring to be a great knight, Rodrigo?"

"I aspire, Your Majesty, but I still have much to learn. Knighthood is the journey of a lifetime!"

The King turned to Alfonso and Garcia. Garcia was the same age as Rodrigo but while Rodrigo looked like a man, both of Sancho's brothers still looked like boys. "You see, my sons, that is what you should be doing and not wasting your time hunting and hawking."

Garcia said, somewhat sulkily, "They help to train for war!"

The King shook his head, "They do not!"

Alfonso had coloured, "If they are so good then why does my brother not take them to the Taifa of Badajoz where our men still try to take Coimbra back from the Moors?"

The land to the south and west of the Kingdom was still Moorish and, unlike Zaragoza, a thorn in the King's side. Men had been trying to take the fortress of Coimbra for some years and had had no success. The King glared at Alfonso, "Enough! You seek to spoil my pleasure on this day by bringing up my failure? For shame! Come, let us retire to the palace before my appetite is completely ruined."

It was as we headed back to our horses that I saw the men who had followed Don Gonzalo Ordóñez. I recognised broad and slow. When he saw me, he pointed at me and drew his finger across his throat. I was not intimidated and shouted, "Any time you wish to face me as a man then I am ready but I expect that you would rather be a knife in the night. As you lumber around like an elephant, I do not fear you."

"I will have you now!"

One of his companions restrained him, "Now is not the time nor place." He pointed at me, "William Redbeard, we have a score to settle with you. It is thanks to you that our friend and leader, Garcia is dead and that Juan here can never father children. We will have blood but vengeance is a dish best served cold!" They left and I wondered if I should have ended the blood feud there and then. I did not and the ripples from the stone thrown in Pamplona continued to spread.

When the Prince returned the next day, he summoned me along with Don Raoul. "My poisonous little brother will live to rue his insults." I had no idea what had gone on but Don Raoul gave a slight shake of his head which indicated that he would speak with me later. "Have my young warriors prepare. We go to raid the land south of the fortress of Coimbra." That was all he said and his terse words forbade me to ask more.

When he had gone, I said. "Don Raoul, what happened?"

"It was his younger brother Garcia and he was egged on by Alfonso and Urraca. When Prince Sancho said that besieging a castle was not the work of a horseman, and that is correct, then Garcia mocked him and said he just sought the glory of a cavalry charge." He shook his head, "What do those two popinjays and their harpy of a sister know of war? They enjoy the pleasure of the peace made by their father and brother. We serve a good man, Will Redbeard, but he is driven by demons from within. We go to war and it is unnecessary. Men will die for no good reason save to make two princes and princesses smile!"

Don Raoul was right but it did not change our task. We had to prepare for war. The land around Coimbra was part of León but the Moors had taken the mighty fortress thanks to incompetence. It explained the King's reaction for he saw it as a failure on his part. I had no doubt that the King would choose a time to reclaim it but now was not the time. I knew that my men would not mind for they were keen to prove themselves but I knew that we should be training and preparing for the real war, the war that had yet to begin.

Chapter 8

I was just a servant of the Prince and I did not decide policy but I did wonder at the wisdom of such an action as we could not force the walls of the fortress which, according to Rodrigo, should never have fallen in the first place; especially not with horsemen! I told my young warriors what was intended and they were happy to put their skills to the test. Rodrigo had become something of a lieutenant and he helped me more than I could have expected. I was amazed at his maturity. While the other young warriors were banging their shields and talking of showing the Muslims the Castilian way of war Rodrigo was cautioning them, for he knew that Prince Sancho had been placed in an impossible position. If he succeeded then even Coimbra itself would not be subdued and, in all likelihood, we would lose warriors with no resulting gain of land. If King Ferdinand was to succeed in taking Coimbra then it would be with the full force of the might of Castile and the swords of each and every warrior who served the Christian world of Spain. I knew this from a gut feeling which came from the blood of the Viking and the Norman. Rodrigo knew from his readings. We worked well together.

Since the bandit attack, Stephen had become a better servant. I thought it was because he had been so close to death and survived that he saw life as something to be lived to the full.

Whatever the reason, our two servants were a positive boon as we prepared to head south. It is only with hindsight that we see that which is before us. Pablo and Stephen were happier with Rodrigo than they had been with Don Diego and that said as much about the father as the son!

I was pleased that our young charges had had the experience of going to war before for it made this so much easier. We were heading far from our heartland against a foe we had yet to defeat and who had held Coimbra against many attacks. Prince Sancho was a sound general and he knew that trying to take the fortress would be a waste of time. Instead, he chose a different route; he would hurt their hinterland for he would raid and take from the people who lived to the south of the mighty fortress. True, it would not take Coimbra but it would weaken that bastion so that sometime in the future it would fall. To that end, wishing to move swiftly, we took no foot soldiers and all were mounted, even the servants.

This time the Prince had learned the lessons from the battle of the bridge and his knights were both before and behind him. I led the cubs and we rode behind the knights and in front of the baggage. The young warriors were not put out by this for they knew that they might not have been able to save the Prince had the Moors at the bridge had a little more luck. They now knew how important was the baggage for it had the food and spare weapons and another valuable lesson had been learned.

The land north of Coimbra was firmly in Castilian hands and we were welcomed and housed, all the way south. These were the borderlands with an enemy who sought Christian land and was prepared to fight for it. This was not like Zaragoza where the Emir was content to keep what he held and leave Castile and Navarre well alone, Badajoz wanted the lands to the north, King Ferdinand's lands! Here we saw armed farmers working their fields and even shepherd boys had weapons close to hand. The farms were walled and many had a small tower; this was a land ravaged by war and it showed.

The local lords kept a presence close to Coimbra but it was not a siege. The roads were guarded and it just kept the people inside the fortress hungry. We stayed at the castle of Don Raimundo of Porto who was a powerful lord, at his castle on the River Douro. Lying to the north of Coimbra it guaranteed that the men of Badajoz could not advance further north than the river which was protected by his stronghold. However, he did not have enough men to take Coimbra. Once again, I was privileged enough to be present, as campi doctor, when the Prince and the Lord of Porto spoke together. "We stop them from advancing north and we control their slave and animal raids. Until your father, King Ferdinand, brings an army here to subdue the fortress then we merely hold them for that is all that we can do."

Prince Sancho was loyal to his father but the frown which creased his face showed that he agreed with Don Raimundo. "And all that I can do with the handful of men I have brought is to be like the biting insects of summer and annoy the Muslim but we shall do so."

"Then you will need a base closer to Coimbra, somewhere to which you can retreat if threatened. Don Luis of Sangalhos has the closest castle to the north of Coimbra. Don Luis hates the Muslims for they killed his parents and took his sister as a slave. He does not have many men but he is a sentinel to the south of us and his men know the land well."

When I mentioned what I had heard to Rodrigo, not as mere gossip and tittle-tattle but because I thought it would help to educate him, he nodded, "Using local men is vital in a campaign. I thought that the Prince's idea of using Berber archers was a good one. It is a pity that, at the bridge, he did not use them effectively."

"Effectively?"

"The Taifa have good warriors and some are better than ours, and, if it is possible, we should use those kind of warriors. Each part of an army has its own strength and they should be used. The horse archers need protection from light horsemen. Foot soldiers are vulnerable to arrows. Knights and mailed men can be isolated and defeated. An army, Will, need not be large to succeed. It just needs to have the right component parts." I could hear in his words the development of the thoughts which had begun when I had been attacked in the narrow street in Pamplona by the six warriors. He was now on a path which I could only follow. His training, education and his eyes had allowed Rodrigo to come up with a way of fighting here in Spain which was new. Until he commanded an army then he would never achieve that which he ought to.

Prince Sancho also used some of Don Raimundo's men to act as guards and guides. We were a small force but a potent one.

Don Luis was an older man than I expected. He was of an age with Don Diego but he had a fire in his eyes which told me that he had not forgotten what his enemies had cost him. He did not have a large retinue for this land, compared with Vivar, was poor; sheep and goats were the main source of income. His lack of income was reflected in those who followed his banner: he had just ten mounted men and none wore mail. All were local farmers who served as his warriors. In addition, there were slingers and a handful of farmers who served as archers. However, they knew the land and they were passionate about what they did. Our servants and some of the men sent by Don Raimundo meant that Don Luis could use all of his armed men to accompany us as the walls of his stronghold would be protected. I felt more comfortable for Stephen and Pablo would be safe whilst we raided.

The lord also had ideas about where we should raid. The land between the Mondego and Ceira rivers was fertile land and far enough away from Coimbra to allow us the freedom to raid and to take animals. We headed south and east to the bridge over the Mondego at Penacova. This was a peaceful part of the Taifa as Don Luis and the other lords did not have enough men to cause the Muslims a problem. The bridge was unguarded but, even had it been, then the river was fordable by horsemen. We clattered across the bridge as dawn was breaking. A handful of men rushed, with weapons, to stop the advance guard but they were slain. Don Luis and Prince Sancho then headed due south to begin to harvest the animals and to take their grain and their treasure.

By the end of the first day, neither the knights nor my young warriors had had to draw their weapons for any opposition had been dealt with by Don Luis' small number of horsemen. They rode before our column to take care of any armed opposition. They had suffered at the hands of the Moors for long enough and now that they had the backing of Prince Sancho, they could be more belligerent and they were. The men sent by Don Raimundo had been left to hold Penacova and the treasure and the animals we had taken were sent back there. That first night we stayed in the Moorish town of Branco. This was the first place we had found which had any sort of defences but they were Roman and they were ruins as the locals had robbed the stone to make their homes. We camped in the remains of the Roman fort on the top of the hill which made it a secure base. We ate well that night for there had been some cattle and they were slaughtered for meat.

Now that we were on campaign once more, my young warriors and I kept apart from the knights. It was deliberate on my part for I needed them all to feel as one unit and to maintain the sense of brotherhood which the separate camp engendered. I knew that when Lord Lain had led us at the Battle of Atapuerca, Alfonso had kept our men separate and it had helped us. As we ate meat, quickly cooked and still bloody with the juices mopped up by fresh bread, one of the young warriors, Antonio, asked, "Campi doctor, why do we not return north to Penacova? We have taken all that there is and we are at risk from the Moor."

I was chewing the meat and Rodrigo answered for me, "Simple, Antonio, we might not be able to take Coimbra but we can raid this land and draw men from Coimbra to battle with us."

"The Prince wants to fight the Moor?" He was surprised but not shocked. The young warriors were keen for a battle and were a little aggrieved that, hitherto, they had been watchers and not warriors,

Rodrigo and I had spoken of this and I knew his thoughts already. He smiled and said, "We are horsemen and cannot assault walls but this is not as mountainous a land as further north and here, if the Moors come to rid this land of us, we can use our strengths and training as horsemen to our advantage."

Another warrior, Carlos, asked, "But what if they bring a huge army? We are few in number."

Rodrigo pointed to me, "Has not William Redbeard here trained us well? He will lead us in battle and if we heed his commands then we will prevail; of that, I am convinced for we just need to fight together as a band of brothers."

I was flattered but I knew that when we did ride to battle then it would be Rodrigo who would lead and inspire the young warriors. I had watched the eyes of the young men around the fire and all had been fixed upon the charismatic Rodrigo de Vivar and not the son of the sword for hire who led them.

It took two further days for the Moorish leader to stir himself and gather men to rid his land of the locusts who had descended upon it. We were already heading north, having sacked a swathe of land ten miles by ten miles when we were discovered. We had taken treasure, animals and food and we had captured more than forty horses. Had we so wished then we could have taken many slaves back but they would have slowed us down and Prince Sancho saw no need. Don Luis' men were border warriors and they knew the land well. It was they who brought us the news of the approaching Moorish warriors. We were in the land which had, until the Muslim Moor had come, produced some of the finest of red wines. Now the vines had been removed and other crops planted. The land still showed traces of the terraces. Had the vines been left then we would not have been able to fight as well as we did. Álvar took this as a clear sign that God was on our side. Once Prince Sancho realised what was happening, we halted on the slopes and he formed us up. The archers and slingers were placed before us as a thin screen while Don Luis and the men of the area were placed on the right flank and I was given command of the left. Prince Sancho kept all of his men in the centre.

He waved me over to speak with him and Don Luis. "Campi Doctor, I know that you will answer me truly if I ask you a direct question that requires an honest answer. Are my cubs now lions? Can they fight but, more importantly, can they obey orders?"

I looked him in the eye and answered him truthfully, "Yes, Prince Sancho."

He pointed to where the Moors were approaching. They were still more than a mile away but I could see that they were a mixed army. There were some on foot as well as the mounted archers and mailed askari. "When they form up, I want you to attack their right flank but as soon as you have hit them, I wish you to turn and flee."

"You want them to follow us."

He nodded, "You will draw them across our front and join Don Luis here. I will attack them in the flank as they pass before us and then drive into the heart of their army. Don Luis, you and William here will then lead your men to attack their left flank. I hope to catch them disordered."

Don Luis looked at me first and then asked Prince Sancho, "I have no doubt that William Redbeard is a good warrior but he is not a knight and he leads young warriors."

I might have been insulted but I knew that Don Luis was right. However, he did not know my warriors. Prince Sancho said, "Watch them Don Luis and, when we have won, ask William here how he trains his men. You will learn much."

He nodded but I could tell that he was not convinced; we would have to prove to him the worth of my young warriors in battle.

I rode back to Rodrigo and the others to explain, quickly, what was intended as we did not have long. "Álvar, you have the horn?" He nodded. "Then you ride next to me. As soon as I give the command then sound it three times and I want every one of you to throw your spears at the enemy, turn and follow Álvar Fáñez. You will lead the men across the front of Prince Sancho and form up behind Don Luis. Rodrigo, you and I will be at the rear!"

No one objected, complained or looked in any way fearful. We used spears and I had practised this frequently as Rodrigo had read about how the Roman Auxiliary cavalry had done the same with their javelins. If it worked for the Romans then why should it not work for us? A spear was heavier and harder to throw but all of my young warriors could hurl them more than twenty paces and their heavy heads would cause many casualties. More importantly, it would buy us the time to turn. We formed up and I was in the centre with Rodrigo on one side and Álvar on the other. We waited for the enemy to make their own battle lines. I was nervous for it would be me who would initiate the encounter. The rest of the army would wait until we charged.

As we waited, I shouted, "I want you all to scream and shout wildly as we charge so that they think we are callow and untried warriors. You look young; let us use that and fool these Moors who will learn the lions of León are a force to be reckoned with!" My words ensured that we were in good heart and they cheered. I saw Rodrigo nod and it was another lesson for him. I saw that the Moors had formed up with their foot soldiers before their horsemen and they were at the bottom of the shallow valley. We would be charging downhill and they would have to charge uphill after us as we raced across their front. Their force was half and half: horse soldiers and foot soldiers, while we were almost all horse with a sprinkling of Don Luis' slingers and archers. I waited until I was certain that they were in position before I said, "Álvar, sound the advance."

The horn sounded and I urged Killer forward. We now understood each other but not as well as Rodrigo and Babieca. His horse seemed like an extension of Rodrigo. The Moors sounded their drums which were intended to unnerve us and they prepared to receive us. We had four hundred paces to cover and the arrows the archers used, both those mounted and those on foot, would be able to reach us when we were one hundred and fifty paces from them. By then I intended to be galloping. I rested my spear on my cantle and looked down the line of young warriors who waited expectantly for my next command. All of our training had paid off and the line of forty warriors was straight. They were all cheering and screaming as I had asked and when I looked ahead, I saw the Moors nervously looking at each other. Fighting wild men was never easy for they were more unpredictable. When the Vikings had raided this land, they had surprised the Moors by the ferocity of their attacks and the presence of berserkers often won the day. I had only heard of such men from Alfonso who, in turn, had heard of them from my father. I wondered what made such warriors leave the protection of a shield wall and race to almost certain death.

Killer was always keen and his pace increased as he smelled the Moors, he snorted and flared his nostrils impatiently. I had no need to order an increase in pace for Killer determined that. The arrows flew towards us but we were mailed and the Moors aimed at men. One arrow hit my shield and another thudded into my shoulder but the mail held; I would have a bruise but that would be all. When we were fifty paces from them and when their arrows should have been causing casualties, their archers fled and, at that moment, disrupted the lines of spearmen. As we hit, they were already broken and the shields were not continuous and my spear struck the open mouth of a spearman whose spear glanced off my leg. I pulled back and skewered another whose back was to me. I saw a warrior with mail and a plumed helmet begin to shout something and knew that they were preparing a counter-attack. I speared another and then shouted, "Now Álvar!"

As the horn sounded, I threw my spear at an eager horseman who was just thirty paces from me. The spear entered his chest and he slid from his horse which careered into the one next to him. I had to drag Killer's head around for he had the smell of battle in his nostrils and was trying to get at the enemy horses, Killer was a warrior too! Drawing my sword, I dug my heels in and he took off after my young warriors who had all obeyed my order and the horn. Babieca was a clever horse and he soon caught up with Killer; I pointed to my right and Rodrigo joined me as we followed my disciplined young warriors who now looked as though they were fleeing to safety. The hurling of the spears had broken the already disrupted line of horsemen. We had not killed many but we had annoyed the Moors who now tried to negotiate their own dead and demoralised foot soldiers as they attempted to get to us and have their vengeance. As we headed at full tilt towards Don Luis on our right flank, I saw that we had empty saddles. We had lost young warriors. It was to be expected but it was not something which sat well with me. I glanced over my shoulder and saw that the nearest Moorish riders were fifty paces from me. I saw that there were a couple of horse archers with them and I felt arrows striking my back. My mail and padded gambeson afforded me protection but it was still worrying. If any managed to develop an arrow that would penetrate mail then the day of the horseman was over.

To my right, I saw the archers and slingers waiting for us to pass close enough to them to begin to rain death upon the Moors. Already Álvar had led the warriors behind Don Luis and it was just a handful of us who had to pass the front of the men of Sangalhos.

I heard as I passed Don Luis' line, the command, "Draw!"

A heartbeat later came the command, "Release!"

I heard the sound of stones striking and arrows hitting flesh and metal. There were screams and cries. I risked looking behind me and saw that Prince Sancho had cleverly used the fact that the Moors had no protection on their right. Those with shields bore them on their left and so men were hit. Those who were not killed were wounded and many died when they fell from their horses. Rodrigo and I wheeled in next to Álvar who was grinning.

"Well done, Álvar, it is good to see that you can obey orders!"

I looked ahead and saw that the wing which had chased after us were broken and making their way north, back to the River Mondego and Coimbra. A horn sounded and Prince Sancho led his knights after the fleeing Moors. They could do so with impunity for the defeated Moors prevented the rest, who had not pursued us, from using their bows and javelins, more than that, they stopped a counter charge so that the heavily mailed men of Castile could tear into the lightly armoured horsemen. I stroked Killer as we followed the rest of the army. We had ridden hard and the next charge would have to be slower but Killer and Babieca could cope. I just hoped that the other horses were in such fine fettle. We no longer had spears but Don Luis and his men did and they would be the ones striking at the enemy. He was a veteran warrior and he waited until Prince Sancho was about to strike the enemy battle line and then he ordered the charge. It did not matter that the men we charged outnumbered us; we were better protected and armed in addition to which we rode downhill and had the increased momentum the slope provided. The men of Sangalhos had revenge on their minds for they had suffered raids like this for some time and this was the opportunity to pay back the enemy.

A gap appeared between our horses and those of Don Luis. It was not a surprise for we had charged and then galloped while they were fresh. In the event, it helped us as, striking a few heartbeats after Don Luis, we were able to mop up those who survived the initial charge. Later Rodrigo commented on the fact for he saw it as a way to exploit a charge and he used it many times when he led the armies of Castile. It was such a simple thing and yet it saved lives and it won battles. Don Luis and his men had unhorsed riders and killed some. As the survivors rose to their feet our swords swept into their heads and bodies. It was like practice except that it was not overripe fruit and vegetables we hit; it was skulls and bodies. Their spears shattered, Don Luis and his men had drawn swords, axes and maces. The Moors best weapon was their bow but here we had Moor and Christian fighting so closely that arrows were unable to discriminate and so we held the advantage.

Rodrigo and Álvar flanked me; they were so close that our boots almost touched. We had trained our warriors to do the same but only the three of us managed the feat. The result was that we drove like an arrow deep into the Moorish lines. Killer was just a nose ahead and that allowed me to stand in my stirrups and bring my sword down. Some Moors just wore a turban but my sword, my father's sword, split helmets and heads in twain regardless of what they wore upon their skulls. Álvar and Rodrigo had an easier time as our three horses forced theirs apart and they fought Moors who were sideways on to them for Killer was a warhorse and drove the Moorish horses from our path.

Prince Sancho was the one who broke the enemy for he reached their standard and he was the one who slew the standard-bearer causing the rest to flee. I think that if I had commanded the right flank alone, we would have stopped for our horses were tiring but the vengeful Don Luis wanted none to escape and so we had to follow and support him. We caught up with some of the Moors but the effort was not worth the cost of blown animals. If the Moors had been leading us into an ambush, we would have been slaughtered! Fortunately, they had not planned ahead and there was no second force of archers waiting in ambush. It was well past noon when his horses were too tired to move. We had slowed to a walk long before the vengeful Don Luis' attack petered out.

I shouted, "Dismount and walk your horses."

Killer was lathered and I took off my helmet, filled it with water from my water skin and allowed him to lap it up. Rodrigo and Álvar saw me and emulated me. Only when Killer appeared satiated did I enjoy the last two swallows of lukewarm water which remained in the skin. Don Luis and his men walked back towards us. "Thank you, Campi Doctor, for following us, I feel that we have had some justice now. Your young warriors will be great knights for they fought as fully-grown men who had many battles to their name."

I saw those who were within earshot swell with pride. "Aye, Don Luis, they are getting there but we still have a journey to make." I had seen, in the skirmish, ways to improve all of them. I did not tell Don Luis of his mistake. He was a lord and would not take kindly to criticism but I saw, as we headed back to our lines, that some of his horses had been broken for they had travelled too far and too fast. They were finished for war and would become pack horses at best.

It was dark by the time we made a rough camp close to the hill of past vines. First, there were the dead warriors to bury. Four of my lions had died and I wished them to be buried with honour. The priests saw that all was done well and they were buried with their weapons. We did not mark their graves as this was, for the present, the land of the Moor. We knew where they were and after we had walked our horses across the tops of the graves to disguise them, I make a silent oath to return and put markers on them once we had taken the Taifa of Badajoz. There had been horses to recover and to collect. We had to find our spears and there were bodies to search. My young warriors thought it was beneath them until I pointed out that if we did not take the weapons then the Moors would and we wanted them weaker. They saw the sense in that. When Rodrigo reminded them that a warrior could never have too many weapons then it was as though he had given the approval to take from the dead.

We left for home the next day. It would be a long journey for we had captured many horses and taken large quantities of weapons. Don Raimundo and Don Luis would have all of the sheep, goats and cattle we had taken, and there were many hundreds, while we would take the horses and weapons. We stayed for a week in Porto and then headed back to Castile and the King's palace. We had not recovered Coimbra but Prince Sancho had shown his brothers that there was a general to replace King Ferdinand and it was he, Prince Sancho. The King was not yet dead but battle lines were being drawn.

Chapter 9

I knew, after our last fight, that we still had much work to do. The cubs we had lost had died unnecessarily. When we had fought they had not kept as tightly together as I would have wished. As I had drilled into them, a knight alone, unless he was incredibly skilled, was likely to lose but if he was surrounded by his shield brothers then he would, in all likelihood, survive. Rodrigo echoed my words and he told them how the three of us had been able to act as one. The winter saw my training regime become even harder for I had seen their shortcomings. When I had first begun to train Rodrigo and then Álvar I had only looked at the two of them. Since I had been given greater responsibility, I saw the bigger picture. It helped that both Rodrigo and Álvar did not need as much individual attention and could now, largely, work on the minor improvements which would see them become knights. As autumn became winter and the hours we trained became fewer, so I sought the advice of Don Raoul.

"Don Raoul, I am just a sword for hire and I am happy to continue as Prince Sancho's Campi Doctor but I have done almost all that I can for some of the men I train. I will continue to train them but if I was one of them, I would wonder if I was ever going to be knighted."

"You are right to speak with me. I have thought the same. You and your charges did well when we raided last summer and I would not like to see your young men disheartened. I will speak with the Prince but he and his brothers are in dispute and this is not a good time."

I nodded, "As I said, Armiger, I am happy to take the Prince's gold and to train the young men. I just worry about their attitude."

To be fair to all of them there was no resentment whatsoever. They all still trained hard. At night, when work was done, they would play games and read with Rodrigo who seemed to have a great knowledge of the past and where to find the books he needed to illustrate a point. They were a well-honed blade and I felt pleased with what they had achieved.

Don Raoul asked, "And you, Campi Doctor? What do you wish?"

I confess that I did not understand the question. I shrugged, "I have been elevated far higher than I could ever have dreamed. When the cubs are all knighted then my work will be done. If you ask me what I will do then I have to say I know not. I think that my future is tied up with Rodrigo de Vivar."

The Armiger nodded, "It is true that there is something which is special about the man. I have never seen such a dedicated warrior and he could become the greatest knight in this land." I knew that but to hear it confirmed by one such as Don Raoul made me more determined than ever to do my part.

Once Christmas had passed and the nights became slightly shorter, once more, Rodrigo asked Pablo if he could find a local Moor or

Muslim who could teach him Arabic. I was surprised and when Pablo headed into the city to enquire about such a teacher, I asked Rodrigo why he had made the request.

"Zaragoza is a vassal state and I doubt that we will need to go to war alongside them, but they have soldiers we do not. There are horse archers whom we could use but I remember when Prince Sancho lost the Berber archers at the battle of the bridge. If he had been able to speak their language then that disaster might not have happened. If we are to retake Spain then we need to harness the men of the Taifa. We will not do this with just Christian soldiers but Moors too. I am just planning for the future. I wish to be able to speak the language of our allies and our enemy!"

And that was Rodrigo de Vivar. He knew what he wanted and he went after it. I had trained him and taught him all that I knew about fighting. Now he was moving on and leaving me behind. He was developing and honing new skills. I felt sad for I knew that I would no longer be needed.

The teacher who was found by Pablo was a Moor who had been blinded as a punishment by one of the lords who followed Prince Garcia and he had been abandoned in the city far from his home. Pablo found the man who was by profession a teacher, begging by the gates to the city. Pablo was a gentle soul and he saw something in the teacher, Hassan ibn Hassan. He proved to be an inspired choice. Not only was he a good teacher but once he had taught Rodrigo his language he remained in his service. He helped me to begin to learn the language and was a very cultured man. Perhaps the fact that he was blind gave him other ways to see for he seemed to be able to pick up inflexions in men's words which were truly insightful. It was almost as though he could read men's thoughts!

My time was taken up with the four new cubs who had arrived. It was harder to train those for the rest had all had the same level of skill when they had arrived. These four were new and they were much younger. I had to spend more time with them and Rodrigo took over the training of the rest of the young warriors. Perhaps this was meant to be for they all became closer and Rodrigo was their leader!

King Ferdinand sent for Prince Sancho in April and when his armiger and myself were also summoned then I knew that war was coming. Prince Alfonso and Prince Garcia were also present with their armigers. I was the only Campi Doctor. The two princesses were not present and that, strangely, kept the conversation and discussion civilised.

"My son, Prince Sancho, has brought us a great prize, Zaragoza, and I would emulate him. I am not getting any younger and, before I die, I would like the Taifas of Toledo and Badajoz under our control. To that end, I wish you to each raise an army for within the month we will invade Toledo. We will invest it and make it a vassal. The money we accrue will enable us to hire more men."

I hid my smile for the King was confident
that we would succeed and yet Toledo was
bigger than Zaragoza and was more belligerent.
Its Emir was al-Ma'mun who was both
aggressive and clever having tried to take
Zaragoza by force of arms already and he would
not give in quite so easily as al-Muqtadir.

This time there were maps for us to use and
I saw that Toledo was a far bigger land and it
had more fortresses than Zaragoza. The King,
much to the annoyance of his two younger sons,
constantly deferred to Prince Sancho. I
understood this for he was the only one of his
sons who had actually had success in war. "My
son, what would be your strategy?"

"We use the rivers. The land to the north of
Toledo, around Magerit, is known as the land of
the waters. We will be campaigning in summer
and we need water for our horses. We do as I did
in Badajoz and take their animals to draw them
to battle. Our strength is in our mounted men so
let us use them."

The King nodded, obviously swayed by the
argument. He turned to his other sons, "And
have you any other suggestions or strategies?"

Alfonso shrugged; it was obvious he did not
but Garcia said, "Why not head directly for
Toledo and take it!"

The King shook his head, "And we would
attack the walls with our knights or would you
spend a month or so building machines of war
while our men bake and disease races through
the camps? Would you wait for the desertions
which inevitably accompany a siege? Your

brother has twice succeeded in raids against the Moor and I am inclined to go along with his idea. Perhaps you can both impress me on campaign and show me how you use your men."

The looks of hatred on their faces were directed not at their father but their brother. I was glad that I was an only child.

As we rode back to Lion's Den, Prince Sancho said, "Don Raoul has told me of your concerns, Campi Doctor. I am disappointed that you did not seek to speak with me directly however, let us put that aside. I agree and when the time is right on this campaign then I will knight some of my young lions for Don Raoul has told me that some of my knights are ageing. We need fresh blood."

"Thank you, Prince Sancho, and I am sorry that I did not speak with you directly but I am keenly aware that I am not of noble blood."

The Prince laughed, "And I care not." he gave me a serious look, "Is this your way of asking to be knighted? Is it in your head to have me elevate you and make you a noble? Do you see yourself as a knight?"

I had learned to listen to men's words and knew that Prince Sancho was not offering me a knighthood for his tone was almost mocking. This was what Rodrigo called a rhetorical question. I heard the message beneath the words and I gave him a diplomatic answer, I shook my head, "No, I do not see myself as a knight, not yet, anyway. Thank you, Prince Sancho, but I am not certain that I am ready yet. When

Rodrigo is knighted then I will consider accepting."

He shook his head, "Who says if there would be an offer of knighthood then and besides, I need you as a Campi Doctor."

As I headed back to the hall I wondered if I had been a fool. Alfonso would have smacked me about the head for my words and he would have told me to take the title with both hands even if the offer was not a real one, but I could not for I still had work to do and I did not believe that I had been offered a knighthood. I also decided not to tell any of their impending knighthoods. It would only distract them. Better they fight as hard as they could and not know that it might gain them their spurs.

The faith the Prince still had in me was shown when he told me that I would command the young warriors in battle for he had been impressed with the way I had obeyed orders and handled our men. I took Rodrigo and Álvar into my confidence and explained to them how we would fight in the campaign. We were not knights, not yet anyway, and our role would be to engage the horse archers and lightly armoured horsemen. It meant a different approach. We would not charge boot to boot for that would just present the enemy with a bigger target. Instead, I had the idea of using knots of men so that the three of us would each lead a third of the men to surround and confuse the enemy. It was just an idea but when Rodrigo thought it a good one then I began to believe in myself.

As part of my reward for the campaign I had been given another captured horse in the raid, Copper, and this one was more of a palfrey. I named her Copper for that was her colour. It meant I had a good riding horse and could save Berber and Killer for battle. That was what they were bred for. We were now quite accomplished when it came to preparing for battle and campaign. All but the four new men knew how to prepare and what to take. The preparation was almost easy and there was a calm air as my young warriors chose weapons, clothes and horses to take. Álvar had taken on much of the training of the four new warriors and he chivvied and chased them so that they were ready. The weather would be hot and instead of a heavy woollen cloak, I took the finer white one I had taken from the body of one of the dead from the Taifa of Badajoz. With a large hood, my head was as cool as the rest of me. I still worried that the Prince did not have enough archers but that was outside of my control. I would just lead my young gentlemen.

This time King Ferdinand tried to make peace with his sons and he allowed Prince Alfonso to lead the army and be the vanguard. It meant that we were towards the rear of the column and just before the men of Prince Garcia. Rodrigo had a critical eye and he could not help but notice the deficiencies in the men who would fight alongside us. He did not speak them aloud then, that came when we camped but I recognised the signs as his sharp eyes looked at the way Prince Garcia's men rode and the careless way they carried themselves. Our men rode in a neat column of four men. I had trained them to do so. They knew what to do if we were attacked and they knew how to look for danger. The fact that we were half a mile or more from the vanguard did not matter. The attack on the bridge when we had lost so many men had been a bloody lesson and we had learned from it. Prince Garcia's men seemed to loll across the road and along the fields which were adjacent. They rode in untidy groups of men so that sometimes there were five or six abreast and sometimes just two. Where our men rode in neat, equidistant lines there were gaps between some of the groups of knights.

I saw Rodrigo shake his head and counselled him, "We cannot say anything, Rodrigo, these are knights and we are their inferiors, more they are the knights of Prince Sancho's brothers and we need no argument with them. There is enough bad blood already."

"That is not right, Will, for you are inferior to no one. You should be a knight for what you have done already for Prince Sancho."

I said nothing for Prince Sancho had tempted or perhaps taunted me with the hint of a knighthood and it was my fault that I had rejected it. I still did not know why except that, perhaps, I wanted to finish my work and that I did not believe that I had been truly offered spurs. If Rodrigo had been knighted then I might have accepted but the moment was gone and would not return. For some reason, I did not dwell upon that and I wondered if it was something to do with my past. I came from a people who had, until only recently, not had knights. I confess that I had always been happy standing in Alfonso's shield wall.

Before us marched the men on foot. Prince Sancho's archers, crossbowmen and slingers, as well as his spearmen, were between Prince Sancho's knights and ourselves. Prince Sancho knew how vulnerable they were but he also understood that, if we were ambushed, then they would be able to protect the horsemen too, so long as their flanks were secure. We were that insurance.

I had seen Alfonso and the rest of my former shield brothers for Don Diego was with King Ferdinand as was Rodrigo's grandfather. Lord Lain had waved at Rodrigo and asked him how he was as they had passed. Don Diego had managed to avoid riding close to us. I had made do with a wave to Alfonso. I knew that when we camped, I would be able to speak with them.

This was the largest army I had been in since Atapuerca and the dusty hot roads made for an uncomfortable ride. I began to understand why the Moors used their turbans for they could wind the ends around their mouths and noses and keep the dust from choking them. I gained some relief from the hood of my light, white cloak. I saw the rest of my men looking enviously at me as they sweated beneath their heavy woollen cloaks. Most had thought it was beneath them to take clothes from the dead; I suspect that they would be less squeamish the next time.

There was no actual border between Castile
and the Taifa of Toledo. Christians and Moors
lived on both sides of the hypothetical boundary.
The difference lay in the strongholds. Before we
crossed the border then we could happily camp
next to the defended villages and towns. We
could use their water and they would provide us
with food; once we crossed then life would
become harder.

It was the second night of the journey when
I was able to speak with Alfonso and Iago. Don
Diego had camped as far away from his son and
Prince Sancho as he could but I had been
summoned, along with Don Raoul and Prince
Sancho, to the King's tent and that allowed me
the opportunity to speak with my former
comrades. The summons had been to give us the
orders for the march. As we were about to cross
into Toledo State proper there were orders given
to protect us. Perhaps the King had noticed the
unruly line of march or perhaps he had always
planned this. Whatever the reason each of the
four parts of the army were to provide a small
number of horsemen to ride along the flanks.

Prince Sancho would stay to speak with his
father but he said, "Campi Doctor, it seems to
me that you are the perfect unit for this task.
Your men are younger, fitter and have the
discipline to follow your orders. I do not want
you chasing off after Moors to gain glory."

I was offended but Don Raoul came to my
defence. He was the armiger and, as such, in a
position to speak more openly, "To be fair

Prince Sancho, William here has never allowed his men to do anything like that."

Prince Sancho nodded, "And long may it continue so."

As we left, he said, "He is ever thus when he is close to his brothers. He does not actually change but he is just a little different."

"Will!"

I turned and saw Alfonso and Iago. They had been searching for food for their camp. I smiled at Don Raoul. "These are old comrades, shield brothers, with your permission I would speak with them."

Don Raoul smiled and nodded, "Shield brothers is a term I have not heard for some time. I will tell Rodrigo that you will be delayed."

When he had gone Alfonso embraced me, "It is good to see you and to find you not only alive but fully grown! Conference with the King eh? Should I doff my forelock and bow a little?"

I smiled and grasped Iago's forearm, "Aye, I was receiving my orders for the morrow."

He looked down at my boots and I knew he was looking to see if I had spurs. "You command?"

"I am Prince Sancho's Campi Doctor and I train all of his young warriors."

The delight on Alfonso's face was obvious and filled me with joy for there was not a hint of jealousy or envy. He was the one I wished to impress, not Prince Sancho. "Then you have come on and done well. Come to the fire and speak with the others. They will be happy to speak with you."

As much as I wanted to return to Rodrigo and begin to plan the next day I had to speak with my old comrades. The young warriors were my charges but these were my friends. "Aye, but it will have to be brief. Tomorrow we are the flank guard and I have preparations to make."

Iago nodded, "I always knew that you would be a rising star. One day, Will, you will be a knight!"

I shook my head and my refusal to Prince Sancho stuck like a lump in my throat, "I am content and you, are you and all well? Maria?"

Alfonso now had more grey hairs than black and his face darkened, "We are all well, as is your foster mother, but Don Diego complains that he has too many servants and I fear that she may lose her place."

"But she has been there for many years and is part of the family."

"Your family, Will. You forget that Don Diego only swore to care for you until you were a man grown and that allowed Maria to live on the estate." He lowered his voice, "We heard that you were Campi Doctor and we have heard of the exploits of Rodrigo and Álvar. We knew that you would be involved but you should know that Don Diego resents his son's rise."

We reached the camp and there was such a roar from the others that those in the nearby camps turned to look to see if there was a fight, such an event was not uncommon in such a large army. I greeted them all and they each commented on the change in my appearance. It was only then I realised that the coin I had earned had allowed me to dress like a lord. I was paid more than Alfonso and that, suddenly, did not seem right. Alfonso and Iago had had to forage for food. Prince Sancho ensured that I had enough coins to buy what we needed. Don Diego had not changed.

As they questioned me, I discovered that they had not been to war since Atapuerca. I told them of the taking of Zaragoza and the raid into Badajoz. That confirmed what I had heard about Don Diego; he would only go to war when he was ordered. When I smelled the food begin to cook, I said, "I must get back to my men for I have commands to give. I will visit with you again for this will not be a swift campaign."

Iago laughed, "Listen to Caesar here!" He put his arm around me, "It is good to see one of us elevated. Remember Will, we live through you."

Alfonso walked me back through the camp, "Your father would be more than proud, Will. You have a reputation that is to be envied. None know the name of Alfonso the Armiger but William Redbeard who serves Prince Sancho is famous."

I shook my head, "It is Rodrigo de Vivar who will be famous, Alfonso. If I am a star then he is a comet and he will flash across the skies of Spain to illuminate it!"

Alfonso clutched his cross, "You are a fortune teller now?"

"I am but a path he walks briefly and soon I will no longer be needed. I am content with that for he will be a true knight that men can follow."

"Well it is good that at least one of us has a true knight to follow for Don Diego is here reluctantly and is already complaining about the coin he is losing. He hopes for a reward when we take Toledo."

"Then he will have to fight. Be safe, Alfonso!"

"Go with God, Will! I will tell Maria that you are well!"

Alfonso was a good man and a professional warrior. Don Diego did not deserve him. I wished that Prince Sancho would knight Rodrigo quickly so that I could ask Rodrigo to request to take on Alfonso and the others. Then they would be treated well, as they deserved.

Chapter 10

The next day we entered the Taifa of Toledo. In theory, being towards the centre of the column, we should not have had much to do. Prince Alfonso had men who watched the fore and one flank. King Ferdinand had other men watching too but the land was perfect for an ambush. Our progress was slow as King Ferdinand insisted upon the subjugation of even the smallest villages and the swearing of an oath of loyalty from all of those within. What worried me was that there appeared to be few Moors who swore such an oath and our slow progress meant that the Emir would have a clear picture of our line of march. Three days into the progress through Toledo we endured our first attack.

We were passing through the upper reaches of the Tajo valley where there were tracks and trails on both sides of the main road. Our task was to guard the right flank along with the men from Prince Alfonso's horsemen who were ahead of us. I had just taken our men behind a tiny hamlet of perhaps eight huts and houses to investigate a flock of birds which had taken flight, when horse archers swept down behind Prince Alfonso's men and headed for the King. His men were guarding the left flank of the vanguard. We did not see them but we heard the sound of their bowstrings as they released their arrows and Rodrigo saw the missiles as they

soared in the air above the trees. I raised my
spear and shouted, "Álvar, sound the alarm!" I
dug my heels into my new horse, regretting that
it was not Berber. Copper was a good horse but
was not a warhorse.

It was the houses of the hamlet and the trees
which masked us that allowed us to fall upon the
flank of the horse archers. There were at least
two hundred of them but they had neither shields
nor mail to protect them. We did not hit them as
I might have wished, in a solid line for the land
did not suit us. There were fences and little plots
of farmed land over which we trampled but
when we hit them it was as though they had
been struck by an axe for they had neither seen
nor expected us. Rodrigo was ahead thanks to
the fact that he was riding Babieca, the best
horse that day, and he drew first blood. I was
just behind him and I was able to admire the
skill with which he rammed the spearhead
between the ribs of the hapless horse archer and
then twisted as he pulled it out. It was a clean,
killing strike for entrails and organs came out
with the spearhead. Twisting the head enabled
him to bring out the spear without causing it
damage.

Then I had my first Moor to kill since the
Coimbra campaign. I pulled back my arm but
the Moor was slightly ahead of me and I had the
high back of his saddle to negotiate. It was not
as good a strike as Rodrigo's but it killed
instantly because I struck his spine and my spear
jarred in my hand. The bone stopped my spear
from penetrating too deeply and the rider slid,

already dead, from the saddle and I was able to pull my arm back. Some of the Moors had the ability to turn and loose an arrow at someone pursuing them and the next Moor did just that. He was less than twenty paces from me and I saw his hand release the arrow and knew that it brought my death. Alfonso's training when I had been a boy, however, saved me and my hand instinctively flicked up to take the arrow on my shield. The metal pieces of damaged arrows I had collected now almost completely covered the shield. It was heavier but that day I was grateful for the hours I had spent making it stronger as the arrow bounced off and I rammed my spear blindly, forward. I felt it strike flesh and, as I lowered my shield, I saw that the Moor had dropped his bow and was trying to hold in his guts. He slipped from the back of his horse.

All of my men were now engaged and Álvar's trumpet call had warned the King and his sons of the danger. A wall of shields and spears were presented and with Prince Alfonso's flank guards and ourselves, the attack was beaten off. As we reined in, for King Ferdinand had sounded the recall, I looked around and saw that we had lost none of my young warriors. Our four new warriors had survived. Each fight in which they emerged without a wound would increase their chances of survival.

I nodded to Rodrigo and Álvar, they were, effectively, my lieutenants and had both done well. "Our lions performed well."

Rodrigo pointed to the empty saddles of the horsemen of Prince Alfonso. "But not all of the men of our army have been as lucky." The lighter armed horsemen had been poorly led and had paid the price. Almost half had fallen although they had helped us to prevent greater losses to King Ferdinand and the main column. At our next camp, we were once again summoned to a council of war. I was the only one who was neither a knight nor a member of the royal family and I saw that neither Prince Alfonso nor Prince Garcia approved of my presence. King Ferdinand was not angry for he had had no losses but he was disappointed.

"We could have been hurt by the Moorish attack. We must have scouts out further from the column to give warning."

"But King Ferdinand that puts our men at great risk!"

"My son, Prince Alfonso, that is the risk you must take. Each of us is responsible for the protection of one part of the column. Our men share the risk."

"But I have the van too!"

Prince Sancho smiled, "If you would have my men do so then we are happy to undertake the task. We did so at Atapuerca where my men acquitted themselves well."

Alfonso's eyes glared at his brother, "We will continue as we are but I think we ought to hang the Moors we find in this land. It will deter them."

Don Raoul shook his head, "It would have the opposite effect, Prince Alfonso, for it would harden resistance."

181

King Ferdinand nodded, "We are not far from Salamanca and that is a mighty fortress. If we can reduce it then the Emir will have to sue for peace and will offer us tribute."

"And if that does not work, father?"

"Then, Prince Garcia, we will take Magerit and threaten Toledo city itself. We have already hurt the Moors of Toledo and not had to fight a battle. This ambush is like the biting of an insect and does not affect our ability to fight. Let us see where we are in September before we talk of hanging." The King spoke to his two younger sons as though they were miscreant schoolboys who needed scolding and in that he was right.

That night Prince Sancho came to see us. "You did well today and my father is pleased." I gave him a sharp look for his father had had the opportunity to say so at the meeting but had declined to do so. Was Prince Sancho making it up? Prince Sancho was well attuned to his men and their reactions. He seemed to read my thoughts, "My brother already feels that I am the favourite and if he had praised my men before my brothers then it would have increased the existing rift. We both seek to heal it for my father has a vision of one Spain and I share that vision."

Rodrigo nodded, "But it will be a land of Moor and Christian, Prince Sancho. How will your father reconcile the two?"

"Have you not noticed, Rodrigo, that we do not persecute the Moors who live in our kingdom? So long as they pay their taxes and swear allegiance to the King then they are allowed to prosper. We will do so once we have conquered the taifas." I understood the policy, I was not certain that the younger brothers were of the same opinion.

I was not looking forward to Salamanca for this meant a siege and from what I had heard they were bloody places. That night I spoke with Don Raoul about it and the potential dangers of a siege. He smiled at me. He was the same age as Alfonso and I think that, as he had no children of his own, he viewed me as the son he never had. Certainly, he humoured my questions. "Do not fear, William, for King Ferdinand is a clever general and chooses Salamanca deliberately. The city guards the western side of the Taifa and once, a hundred years ago, it was a mighty fortress for there were great churches and a cathedral there, but once the Moors captured it then the Christians left and the town became unimportant. There are walls but they are not the walls of Toledo and the garrison will not be a large one. It will not be easy but it will fall and once we have it, we can demand tribute. Magerit is also somewhere we can reduce. By taking places that are easy then we weaken the enemy and give our soldiers more confidence. Toledo is the jewel in the crown and as such would be hard to take if it was fully garrisoned. By taking the smaller places we diminish the number of men who can man the walls of Toledo. Do not be afraid of the siege for you and your men are well trained and it will do you good to fight at a siege for you are a warrior, I can see that, and you will have to scale a wall sometime. Better an easy one than Toledo or Valencia!"

Heartened by the conversation, I spoke with Rodrigo. He was as interested as I had been for, like me, he had wondered at the wisdom of taking a city with an army made up of horsemen. "Don Raoul is right and we are still enjoying an education. I am pleased that I am yet to be knighted for I see knights who stop learning and I have a hunger for knowledge. I would be the complete warrior." He smiled at my face, "I am noble-born but I am not like my father and I do not choose commerce and farming. I choose the sword." He took out his sword. "This is a good sword and has served me well but, when I become a knight, I will find a weaponsmith, probably in Córdoba where they make the best swords and have a weapon made which serves me. To do that I need to know as much about war as I can."

That was Rodrigo de Vivar all over; he was a perfectionist in all that he did and he would not compromise. Perhaps that helped to contribute to his downfall. But I get ahead of myself. The man who became known as El Cid, El Campeador, was not yet even a knight of Castile!

When we reached Salamanca, I saw what Don Raoul had meant. The castle and town walls could only keep an enemy away if they were maintained. The Moors had let the walls fall into disarray. Mortar dried in the hot Salamancan summers and the freezing winters made them crumble. I saw large pieces of masonry in the ditches which surrounded the town. Only the gatehouses had been maintained but the walls circumnavigated the town and there were weak places where we could attack. Beyond the walls, we could see the cathedral and the churches as well as the mosque. They were a symbol of what had been and what could be again; if the town was returned to Christian rule.

King Ferdinand had heralds who could speak Arabic and they rode to the gates to demand the surrender of the town. The mighty host which surrounded it should have been enough to persuade them but, perhaps, they thought that their walls would keep us out or they may have had word that relief would come their way. Once again, as Rodrigo and I helped to set up our camp, after the rejection by the town of our demands, we spoke of the genius of King Ferdinand. When we had left the Tajo valley we had headed west, away from Toledo and the move had caught out the Moors. There might be an army heading west to fight us but there would be a delay for we were no longer where they thought we were, heading for Toledo, and King Ferdinand hoped to take Salamanca before they could reach us.

The town was surrounded and each of the four segments of the army was given a section to watch and then to assault. The three princes urged their men to complete their ladders first for there would be no siege engines and each wanted the honour of being the first over the walls. This would be a simple attack using ladders and men climbing through a storm of arrows, javelins, stones and, perhaps, boiling oil!

Don Raoul showed his experience by ordering great pavise to be made. These were man-sized shields and would allow us to walk close to the wall without risk from arrows and stones. Our small shields would be of little use against a rainstorm of arrows.

Hassan ibn Hassan had accompanied us for Rodrigo still wished to continue his lessons. He proved to be useful for he had once lived in the town and the fact that he had no eyes did not impair him for he was able to describe what he remembered. He told Rodrigo that the fighting platform was just the height of two men and that the access to the walls was up ladders and not stone staircases. He said that the gates would be strong for they could continue to hold out after the walls had fallen and that within the town was a keep, a bastion, into which the garrison could retire. Rodrigo told Prince Sancho and we were better prepared than some of the men who would attack.

Prince Alfonso's and Prince Sancho's men were ready first. The two brothers would attack the opposite ends of the town. Next to our men and ladders were the men of King Ferdinand and, as we prepared to assault, we saw Rodrigo's father, Alfonso and the rest of his retinue watching us. Alfonso and Iago waved cheerily to me but Don Diego was impassive. Prince Sancho would lead his knights on the left of our line. His foot soldiers would assault the centre and we would take the right, closest to the King. We had just one ladder for our young warriors to climb. The Prince had three ladders and the foot soldiers and peasants, four. I had already decided that I would lead with Rodrigo behind me. Álvar would be the tenth man up in case the others needed encouragement. He would be the anchor.

Prince Sancho sounded the horn and, as we advanced behind pavise made and brought to us by our servants, King Ferdinand's men gave us a cheer and I, for one, felt heartened. I knew that my former shield brothers would be willing me on and, more importantly watching me. This would be the first time they had seen me fight since Atapuerca. Then they would attack for I saw the preparations being made to advance next to us. We had three hundred paces to march over steadily rising land before we would reach the ditch. The first hundred paces were eerily silent except for the grunt of the men to the side of us. My lions were silent for they were well trained. Then the arrows began to thud into the pavise. The shields were crudely made things but effective for they were thick planks and boards hammered together. They were heavy but with two men carrying each one, the load was shared. Rodrigo and I carried ours. The closer we came to the walls so the cacophony grew for stones and arrows clattered into them. To our left, I heard a cry from a careless carrier; the safest way to carry was to be as close to each other as possible and keep bent over. Our line marched in a straight line.

I had examined the ground before the attack and knew that just before the ditch there was a line of rubble and fallen masonry from the walls and when I neared it, I shouted, "Prepare to cross the ditch!" We had warned the lions about the dangers of the ditch and they all knew what to do. The worst thing to do would be to rush. I had told them that we would go slower there than on the approach. The decision proved to be a good one for to our left five men on the next ladder fell as they hurried and their pavise was dropped. Moorish archers knew their business and a gap appeared on our flank as they poured arrow after arrow into the men. The pavise Rodrigo and I carried was becoming heavier for it was laden with arrows. Behind us, our men carried our ladder with their right arms whilst holding their shields above their heads. It was why Rodrigo and I had taken on the onerous task of carrying the pavise for we had our shields held over our heads as well. The fallen masonry helped us to negotiate the ditch but when an arrow clanged off my helmet, I knew that I had been lucky.

Once we reached the wall then Rodrigo and I laid the pavise against the wall as the ladder was brought up. We held our shields above our heads and it proved to be a wise decision as stones were dropped from above. The foot soldiers, to our left, were suffering and I knew that we had to begin to climb quickly to give them heart for my men were the sons of nobles while the ones to my left were swords for hire. If they were wounded then their lives as they knew it would end for no one wanted a wounded soldier. I put my dagger in my left hand and, as the ladder was placed and then braced by our

strongest warriors, protected by two men
holding the pavise, I began to climb. There was
a temptation to draw my sword but I knew that I
would need my right hand to grip the ladder. I
would have to endure whatever missile and
weapon came my way.

Don Raoul had explained the technique I
would need and I employed it now. I placed my
left hand as high up the ladder as I could manage
and I angled the shield to afford as much
protection as possible. Then I used my right
hand to pull me up until my head touched my
shield. I repeated that and slowly climbed.
Hassan ibn Hassan's description helped me for I
was able to estimate where the top of the wall
and the ladder lay. I knew that they had men
trying to push the ladder away from the wall but
the moment for that to work had passed. Now
there were four mailed men on the ladder, we
would be too heavy to push and our archers and
crossbows were hitting the men holding the
poles. The closer I came to the crenulations then
the more parlous became my position for they
were able to thrust spears at me from the side
where I had just my mail to protect me. Even as
one spear was rammed into my right side and I
felt the trickle of blood where it had broken flesh
the spearman was hit by a crossbow bolt and
tumbled to the ground. The foot soldiers to our
left had not managed to make the wall yet and so
we had to endure the full force of the Moors
attack.

When I felt the top of the ladder, I knew
that I could use my right hand again. I drew my

sword and then had the hardest task of all, I had
to walk up the last few rungs unaided and it
would be when I was the most vulnerable. The
fact that Rodrigo was below me calling out
encouragement helped me and as I raised my
sword, I almost raced up the last few rungs. I
swung my shield and dagger as I cleared the top
of the wall and, leaning forward I swung my
sword. It almost proved to be my undoing for I
overbalanced and began to fall but that,
ironically, saved me for the two spears did not
strike my side, where they were aimed, but slid
over my back. Even more fortuitous was the fact
that, as I swung my shield, I connected with the
side of one spearman's head and as I fell, I
landed on the other. My sword was between us
and whilst one edge was pressed against my
mail and did no harm, the other was across his
throat and he was almost decapitated by my
weight.

As I was rising, a sword cracked across my
back and I flailed with my sword to give me
time to regain my feet. I was on the fighting
platform and facing three men. Rodrigo was still
climbing, I remembered the words of Alfonso,
'*if you are fighting more than one opponent then
take the strongest first*'. The sword which was
swung at me came from a huge mailed askari. I
flicked it aside with my shield which I angled
down. At the same time, I used my sword to
block the weaker blows from the other two.
Then I lunged with my dagger held in my shield
hand. My dagger had a needle tip, it was almost
a stiletto and it burst through the mail links and

into his left side. I am not sure if it was a mortal wound but his fall to the bailey below was. As he fell, I swung my dagger around while slashing with my sword. One Moorish sword struck my helmet but I kept my feet and one of the Moors fell.

Behind me, I heard, "Will, ware right!" Rodrigo stepped next to me and the two of us had a foothold on the wall. I stepped to the side and blocked another blow. I had had enough of being outnumbered and I roared as I stepped forward and brought my sword into the neck of a Moor. Three others fell back and that allowed Carlos to step to the other side of Rodrigo. With a section of the wall in our hands then we had changed the balance of power. Now those on either side of us, fighting the foot soldiers of Prince Sancho and the men of King Ferdinand were looking over their shoulders. The fighting platform was a narrow battlefield and their defence was to their front.

I saw that the first ladder to our right was at the wall, it would be King Ferdinand's men, and I took the decision to go to their aid. "Lions, form a wedge behind me!" There was logic to my choice for this meant our shields were on our left and the archers in their keep and on the ground below us had less of a target. Rodrigo locked his shield with mine and we angled our swords over the top. I still had my needle-pointed dagger in my left hand and Carlos slipped his shield to lock with mine. We stepped forward.

I learned a lesson about defending walls that day as there were few mailed men for us to fight. Had there been we might have struggled. As it was the men we faced were lightly armed and wore no armour. Some did not even have helmets. To defend walls well and effectively, you needed a sprinkling of mailed knights. Had there been more on the wall then we might have been beaten back, as it was, we were able to progress. We moved towards the nearest Moors and they were attacking four of the ladders belonging to King Ferdinand. When I heard the cry, 'Vivar! Vivar!' then I knew that my shield brothers, led by Alfonso, were ascending and it added impetus to our attack for Rodrigo and I were close to them. We were not slashing for there was little room. Instead, we used the tips of our swords and lunged. Against mailed men that would not have worked as well as it did but the men we stabbed wore no mail and sword tips slid through cotton and even thin leather easily. Once in flesh, the three of us turned our blades to enlarge the wound and blood flowed before withdrawing them to add to the damage and the likelihood of death. I saw the men of Lord Lain clamber over the wall and we moved on. The next ladder was being attacked by four men, one of whom had an axe. I saw Ramon clamber over and stand on the crenulations. Even as he brought his sword into the head of one Moor a mailed warrior with a two-handed sword swung at his legs and took them both. Ramon seemed to hang there for an instant and then tumbled back, down to the ground. To my horror, it was

Alfonso who raised his head next and the mailed
Moor back swung and took the head of the man
who had raised me. I had no time to shout,
scream or do anything. I just stood as though
petrified. Later I would realise that it was a
quick death but that would be later when the
blood had left my head and I had become sane
once more.

I know not what happened next for a red
mist descended and I screamed in rage and
hurled myself at the three men who remained
before me. I forgot my own fighting instructions.
I ignored every rule by which I had lived and I
tore into them. I back-handed one with my
shield as I brought down my sword onto the
helmet and head of a second. I was lost in the
moment of battle and all I saw was Alfonso's
head flying through the air and all I wanted was
to butcher the huge mailed Moor who had killed
him. This was, for the first time in my life,
personal. I rushed at him and he swung his
sword with all of his might to repeat the blow
which had killed two of my shield brothers. It
smacked into my shield and was so powerful a
strike that I reeled but I kept my feet and I threw
myself at him using my shield and body as a
weapon. He was a big man but I knocked him
from the fighting platform. Unfortunately, in my
anger I went with him for I could not stop
myself and I sailed over the open side, too. I
know not how I survived except that I landed on
his body. As I crashed into the ground and the
Moor my shield took some of the force and my
dagger sliced through his neck spraying me in

blood. I was winded but I was alive. I looked around and saw Moors running at me. I forced myself to my feet, acutely aware that I had hurt myself and I was finding it difficult to breathe. Alfonso was dead and soon I would join him but I would take as many Moors with me as I could. I saw the gate was just forty paces from me and, remembering the words of Hassan ibn Hassan, I ran at it. I could hear voices behind me calling my name but they seemed to be coming from another world and I ignored them. Alfonso and Ramon would be avenged.

I had no idea what were the wounds I had suffered and I did not seem to be slowed as I hurtled towards the gatehouse. I was in pain but, strangely, it did not slow me as it should have done. Moors ran at me but while I saw enemies to kill, they saw a mighty, undefeated warrior covered in blood and gore. They saw a man who had fallen to his death and risen, like Lazarus. They hesitated and I did not. I used my small shield to step inside weapons knowing that the dagger I still held in my hand would gut them as I ran past them. I was now able to use the blade on my sword and I ripped through thin leather and flesh as though they were parchment. I do not know if their weapons touched me but if they did then they neither hurt me nor slowed me. I saw four Moors turn to face me but I did not slow nor was I daunted by their weapons. When a Moorish spear was thrown from behind me to embed itself in the chest of the largest warrior, I took that as a sign that God was on my side. I held the shield before my face and punched at the warrior to my left as I hacked across the other two. I connected with flesh as a sword rang against my helmet. One warrior remained and I hit his head with my sword as I rammed my dagger into his middle. Rage took over and I hacked and slashed into him long after life had left him.

Rodrigo almost lost his life when he grabbed my shoulder and tried to speak to me. I whirled with a weapon ready to rip out the throat of another enemy and then I saw that it was Rodrigo. It was almost as though I could not hear him. Carlos restrained my sword arm and I finally heard Rodrigo's voice, "Peace, William, we have won. Let us open the gate and let in the King's men!"

With the blood no longer boiling in my ears I nodded, "Aye!" I could barely speak.

There were just three men left at the gate and seeing us they dropped to their knees with their hands held up in supplication. A few moments earlier and I would have slaughtered them but Rodrigo' arrival had calmed me, a little. We opened the gates and stood back as King Fernando's men flooded in.

I looked at the man with the Moorish spear in his chest, the spear of God, and I turned to Rodrigo, "The spear? You threw it?"

He grinned, "It was a lucky throw for it could just as easily have hit you as the Moor but God guided my hand." He shook his head, "What madness overtook you? Were you possessed by the Devil?"

"I know not but when Alfonso died, I saw red and all that I wanted to do was to slaughter."

The great mass of men had entered and King Ferdinand and Prince Sancho stood there. Both were smiling but Prince Sancho had the biggest grin I had ever seen. The King said, "And you three took the gate?" I nodded, dumbly, and the King waved a hand down my blood-covered surcoat and mail. "Are you wounded?"

I shrugged, "In all truth, Your Majesty, I know not for the blood was in my head too."

"Rodrigo, take the Campi Doctor to the healers at our camp! We will speak more of this later."

"Yes, Prince Sancho!"

Chapter 11

We trudged back over a field still littered with most of the dead. That there were not as many as there might have been was a result of Don Raoul's suggestion to use pavise. As we neared the tents of the healers and doctors, I saw some of the lions who had been wounded. They must have fallen climbing the ladder and they were having their injuries tended. The healers were all occupied and so Rodrigo said, "Let us take off Will's mail and surcoat, Carlos. There is so much blood and damage that it is hard to see where he is wounded."

I did not mind for I was exhausted and my mind still reeled that Ramon and Alfonso had both died. When I had been fighting, I had felt as though I could have fought all day and night but now it was over, I felt as weak as a newborn babe. Carlos handed me a wineskin and I drank. I had not eaten for some hours and I knew that I would soon be drunk. I began to feel a little light-headed and dizzy and so I put it down to the wine.

Rodrigo shouted angrily, "I need a healer, now!"

And then all went black and I saw nothing more until the face of my father came into my head. I had been barely a child when he had died but I remembered his face and his red beard. It was my father and he was smiling. Behind him, I

saw a fleet of Viking ships and then all went
black again.

When I opened my eyes, it was dark and I
was in a tent with candles burning. I looked up
and saw a man I did not recognise and assumed
he was the healer for he was wiping his bloody
hands on a cloth. Then I saw Rodrigo and Álvar
and, finally, Iago. My old shield brother had a
bandage across one eye. It was he who spoke,
"The Viking returns!"

I croaked, "Viking?"

He laughed and gestured to the others, "I
was telling these young warriors of the stories
your father told us about his grandfather and the
Vikings who raided Paris and the Seine. They
told us tales of warriors who went berserk when
the red mist descended. That was you. I reached
the top of the walls as you leapt at that Moor and
I was trying to get to your side when you and
Rodrigo took the gate. You, my friend, went
berserk and this day I saw a Viking fighting. I
confess it terrified me. I helped to train you but I
would not have faced you when you fought on
the fighting platform of Salamanca!"

The healer spoke, "And I would not
recommend it again, Campi Doctor, for you
have several wounds. You were lucky that none
were serious but I would not recommend that
you fight for the next few days. Blows to the
head can be dangerous and you took a hard hit.
In addition to which you have broken ribs and I
have had to stitch a larger number of wounds
than I would like. You are lucky!"

Rodrigo nodded, "I, too, thought I had lost you but it just shows what determined men can do. We would still be trying to take the gate had you not thrown away all reason. The rest of our men, Prince Garcia and Prince Alfonso, failed to take their sections of the walls."

Iago said, "Aye, and I had better leave you two for Don Diego will be seeking me."

Rodrigo asked, "Did my father climb the ladder and fight?"

Iago was an honest man and could not lie, especially not to a true warrior. He shook his head, "Your father said that he turned his ankle as we left the camp which was why Ramon and Alfonso were leading. I am the new armiger which means that, in all likelihood, I will be following Alfonso and enjoy an early death!"

"Is the wound to your eye serious, old friend?"

He shook his head, "No, Will, a dagger cut my forehead and the pommel hit my eye but I am not blind if that is what you fear. Old Iago is not done for yet!"

When he left Rodrigo's face became dark, "My father never changes. I keep hoping that he might but it is a false hope and good men die while he squats like a toad and watches them."

"If it is any consolation, Alfonso and Ramon would never have expected to live so long. How many white-haired armigers have you seen?"

He nodded, "Can we take him back to our camp, healer?"

"Aye, and if you can find fresh liver for him to eat, I believe it can be efficacious for he lost much blood but keep his sword sheathed for a few days I beg of you."

"We will do so. Come, William, let us help you. Carlos took your sword, helmet and mail back to the camp. There will be food waiting for you and we will try to get some liver!"

My men made a great fuss of me for they thought when they had seen me fall from the fighting platform, that I had died. When they heard of what we had done they were even more impressed and determined to become better warriors. I enjoyed the liver which was cooked rare but the wine was even more of a pleasure for it dulled the pain from the stitches and the broken ribs. Don Raoul arrived at our camp shortly before I was about to say that I intended to retire to bed.

He smiled at me, "I did not witness your act but I have heard it was reckless in the extreme. I would not recommend that you have your lions emulate you! There is only so much luck which is available."

"I lost a foster father and the man who trained me, the result was that I lost my head." That was as simple as I could make it and Don Raoul understood.

"Tomorrow the King and Prince Sancho wish to thank the three of you for your actions today. You won the walls and saved many lives."

I was about to nod and remembered my head wound, "We will be there although my armour, helmet and surcoat may need cleaning."

Rodrigo said, "Fear not, Pablo, Stephen and Hassan have cleaned your mail and polished your helmet although they cannot repair it and the dent will need a weaponsmith."

"They are badges of honour and courage. Wear them proudly and worry not about how you look. It is that which is in your heart that the King wishes to reward." Don Raoul smiled proudly at me.

I slept surprisingly well but, when I woke, I felt each and every wound. My body ached all over. The Moor's body may have saved my life but I still had broken bones and bruises. Pablo and Stephen helped me to dress and when I donned my mail it was agony. As we headed towards the open gates of the town, I saw that our dead were being buried. I suddenly felt guilty that I was not there to see Alfonso and Ramon placed on the ground. I could not refuse the command of King Ferdinand but I knew where I would rather be. I saw that all of the knights and leaders had been summoned. The Archbishop of León had accompanied the King and we would all gather in the cathedral to thank God for our victory.

After the service the King stood, bareheaded before the altar. He raised his hands for silence. I saw that his three sons had joined the Archbishop. When he spoke it was with a powerful voice that carried across the nave of the cathedral, "We had a great victory yesterday and God came to our aid. We can now move towards Toledo where we will bring the Emir of that Taifa to heel. It is not only God that we have to thank. Step forward William, known as Redbeard, Campi Doctor to Prince Sancho."

Standing and walking towards the altar took longer than I would ever have dreamed before I had been wounded and I was sweating by the time I reached the King.

"Let all know that William known as the Redbeard is to be given five-hundredths of the treasure which we will take on this campaign and that he is to be accorded the title of Hero of Salamanca." There was cheering although it came mainly from Prince Sancho's men.

I bowed, "I thank King Ferdinand but we all serve God, León and yourself and it is an honour to do so."

When he smiled, I knew that I had done and said the right thing. As I walked back to my place, I knew that he had given me a small fortune. The King would take six-tenths of what we collected while the church and his three sons would each receive an equal share of three tenths. The last tenth was for the rank and file and I was to be given half of that. It had not cost the King nor his sons anything as my share came from those who had not fought and would be seen by the others as a punishment. Apart from the men of Prince Sancho there would be resentment and I would have to endure looks, stares and comments, more, there would be men with murderous intent.

King Ferdinand spoke again, "William, the Hero of Salamanca has his reward but there are others who need one too. When the young warriors who followed their brave leader claimed the walls, they showed courage every bit as much as the man who led them. For that, we will knight those who were first over the wall: Rodrigo de Vivar, Carlos of Burgos, Ramon son of Ramon, Ricardo of Palencia, Fernando of Oviedo and Rafael of Benevente. All of you, step forward and receive your reward."

It was only as they stepped forward that I realised Álvar was not named. Then I remembered that he had been tenth in the line of warriors waiting to climb the ladder and was not the first one over. He would not be happy and I did not blame him. To be knighted after a battle was a great honour, probably the greatest one any warrior could receive and to be knighted by the King was the ultimate accolade. After each had been knighted, they were embraced by Prince Sancho. I was losing six of my men for they would now join Don Raoul. I realised that I would have to call Rodrigo, Don, as would Álvar. I wondered how this simple ceremony would change our lives and the way that we would fight in the future. I would now have far fewer men to command and we would not be as potent a force as we once had been; adjustments would need to be made. The King, Archbishop and the three Princes all left the cathedral first and then the rest of us followed.

Lord Lain was waiting for his grandson as was Peyre Pringos. They also embraced Don Rodrigo and showed their unbridled joy. We crowded around the others to congratulate them and as Lord Lain led his grandson off, I noticed that Don Diego was not there. I did not think for one moment that he would be with his men and so he was deliberately ignoring his newly knighted son. I suppose I had thought, until that moment, that there might be some sort of reconciliation between father and son. I knew that Don Rodrigo would have happily buried any animosity. It was sad. I had a father I could never see for he was dead and Don Rodrigo had a father who chose not to see him.

Álvar sidled up to me, "Will, why were you not given a knighthood?"

I knew the reason was that I had hesitated when Prince Sancho had mentioned it that first time now so long ago. Thinking back, I realised he had never actually offered me one. He had asked, hypothetically, if I would have accepted one. Prince Sancho knew the value of nobles and I was a peasant. I shrugged, "It is a title, Álvar, that is all. With the treasure King Ferdinand has given me I will be a rich man and I can retire should I wish to."

He laughed, "And you will not retire, for you are a warrior. But it is still not right."

I knew then that he was not just talking about me but about himself. "Álvar, you should have been knighted. If I had been asked, and I was not, then I would have given your name before some of the others."

He nodded, "Aye, Will, for normally I would have been where Carlos was but I was bolstering the weaker ones in the centre." He smiled, "But from now on I shall be at the fore, will I not, Campi Doctor, for in your eyes I am senior, despite what Prince Sancho might think?"

"Of course."

After that day there was a slight change in Álvar. His loyalty to Rodrigo and myself never wavered but he no longer blindly followed Prince Sancho as he had done before. It was a subtle change and I believe that I was the only one who noticed although Rodrigo was such an astute leader that I am sure he would have noticed too.

We did not see Rodrigo again until the evening when he arrived back at our camp, slightly the worse for wear. Álvar along with Pablo and Stephen put him to bed. Don Raoul arrived shortly after Rodrigo's snores could be heard from the tent. He smiled and gestured for me to walk with him.

"Campi Doctor, the knighthoods those six received were down to you and I hope that they know that. They are all incredibly young to be knights but they deserve it," he hesitated, "as do you. Know that I urged Prince Sancho to knight you, as did his father, the King." He shrugged, "I am sorry."

I had had all day to think about this and I had come to the conclusion that it made no difference to me. I was still Campi Doctor and that was a position of great authority. I was rich and I could buy land. The only difference which I could see was that I would not have the title of Don. "Armiger, do you think this will make any difference to the way I do my job or live my life?"

He looked at me, "In all truth I can say, no, and that is remarkable for most men would resent it." He pointed to Álvar who sat alone at the fire, "There is one who does resent that he was overlooked."

"Do not worry about Álvar, he will become a knight one day. I honestly believe that all of the men I train will become knights. Prince Sancho has created a good system."

"You have created the system but I am here because you know that this will precipitate a change. Those six knights will leave your side tomorrow and ride with me and the Prince. Those six are selected to help me to guard the body of the Prince. I came to tell you that to your face."

"And I knew that. You and I have no children, Don Raoul, but this is the moment that every parent expects; it is the moment when the fledgeling leaves the nest and flies off. It is inevitable and we can do nothing about it. It is life."

He clasped my arm, "And you are a good man with more knightly virtues than many who have been knighted. I will see you on the morrow when I come to fetch my charges."

That night was the first and only time I saw Rodrigo drunk. He was ill for most of the night and my wounds kept me awake too. It meant that I was with him when he groggily rose well before dawn and the call to wake. Pablo washed him and I sent him to fetch food.

"I could not possibly eat and keep the food down, Will."

"Don Rodrigo, it will help you, trust me I know."

"What is this Don Rodrigo? I am Rodrigo and nothing has changed."

"Everything has changed, Don Rodrigo. Later this morning you and the others will leave the lions and join Don Raoul. When next we go into battle you will follow him and not me. I am proud for you have become a knight and I swore that I would make you one."

"You should have been knighted."

"But I was not and I am content."

It was almost as though he suddenly sobered up and the night of drinking had vanished, "Minaya! He should have been knighted!"

I nodded, "Aye, but no one asked me. Fear not, he will become one in the fullness of time."

I saw the distress on his face, "But he and I were destined to be together. I saw the three of us leading King Ferdinand's army to victory."

"And that dream may come true, although I doubt it. Your future has changed and you will be a great lord."

Pablo came back with food and Rodrigo ate it, albeit reluctantly. I smiled at the servant, "I shall miss you, Stephen, Pablo and even Hassan."

Rodrigo looked up as Pablo said, "And we will miss you too, lord, for we owe you our lives."

"I am not a lord!"

He smiled, "You may not have the title but those who know you accord you that title."

Rodrigo said, "Why will Pablo not see you later?"

"Because this morning you will leave this camp too. You did not think that you would just follow Don Raoul in the day? You will now camp with the knights. Back at Lion's Den, you will be housed with the Prince. Our world has changed, Don Rodrigo, and we must change with it."

Don Rodrigo had no time for a long farewell. He was fetched, along with the others, and we packed up our camp to head east. The rest of our men were delighted for the six who had been knighted for they saw their future there. For Álvar and me it was different and we were quiet as we mounted. I realised that I would have to hire servants when we returned to León for we had used Pablo and Stephen. As we rode west, Álvar and I were side by side and we could see just ahead, our six former comrades riding close to the Prince. It was as though we had been left behind.

I had much to think about as we rode. My injuries made concentration difficult but I forced myself to make plans as we slowly made our way east. It would take the better part of eight days to reach Magerit and I had things to reorganise. I gave the horn and our standard to

Iago of Astorga. He was a reliable man. I needed
Álvar as my lieutenant. We spoke each and
every mile for I knew that I had not spoken to
him as much as Rodrigo and he needed to know
my mind as well as I knew his.

By the time we reached Magerit most of my
wounds had healed and I was able, for the first
time, to ride Killer. It was not before time either
for the Emir of Toledo had refused to become a
vassal of King Ferdinand. Our successful attack
on Salamanca might have isolated him from
Badajoz but his army had yet to suffer a defeat
and so we prepared to begin another siege. Álvar
and I had spoken of this as we had headed east
and neither of us wanted our men to be the first
up the ladders. Magerit was no Salamanca.
Although the walls were smaller, they were also
well maintained and newer; worse, the garrison
and its inhabitants were well prepared. We
might have caught them unawares at Salamanca
but our slow progress east had told them that we
would either attack Magerit or Toledo.

I was summoned by Prince Sancho to the
council of war. I was now the Hero of
Salamanca although few, if any, used that title. I
was still William the Redbeard or simply
Redbeard to my friends while to my enemies,
and there were many, I was the peasant or the
barbarian. After my berserk attack, the latter was
more commonly used! The men of Prince
Sancho's retinue were friends and they called to
me as I walked through their camp. Rodrigo
came racing to see me. I had not spoken to him

since he had left our camp. "Your wounds have healed?"

"Thank you for asking, Don Rodrigo. I am healed and I am eager to serve the Prince again."

He frowned, "None of that!" he lowered his voice, "We both know what you truly feel." I nodded, "How are Álvar and the others?"

"You and the others are missed but you have given them the spur to prick them and they will soon be knights and then I will be able to retire and use the King's money to buy an estate where I will grow old and fat!"

He laughed, "Others may believe that but I know you better."

"I had better go for I am summoned and I dare not upset Prince Sancho."

The area outside the King's tent was guarded by his bodyguards so that none could hear his words save those in the centre. I stood with Don Raoul. The King smiled ruefully as Prince Garcia arrived last, "Now that we are all gathered, we can begin. This will not be an easy assault. This time they have prepared and there are clean ditches and strengthened defences and we cannot count on luck nor a wild man who cares not if he lives or dies." He and everyone else looked at me.

Don Raoul said, out of the side of his mouth, "I think you can expect this for some time!"

The King frowned and then continued, "However, I see no reason to change the method of attack except in one respect. This time we all attack together. Had we done so the last time we might have lost fewer men. I want each and every man in his position an hour before dawn. When the signal is given to attack then we all march to war, together. They might know that we are coming but they have split their men between here and Toledo and that means we will face fewer men. We should prevail and then I have no doubt that they will accept my demands."

As we left Don Raoul said, "Come to the Prince's camp for he wishes to speak with you."

The Prince was ahead of us and by the time we reached his camp, I could hear laughter from his knights. They were all in good humour. He saw me and began to clap his hands together, the knights joined in, "I realised I had not seen you since Salamanca, Campi Doctor. You are a credit to us all." He waved at Rodrigo and the others I had trained. "And now we see the benefit of your methods!" He put his arm around me, "Come, let us go to my tent."

Once inside his servant poured wine and then hurried outside. The Prince raised his goblet, "The Hero of Salamanca."

"Thank you, Prince Sancho." I knew not what else to say.

"I have a number of reasons for bringing you here not least the fact that Don Rodrigo and the others have been pestering me to demand that you become a knight. I pointed out that you were offered that once and refused." I did not say out loud that it had not been offered I merely nodded. "I wanted to clear the air. Do you resent the fact that you are not a knight?"

I shook my head, "No, Prince Sancho, for I am happy, for the present, to be Campi Doctor and when your father gives me my reward, I may be in a position to buy some land."

"And leave my service?" I heard the anxiety in his voice.

"You made me Campi Doctor to train your young warriors. Most are almost trained and then I will no longer be needed."

"I would not like that." This time there was the hint of a threat in his voice which I did not like. Then he smiled, "However, that is for the future and I hope I can persuade you to stay. You and my lions did well when we assaulted Salamanca but you are fewer in number and I have a different task for you this time. The Moors will have spies and scouts watching our progress. I wish you to deter them. I would have you ride the road twixt Toledo and Magerit to dishearten and discourage the Moors."

I nodded, "That we shall do."

"Good and think hard about your future. One day I shall be King and if you stay with me then the rewards given by my father will seem as nothing."

Álvar had mixed feelings when I told him of our role. Part of him was excited at the prospect of independent action but he wished for the opportunity to perform a heroic act whilst the King or the Prince was watching. I knew that and so I added, "Do not worry too much about where you fight. You will become a knight. Know that I intend to press the Prince to knight you once we return to our home and Lion's Den.

I have fought a number of times since Atapuerca and Rodrigo and the others were the only ones knighted after a battle. You have a better chance of knighthood through hard work and it will come. You have my word on that."

He beamed, "Then I am happy for you are never forsworn and you are a man of your word."

We spent the rest of the day preparing the men. I would ride Berber for he was best suited for this role and being a Moorish horse was less likely to spook the enemy. I knew that the disadvantage we had would be that we were mailed and the enemy horse faster. To that end I had Álvar choose six good men to ride half a mile from our right flank. He would lead those men and if Moors tried to flee away from us then he might catch them. I had another six men who would ride to the left remaining in clear sight of us. They would encourage any scouts we met to ride to the west and Álvar. We left a camp filled with the sound of hammering as rams and ladders were built and we headed south.

This was not a mountainous country. There were hills and there were valleys but they were gentle and it was fertile and filled with farms. Olive and lemon groves lined the road. Animals grazed on the hillsides. More importantly, there were no strongholds between the two towns and as the distance was fifty miles between the two it was unlikely that we would have to deal with garrison troops. There would be scouts and they would ride fast horses. I was not hopeful that we would either fight or capture any but our very presence might discourage them. On the first day, just as we were about to turn and return north, Garcia pointed ahead. There was a flash of white. It was little enough but as we had seen no one all day, I gave the command to investigate. It soon became obvious that it was Moorish scouts and the odds were that they were in Toledo. There were three of them and they each led a spare horse. Seeing us, they turned and galloped away. The six men to our left were led by Juan and he was keen and young. He urged his horses and men on to follow the scouts and they began to pull away from us and draw closer to the Moors.

The Moors were four hundred paces from us and I saw faces turned to see how close we were. Juan and his patrol were less than three hundred paces away and I saw the Moors' skill when they jumped on to the backs of their galloping spare horse and then let go of their first horse. Soon the three scouts were five hundred paces from us and drawing further away with each hoofbeat. As we drew next to the three spare horses I said, "Raoul, sound the recall. We will not catch them."

As we led the three horses back into our camp, I knew that most of my men would see this as a failure while I knew that it was a victory. We had denied the enemy the knowledge they needed. That they would come again was clear but we now had a better idea of what we would see. I had not thought that they would bring spare horses but now it became obvious. Toledo was not that close to Magerit.

When we neared our camp, I saw that there was hustle, bustle and defences were being built. The attack had not yet begun but I saw the completed ladders and rams. I knew from the counsel of war that they would be in position before dawn and that when we left the next morning, the attack would have already started. I sat with Álvar while we ate and studied the map.

"They will not send scouts up the same road tomorrow for they know that we are watching it. We will take this other road, the road to Valdemoro. Now we know how they work you can take your patrol ahead of us. When I sound the horn then you will know that we see them."

"A good plan." There was a sudden burst of laughter from Prince Sancho's camp and Álvar said, "Rodrigo will be getting ready for the battle."

"Álvar, we have our own battle to fight and our own duty to perform. It may not be under the eyes of kings and princes but it is important. Had we not stopped those scouts this morning then they would be riding back to Toledo to tell the Emir that we are beginning our attack. So long as the Moor is blind then we are winning!"

My words were for Álvar and to make him put his resentment about the knighthood behind him. I woke well before the assault was due to begin to see them array themselves. I was pleased to see that Rodrigo and the others were not with those who would assault first. I stood, hidden in the shadows and watched Rodrigo as he spoke to his shield brothers. While the other household knights laughed, joked, and bantered I saw Rodrigo pointing out features on the wall. He was looking for the weakness which could be used. The fact that the other five all paid him close attention showed his power even then. I watched and waited while they advanced to their starting positions. They would be seen from the walls and that was to be expected. Those who had never assaulted the walls would now feel their bowels loosen. They would feel the need to pass water while the ones who had made the buttock clenching climb up ladders before would already have emptied both bladder and bowels.

As dawn broke, King Ferdinand's horn sounded three times and this time the men who would attack were accompanied by drummers who kept the beat as they marched forward. I was aware that I could not wait long for I had a road to ride but I wanted to see the defences. That they were better than Salamanca became obvious when a couple of stone-throwers began to hurl rocks and I saw one take out four of Prince Alfonso's men. Arrows followed and the walls were well manned. I headed for our camp; the walls would not be taken in a day this time!

I headed to our horses where Álvar had the men and mounts ready for me. He handed me some stale bread and a hunk of cheese. He had an ale skin slung around the cantle. He cocked his head, "You were watching the attack?"

I nodded and pulled myself up into the saddle, "And it will be a longer siege than Salamanca. They have stone throwers."

Although Álvar had never seen one in action Rodrigo, who had read of them, had explained how they worked, Álvar nodded, "I do not envy them."

"No, but we have a task to perform. Let us be about our business."

I would eat as we rode and I would dwell on the fate which awaited the men who would attack the walls of Magerit as they were assaulted with rocks, stones, javelins and arrows. I was just pleased that I had not seen the tell-tale smoke which would have shown me they had boiling oil or water waiting. Those were weapons you could neither prepare against nor fight. They were the weapons of the devil and I shudder just thinking about them.

Chapter 12

The sun soon baked the road upon which we rode and made an already long road interminable. After Salamanca, many of those I led had emulated me and taken the thin white cloaks from the dead Moors. Others had found dead warriors wearing the voluminous garment called a bisht and they wore those. We did not look like a Christian army and I dare say that King Ferdinand would be less than pleased with our appearance. However, it meant we could ride for longer and approach closer to Moors who might mistake us for Mamluks, the Christians who had converted to Islam and fought for the Moor. We were, effectively, behind enemy lines and we needed every ruse and trick we could find.

I got on well with all of my warriors but there was no doubt that I enjoyed the company of Rodrigo and Álvar best. Rodrigo was at Magerit, scaling walls, and Álvar rode out of sight. I felt lonely and I wondered if it was because of the death of Alfonso for there was a void in my life. I had only seen Alfonso once since I had left Vivar and yet the simple fact that he had always been there gave me an order to my life. Now he was gone and my mortality had appeared like some spectre at my shoulder. Until he had died I had not thought about death but now I did, constantly, and the dark thoughts threatened to consume me. I suddenly thought of

Maria. What would she do and how would she cope? Her loss would be greater than mine for she had lost me and now she had lost her protector.

I forced myself to stop dreaming and to concentrate on the road. I was acting as a scout and I was looking at the road and the margins of the land to see if there were signs of riders. I sought out animal dung. Horses leave a clear sign and, as far as I knew, none had been down this road for some days. As I looked for signs the lack of animal waste seemed to confirm it. My choice of horse proved to be a good one for Berber was a Moorish horse. We rode south and all appeared to be peaceful until Berber pricked up his ears and began to stamp and as he had not done this for some time, I raised my spear. It was the sign for my men to be on the alert and prepare to stop. I looked to the left and saw that Fernando was riding normally and there appeared to be no danger from that quarter. I knew that I would not be able to see Álvar but I looked anyway. I waved Iago of Astorga forward as he carried our horn and, in the absence of Álvar, acted as my second.

"Ready your horn."

"Is there danger, Campi Doctor?"

"Berber is unsettled and that makes me nervous so let us be cautious, eh? Have your weapon in your hand for if there is danger then we need to strike quickly." Berber snorted and something made me move my shield before me. The arrow which thudded into it told me that we had been ambushed. "Sound the horn and the charge!"

The arrow had come from my left and I hoped that Fernando was already leading his men towards the danger. I kicked Berber in the ribs and he leapt forward. His instincts were better than mine and I allowed him to take me towards a stand of trees. My standing orders were for my men to follow me in the absence of any other command. The horn had given the order and my men would follow me. When two more arrows slammed into the shield which I still held before me then I knew where lay the enemy. I risked lowering the shield a little so that I could see over the edge and as I did so, I saw the Moors. There were mounted archers but I could not ascertain numbers. Álvar was the one who would win the day for us as they could not know yet where he was and all we had to do was engage them and that would allow him an attack towards their rear and that horse archers hated.

The Moors made a mistake; they wounded Berber. The arrow struck a glancing blow along his side but it enraged him and he lunged into the trees with snapping jaws! The Moorish horses who were there reared and tried to flee. It meant the eight archers who had bows drawn ready to send deadly missiles at us were disrupted and their arrows were wasted, for you cannot loose an arrow accurately from the back of a rearing horse, even if you are a Moor! I rammed my spear at the nearest one. My broken ribs complained and it hurt me but I was a warrior and I ignored the pain. My spear sank

deep into flesh and I withdrew and rammed it
again at a second Moor who was trying to
control his rearing horse. Iago was at my side
and he drew blood too. Fernando was leading his
handful of men into the flank of the horse
archers but we were still outnumbered as the rest
of my men were hurrying to get at us and they
had dead men and wounded horses to negotiate.
An arrow clanged off my helmet but I ignored
the ringing and lunged at the face of the archer
whose bow was ready to send an arrow into Iago
of Astorga. My spear entered his mouth and
emerged through the back of his helmet. He fell
from his saddle.

It was then that Álvar made his charge. He
only led six men but the noise they made as they
struck made the Moors think he led an army. A
close battle is not the place for a bow and our
spears found flesh each time they were thrust.
Our mail held despite the arrows of the Moors
and the Moorish leader had no choice but to
order the retreat. I saw him, for he had a plume
on his helmet, as he turned to give the command.
He never gave it for Álvar's spear cut him down.
Some of those fighting must have been kin or
had fought with him for a long time. They
fought on, using their swords long after it
became clear that they had lost while others fled.
Their swords were good but they could not
penetrate mail and the Berbers had no shields.
Barely twenty managed to flee and thirty more
lay dead or dying.

I shouted, "Sound the recall!" as I saw some
of my younger knights racing after the fleeing

Moors. It would avail us nothing save to exhaust horses and risk over-excited warriors. I turned in my saddle and roared to those closest, "Secure the horses, despatch their wounded." I scanned the scene and saw loose horses but none appeared to be ours. "Are any hurt?"

Fernando shouted, "Diego has an arrow in his leg."

Iago, after he had finished with the horn, shouted, "Rafael has a wound but it is nothing."

"See to them." I rammed my spear into the ground and took off my helmet. Nudging my way towards Álvar I said, "Perfect timing."

"It was a good plan. How did you know they were there?"

"I didn't, Berber did." That reminded me that he was hurt and I dismounted and saw to his wound with vinegar and honey while I spoke with Álvar. "They knew of Fernando but not you and that made all the difference."

He smiled, "I thought the plan would not work. I wondered if we were too far away or that we would be seen. I was wrong."

"And I could have been wrong too. Just because I was right this time does not mean that I will always be so. Rodrigo's readings have taught me that. Many times, a leader plans well but fate intervenes and he loses. It does not make his plan a bad one. Unless one can see into the future then a leader cannot predict the outcome of events."

We recovered fifteen horses, weapons, some coins and, most valuable of all, a map. I could not read the writing on it for it was in

Arabic script but I knew that there would be those who could. I recognised some of the symbols and it gave me an idea of the position of their garrisons. No matter what the outcome of the attack on Magerit's walls we had had a victory of sorts. The wounds we had suffered were not serious and were offset by the good feelings which permeated the conversations on the ride back as my men celebrated, this, their own victory. I was able to speak with Álvar and we both commented on the confidence of our men. Álvar was ready for knighthood and the way he spoke of the others most ably demonstrated that. He could easily lead other knights far more competently than someone like Don Diego!

When we neared the camp the number of healers dealing with the wounded and the piles of bodies awaiting burial told us that the attack had not gone well. Iago asked if he could look after Berber. I knew why he had done so; it was to allow me to find Rodrigo and see how the day had gone. After shedding my mail, for I was still not fully recovered and wearing the mail made my aches worse, I headed for Prince Sancho's camp. Don Raoul had been wounded and he had his arm in a sling. He gave me a wry smile. "I was careless or perhaps I should have copied you, eh?" He nodded to the far side of the camp. "Rodrigo and your lions all survived and they did well today."

"What went wrong?"

"Some of the men attacking did not do so with the same effort as we did. A third of the men did not even reach the ladders. We made the walls but they were able to bring other forces from the walls which were not attacked. The Prince and his father are less than happy with the way half of the army performed this day."

That meant another rift between the princes. I nodded, "I will speak with you later." I headed for Rodrigo. He was with my other former warriors and they were sharpening their weapons at the grindstone. Their delight when they saw me was obvious. "I am sorry that you did not succeed. The Armiger is pleased with you."

That was praise indeed and Rodrigo swelled with pride at my words. "Until everyone fights as hard as we do, we will never achieve our objective."

I nodded, "We fought Moorish horse archers today." I waved a hand around the knights I had trained, "Your former comrades did well."

They all wanted to know every detail and I was happy to tell them. Rodrigo said, "Could I see the map?" I showed it to him and his face lit up. "You should take this to the King. It may be crucial. I think these figures give the numbers of the men in each garrison but it would need someone who can read them."

He was right and as much as I wished to stay and speak, I had a duty. I took it to the King and made my report. He listened and nodded and then he took the map to look at it. He conferred with his Arab translator and his face went from the depths of despair to a look of pure joy. "We have them! We could have saved ourselves a wasteful and costly assault today if we had had this."

"I am sorry, King Ferdinand, I brought it as soon as I could."

He laughed and clapped me about the shoulders. "You have nothing with which to reproach yourself for you have done well." He pointed to the map, "This tells us that he has fewer men in Toledo than here. I now know what to do! You have earned your gold many times over."

I was confused but I took the praise and headed back to the camp.

It was the next morning that I discovered what the King had meant. Rodrigo came to speak with me. "We can leave a token force here to stop the garrison from escaping and we can make a forced march to Toledo. The fact that they sent horse archers in such numbers means that they planned to watch us and the King can take the bulk of the army to take Toledo. The Emir might be persuaded that we have taken Magerit for, thanks to you, no words will have reached him of the battles."

That made perfect sense even to a peasant such as I. "Ah! And who will watch the walls?"

He looked down, "That is why I am here. Prince Alfonso will command and there will be men from all four commands. You will represent Prince Sancho along with our foot soldiers. You will command them."

I think he added the last part to give me a crumb of comfort but I did not mind staying at

the siege for the battle I had fought had told me I
was not yet ready to fight in a real battle again,
at least not for a while. However, I knew that
Álvar and the others would be disappointed. He
told me the rest of the plan when it became
obvious that I was not upset. They would make a
forced march to get as far south as they could in
one day and then camp, briefly, before travelling
overnight to be at the gates of Toledo by dawn.
King Ferdinand hoped that the large numbers he
would take and the surprise of such a mighty
host arriving at its gates might win the day. They
left within the hour and I was summoned by
Prince Alfonso. I could see that he was less than
happy to be left behind. However, he used it as
an opportunity to try to suborn me.

"William Redbeard, it seems that we have
been left to watch the walls. Your men and my
bodyguard are the only horsemen we have and
so I would have you camp close to mine." I
nodded. He was in command and I had to obey
him despite the fact that I wished to be close to
the foot soldiers I commanded. "It is a pity you
and I got off to such a bad start. You know you
could always command my warriors for I
recognise your skill? I would happily knight
you."

I was being tempted and I knew it, I bowed,
"And that is an honour, Prince Alfonso, but I
promised Prince Sancho I would finish training
these young warriors. When that is done, I will
happily consider your offer, if you still want
me." I had not refused and that was enough to
satisfy him although I had no intention of

deserting one brother for another. He must have known that I could not give him a positive answer while I was still his brother's man.

"Very well, now you had better shift your camp before dark."

I headed back to the camp and I was grateful that Pedro, my old friend from the Lion's Den, commanded the foot soldiers. I told him of the arrangements and he sniffed. "We both know, Will, that we need the horsemen around the whole perimeter but I suppose he knows best. Do not worry about us. We have the west gate to watch and none shall use it. You have the harder task for you have the south gate and I cannot see the men who follow Prince Alfonso being any good. I may be wrong but I should sleep with one eye open if I were you!"

Pedro was one of a dying breed. He was a loyal and hard-working soldier who knew his business. He was a journeyman like my father and Alfonso the Armiger had been. He had much in common with Roger of Bordeaux. He knew more about soldiering and battles than most of the knights I had met and a good leader would have sought his advice. I spoke with him at length and, by the time I had left we were both clear about what we would do. By the time I returned Álvar, my men and the servants had packed up the camp. None were happy about the fact that we had been left behind. Even the servants had been abandoned. It did mean that we would eat well for the cooks had been retained and Prince Alfonso was already organising a victory feast which I thought was a little premature. I had Álvar build a defensive camp for we had far fewer men to defend it. I noticed that ours was the only defensive camp save the one built by Pedro. It was as though they all thought that the siege was over and we were merely caretakers! While he completed the defences, I went to see the Prince.

"My men and I are happy to keep watch this night."

He laughed, "That is why we have foot soldiers. Your men may not be knights but they are noble-born and one day they will be knighted. Sentry duty is for peasants." He did not seem to notice that I was of low born stock. I tried to persuade him to have some knights watching too but I could not dissuade him. "You must bring your horsemen to the feast for I am keen to meet with them. I might try to develop my own cadre of young warriors."

I told my young warriors that we would be dining with the knights of Prince Alfonso but I was stern with them, "Eat as much as you like but drink sparingly! Even if they try to force wine upon you do not drink so much that you are incapable of being roused in the dark of night. I want all of you to be alert until the King returns!"

I frightened them enough with my tone so that they all nodded. They would obey and I was relieved.

At the feast, Prince Alfonso had me on one side of him and his Armiger on the other. Álvar sat next to me. Prince Alfonso questioned us both at great length about Prince Sancho and

Lion's Den. He was most interested in Rodrigo for he had gained a good reputation as a brave and skilful knight and spent a great deal of time asking Álvar about his cousin. Álvar was loyal and gave away no secrets.

"Prince Sancho is lucky to have you, Álvar, and yet he did not knight you. Why not?"

"Simple, Prince Alfonso, I did not make the wall. All that I did was to control the young warriors."

"But you have performed great deeds. Did you not carry my brother's standard at the bridge where he almost came to grief? Did I not hear that it was you two and Rodrigo de Vivar who saved the army? That alone deserved three knighthoods."

Álvar's face belied his answer, "We are content, are we not, Campi Doctor?"

"We are and now, Prince Alfonso, you must forgive us. We have had a hard two-day patrol and I have yet to check on our men at the gate."

He laughed, "The garrison will not come out for they are surrounded. Enjoy yourself for my father left good wine."

I smiled, "Then tomorrow, when we are rested, we shall join you!"

He was already in his cups and seemed satisfied. I led my men, who in comparison to the Prince and his knights were sober, back to our camp. As we walked, I said, "I know that he has guards but tonight, Álvar, you and I will take it in turns to watch this camp. While I see Pedro, I would have you divide the men into two watches. I will take the first watch and you the second."

Álvar was a good warrior and he never complained no matter what the duty. He knew how to obey orders. Pedro agreed with my assessment and after I returned, I watched Álvar and half of the men go to bed. I had Iago of Astorga as my deputy and I gave him half of the men and sent them to watch the road from the city. I took the other half and after checking the horse lines I had them place themselves in the woods where we could watch both the camp and the road from the south. It had disturbed me that Prince Alfonso had ignored the possibility of an attack from outside the walls. It was almost as though he thought we had won the war already. I was happy for myself and my men to endure the night watch. It would do them no harm to suffer a night of sentry duty. When they became knights, they would understand their men a little better.

I woke Álvar and told him what I had done and he nodded both his understanding and approval. His men relieved mine in the woods and we went to fetch Iago from his perilous position close to the guards who were nearest to the wall.

"How was your duty?"

"Quiet, perhaps too quiet. Call me stupid, Campi Doctor, but I expected more noise from within the walls. We are less than four hundred paces from them and you would expect to hear sentries talking for it is obvious that we are not going to attack. And I didn't hear Prince

Alfonso's men talking either! They were closer to the walls and I expected them to chatter like magpies!"

"Did your men talk, Iago?"

He laughed, "While they waited for you to catch them doing so? There was no chance of that!" He shrugged, "Obviously, I was wrong for nothing happened and I shall enjoy my bed now."

When they had been relieved Álvar said, "I will set the other sentries and then return here. It may be nothing but I will walk to the men of Prince Alfonso who have the watch near to the walls and see if they have seen or heard anything. We may be doing them a disservice and they might be reliable and committed warriors."

I went to my tent but before I retired, I decided to apply some of the liniment the doctor had given me for my broken ribs. It stank but it seemed to give me some relief. I took my tunic and gambeson off leaving just my breeks and boots for I knew that I would have to make water again before I slipped into my cot for a few hours sleep. After rubbing it on, the liniment began to work immediately for I felt a lessening of the ache and I wiped my hands on an old piece of cloth. It was at that moment I heard Álvar's voice call out, "To arms! To arms!"

I did not hesitate but, grabbing my sword and dagger, ran out, half-naked, into the night. I heard the clash of steel in the dark towards Álvar and his men and I heard cries too. Prince Alfonso and his men still lay abed and I could

not hear them stirring. They had drunk too well.
I bellowed, "The Moors attack! Sound the
horn!"

Iago must have been roused and heard my
words for he sounded the call to arms just as ten
armed Moors burst through the camp towards
me. I know not what they thought when they
saw a half-naked man before them but they
dismissed me as a threat quickly and one
shouted a command which sent four of them
towards me while the rest ran to the tent with the
Prince's standard outside it. These were
assassins sent to kill the Prince! Perhaps it was
my sword which dictated that they give me the
respect of four men or it may have been that
they had seen me give commands. Once again,
my mentor's words came to me and I rushed at
the four of them.

I had no shield but they were not mailed and
I had no confining mail and gambeson about my
upper body. The liniment had worked and I felt
little pain from my ribs. If I was to survive then I
had to strike quickly. My move took them by
surprise for they were not yet in a position to
surround me. Two were negotiating the fire
which lay before Prince Alfonso's tent and the
other two ran directly at me. I heard the clash of
weapons from within the Prince's tent. The
Prince was being attacked. There was a
terrifyingly loud scream which rent the night and
one of the Moors involuntarily glanced to his
left. He happened to be the leading warrior and
my sword hacked into his side, tearing a wide
wound there. While two of the Moors were still

navigating the fire, I lunged beneath the swinging sword of another Moor and my dagger tore up under his ribs.

I saw Álvar and four of my men and I shouted, "The Prince! Get to him for he is in danger!" Iago was close by and he and I would have to deal with the others. I could hear the clash of steel all around the Prince's camp. This was a major attack.

Álvar nodded and ran towards the Prince's tent. I whirled, without knowing if there was danger behind and my dagger connected with the swinging sword which was aimed at my back. I was now alert and wide awake. My sword rose to block the other sword but I could do nothing about the shield which was punched at my face. It hit my nose and knocked me to the ground. The blow made my eyes water and sent a flood of blood, which erupted like a fountain from my damaged nose. I hit the ground and even the liniment could not prevent the pain I felt as I hit hard but I had no time to lie there for if I did so then I would be dead as the Moor was swinging his sword to rip me open. I swung my right foot and was rewarded when I connected with his shin causing him to fall down towards me. I just had the wit to hold up my dagger and he drove his own throat onto the blade and I was splattered with his blood. My clearing eyes saw the last Moor raise his sword to split open my head and then I saw the sword of Iago of Astorga ram through his back to emerge from the front.

Ramon appeared and pushed the dead Moor from me. As he helped me to my feet I said, "Moors are in the camp. Get to the Prince."

Just then Álvar and the Prince emerged from the tent along with the other men who had gone to his aid. The camp was now fully awake. I turned to Iago who had his shield and sword. "Have our men come here and we will drive the Moors back to Magerit."

"Aye, Campi Doctor!" He shook his head, "I knew something was wrong and I should have investigated."

I saw that Prince Alfonso looked to be in shock and although Álvar and Fernando flanked him he cowered. "Protect the Prince!" The Prince's household knights had risen and they staggered into the open. They were disorientated and disorganised. "Prince Alfonso's knights, form a shield wall!" It was a basic command and every warrior knew what to do. Even if you had no shield you stood next to a warrior and made a wall of steel. Their training came into play and they shuffled into a line. By the time they had achieved some semblance of order, Iago had fetched my half-dressed men and I shouted, "Advance!"

The Moor's surprise had evaporated and we now outnumbered the survivors of their night attack. As we marched steadily towards the south gate of Magerit we passed the dead Moors Álvar and his men had slain as well as at least two of my men. One group of fanatical Berbers charged at us as we drove the would-be killers back to Magerit but the eight of them could do little against the wall of men who approached. Prince Alfonso's men had now gathered their wits and the fact that it was my men guarding their leader made them ruthless and they butchered the eight. When we neared the gate, we came to our siege lines and I saw why the guards had said nothing. They had all had their throats cut.

In the absence of any other leader, for the Prince was still in shock, I took command. "Stand fast!" I looked down the line and saw that less than ten men had mail. "One in every two of you go back and dress for war!"

Iago was keen to make up for what he thought had been his error and he tapped the warriors I led on the shoulder. He counted them out so that one in two hurried back to the camp. He came to me, "You go back, lord!"

"No Iago, I stay here, you go!" He nodded and I was left with the ten men who, like me, were dressed in little else than breeks and tunics. I turned and laughed, "Well the Moor must be a poor opponent if he can be driven back by half-naked men with no shields! I think this town may surrender out of embarrassment!" I knew it would not happen but I wanted them to laugh and to feel more confident. They did so.

Behind me I heard the jingle of mail and one of Prince Alfonso's household knights, Don Garcia appeared. That he had donned mail before coming to the aid of his Prince disturbed me, "Campi Doctor, the Prince has sent me to take command. He wishes to speak with you."

I nodded, "Carlos, take charge of my men and when Iago returns hand over command to him." I was making it clear that these were my men and not to be commanded by Don Garcia.

Back at the scene of carnage there were now ten knights guarding the Prince and both servants and priests were also there. Someone had built up the fire and I could see by its light that the Prince was the only survivor from his tent but, miraculously, he had not been wounded. His Armiger, Don Raimundo, lay butchered as did the rest of his oathsworn. His limbs were severed and he had put up a mighty fight as had his other knights and they had bought the time for the Prince to be saved.

The Prince was visibly shaken, "How could this happen, William Redbeard?"

I looked at Álvar who answered, quietly, "The Moors sent killers over their walls and they slit the throats of the men you had guarding the gates. Iago of Astorga had kept our men quiet and they did not know we had a second line of guards." He nodded towards me, "That was the Campi Doctor's decision and was a wise one." I saw the Prince nod his unspoken thanks. Álvar continued, "We found the dead guards just as the Moors sortied from the town and that was when I sounded the alarm."

I nodded, "You have done well, Álvar, now go and take charge of our men while I don my mail."

The Prince looked panicky and shouted, "No! He stays here until daylight. Álvar Fáñez saved my life and I must reward him. You take

charge until daylight for I am also indebted to
you, Campi Doctor. Your advice was sound and
I ignored it."

I never really liked Prince Alfonso, even
now I find it hard to think well of him but he
changed a little that night in the camp outside
Magerit and he became a better leader. He was
never as good as his older brother but he became
a leader that men could follow.

When dawn broke, every man who
surrounded the walls of Magerit was armed and
was facing the enemy. Prince Alfonso, still
guarded by Álvar, rode his horse to the south
gate. I had dressed and returned to my men.
Once there was enough light to see I had Iago
count the enemy dead. There were just forty of
them but they had slain over sixty men including
three of mine. They had been elite warriors. I
recognised that in the quality of their weapons.
We had hurt them even though they had come
close to ending the siege.

I walked over to the Prince and spoke with
him, "Prince Alfonso, may I offer advice?" He
nodded and dismounted so that I could speak
with him without others eavesdropping. "Send
an emissary to demand the surrender of the
town. Tell them that your father has taken
Toledo and if they surrender now then the
warriors may keep their arms."

"But my father has not taken Toledo!"

"They do not know that! It is a ruse of war."

"But leaving them armed?"

I shook my head, "Will not change
anything. We still remain without but it may

persuade them that we are reasonable men who will not be vindictive. Your father cannot return here before tomorrow at the earliest. If they give their word then I believe they will keep it."

"They are Muslims!"

"And just as we swear on the Bible so they will swear on the Koran. What have we to lose?"

I think that the fact that I had been proved right once before and that Álvar had saved his life made him follow my advice. He rarely did so again but on that morning, after the potential disaster of the attack in the night, he did. It proved to be the right thing to do. The Moors had been shaken by their failure to end the siege and they believed Prince Alfonso that his father had taken Toledo. The Prince, along with our bishops, priests and his household knights met the lord of Magerit and his mullahs. They agreed to surrender and swore on the Koran. This time Prince Alfonso left his best warriors on guard with fires burning brightly.

I went to the healers with my nose which was, as I expected, broken. The healer was a good man and he tried to straighten it but too long had elapsed since I had been struck and it was not as straight as it might have been and I would be left with a permanent reminder of the day I fought half-naked!

As we had the gates being watched and the Moors had sworn an oath, we had a second feast organized for those not on duty and all of my men were invited. This time Álvar sat on one side and me on the other. Before the food was served, the Prince stood and said, "I wish to thank publicly, William Redbeard, Hero of Salamanca and Campi Doctor. It is thanks to his vigilance and sound advice that we have secured the surrender of Magerit." He waved forward a servant who handed me a small chest. I opened it and saw that it contained jewels and coins. I knew what it was. It represented a small portion of the loot Prince Alfonso's men had taken.

I bowed and smiled at the Prince, "Thank you, Prince Alfonso, but I was just doing my duty."

"And had others done their duty then there would be no need to reward you!" He smiled, "Take it." I nodded and sat. "There is another I would reward, Álvar Fáñez, who saved our life. Álvar, take a knee for I would do that which should have been done before now, I shall make you a knight." Álvar did so and Prince Alfonso knighted him.

This was a strange twist of fate. He had not been knighted by Prince Sancho but his brother!

Don Álvar stood, stunned, "My lord I…"

"You deserve it and my brother should have done this long ago. Now I would have you join my household and become one of my knights!"

Men have said many things about Álvar Fáñez and most of them are untrue. He was ever loyal to both Rodrigo and Prince, later to become King Sancho. What he said next made me proud of him and I knew that I had contributed a little to make him the man he was. "My lord, I cannot join your household for I am still oathsworn to your brother. I cannot undo a holy oath. If you wish to rescind the knighthood,

I will understand, but until I can speak to your brother then I cannot join your retinue."

The old Prince Alfonso would have erupted like a volcano but this was a different Prince. He had been chastened by the events of the previous night, coming close to death will do that to a man. He smiled and nodded. Turning to me he said, "Campi Doctor, you train your men well for they have honour and integrity. I understand, Don Álvar, and while I am disappointed, I hope that you will join my household. You are young and there is time." He clapped his hands, "Now bring on the food!" He smiled at me, "Let us hope that my father is as successful as we have been, eh, William Redbeard?"

Chapter 13

The King returned a week later but we had
had the news already that the sudden attack on
the capital of the Taifa had been successful.
Toledo was now also a vassal and would pay
tribute to King Ferdinand. Prince Sancho had
remained in Toledo to collect the first instalment
of the tribute and so we remained outside
Magerit awaiting the return of our comrades. It
was an easy duty. Magerit was a lovely town
and although we were not made particularly
welcome our victory meant that we could stroll
its streets and markets. I had a chest of gold and
jewels and I used some to buy gifts for Maria. I
also went to the market of servants and hired
two, one was a Christian, Geoffrey, who would
look after my horses and Abu Mohammad, a
Moorish warrior who had lost the use of his left
arm. He would act as my translator. Since
Hassan ibn Hassan had followed Rodrigo, I had
been in need of someone who could translate for
me.

When I approached them, I did not demand
that they served me I asked them. I did not ask
their rate of pay I just asked if they wished to
follow me, making it quite clear that I was one
of Prince Sancho's men. Both accepted. I asked
Abu Mohammad if he was certain and he had
smiled at me. "Lord, after the failed attack many
of those who returned spoke of the warrior who
fought against many men and was half-naked. I

thought then that I should like to serve such a man. I was a warrior once but the war against Zaragoza cost me my arm. I am happy to serve."

I had to buy two horses for them but they were cheap enough for the Emir of Toledo would have to raise taxes to pay the tribute demanded by the King. I was happy with the two palfreys.

Our men had stripped the bodies of the dead attackers and, as they had been good warriors, they all had coins, jewels and weapons to sell. Álvar profited the most for he was the only one to have searched the bodies in the Prince's tent and he became even wealthier than he had already been. He used the money to buy a better warhorse as well as a new sword and fine clothes. The night before Prince Sancho was due to return, we sat around the campfire with the rest of my men. We were an increasingly smaller number.

Álvar looked up to me as a sort of surrogate, elder brother and he confided all of his secrets to me, "If Prince Sancho is unhappy that his brother has knighted me then I will have to leave his service and join Prince Alfonso." I nodded for I had already worked that out. "That means I will be leaving these warriors."

I drank some of the wine which the King had left us. It was good. "You will be leaving them in any case. I have no doubt that Prince Sancho will wish you to follow his banner and he will accept the gift of knighthood for we both know that the Prince is many things but a fool is not one of them. Whatever happens, this is your last night with the lions."

He nodded and I saw the sadness in his eyes, "And after the losses we have suffered and the men who have been knighted, you will have less than twenty men to train."

I knew where he was going with this series of logical thoughts and I pre-empted him, "Unless Prince Sancho specifically asks for me to remain in his service, and I doubt that he will, I shall buy a small estate and bring Maria there. She shall enjoy retirement without work and I shall become a landowner. I will have coin enough when the King has paid me my dues."

Álvar laughed, "I cannot see you becoming a Don Diego!"

"That I can guarantee but I cannot just follow Prince Sancho around hoping for crumbs from his table."

It was late in the afternoon of the next day when the triumphant Prince Sancho arrived back at Magerit. I saw that Don Rodrigo now rode next to Prince Sancho. It demonstrated his rapid climb up the pecking order. It meant that, already, he was seen as the second-best knight who served and followed Prince Sancho.

I was the senior warrior and so I reported all to Prince Sancho. Although I told him of the attack and how we had repulsed it I did not mention Álvar's knighthood. That was something between Don Álvar and his Prince. While I was talking with the Prince, I saw Álvar being congratulated and knew that the news was out. To buy Álvar and Rodrigo time to speak with each other I spoke to the Prince of my concerns for the future.

"Prince Sancho, we now have fewer men for me to train and I believe that those who do not choose to return to their families would be ready for knighthood."

The Prince glanced, involuntarily at Álvar, "Aye, you are right and from what you say all but the four who are recent recruits would be ready for knighthood."

"Then I would ask to be released from your service, Prince Sancho. I came to you because I was the trainer of Rodrigo and Álvar. Thanks to your generosity and your father's, I now have enough money to buy an estate."

He gave me a sharp look, "Is this because I did not knight you?"

I shook my head, "Once, it might have been but the loss of Alfonso the Armiger and the meeting with Roger of Bordeaux has set thoughts in my head and I need to plan for my future. I am hale and I am hearty but as the last attack proved I could be maimed or killed just as any warrior. My foster mother is now alone and I need to make arrangements."

For the first time since I had known him Prince Sancho looked at a loss for words, "William, I am grown used to you. I cannot let you leave my service." I said nothing but looked him in the eye so that he could see into my soul. I saw, in his eyes, fear, and I knew that he was worried that I would serve another, perhaps his brother.

He smiled as he spoke to me but the smile was not in his eyes for this was almost like begging and a royal prince did not beg! "I tell you what, I will give you a month to reconsider your decision. Álvar can train the four new recruits while you are away and you can visit Vivar and spend your money. Return to Lion's Den in four weeks' time and we can sit and discuss your future. I know I have asked much of you and, perhaps, I have not always given you either the reward or respect that is due to you. Certainly, I have learned more about you and your skills since Rodrigo was knighted. What say you?"

"I owe you a month, Prince Sancho, and I will take you up on your offer but before I leave, I would ask you to speak to Álvar Fáñez. He has things he must say to you."

He frowned for he had come back in good humour and it sounded like he was being assaulted by nothing but bad news. "What is it?"

"Something he, alone, must tell you. I will not leave until the morrow, Prince Sancho."

I returned to my tent and told my new servants that we would not be staying with the army but heading to Vivar. They seemed happy about the prospect. I was still unused to servants and so I began to pack for myself.

Rodrigo burst in and looked genuinely distressed, "Is it true? You are deserting us?"

I shook my head and sat on my cot, "Deserting is something I would never do. Let us say I am taking a new path."

"But why? What have I done to offend you? Tell me that I may undo the hurt!"

"Álvar has told you his news?" He nodded. "Then you know that soon there will be none for me to train. What would you have me do, shuffle around the gyrus watching the knights I trained joust and fight like an old man who carries the cadge? I am a warrior but I also have a family. I have been given a month to set my affairs in order and I will do so. I promised the Prince that I would return to Lion's Den in four weeks and you know that I am a man of my word and I will return. I have a month to plan my life and a future after service to you and the Prince."

Geoffrey entered the tent and Rodrigo snapped, "Leave us! I do not wish to be disturbed." Poor Geoffrey fled.

"And there is another reason." He gave me a quizzical look. "Before you were knighted you would not have spoken that way. Geoffrey is my man and this is my tent yet you gave commands as though I was your man and I am not. That duty ended when you became a knight."

I saw the hurt in his eyes, "I am sorry, William, and you are right! Have I changed so soon? Am I on the road to becoming my father?"

"That will never happen but you can see my dilemma. When we were in Pamplona I spoke with Roger of Bordeaux and I saw my future. I have spoken with Old Pedro and he has confirmed that which I already know. Unless I take charge of my life now then I shall become like them and I know that both warriors regret decisions they made when they were younger, I

shall not look back with regret. I will take a
month but I will return."

"You swear?"

I took out my father's sword, kissed the
crosspiece and said, "I swear!" He looked
relieved. "And Don Álvar, what will he do?"

Rodrigo was on more comfortable ground
and he smiled, "He will serve Prince Sancho but
he was torn and I fear that he will always have
an allegiance of some sort to Prince Alfonso."

Shaking my head, I said, "He will always be
loyal, first, to you and then to Prince Sancho. He
was another who was taken for granted."

"By me."

I shrugged, "Perhaps but, as they say in
Normandy, the carrot is out of the ground and it
cannot be replaced. A month apart may see a
new beginning and besides it will give the young
warriors the opportunity to see life without me.
Apart from the new four, they are almost
trained."

I could tell that Rodrigo was upset for he
left me without a smile and without a salutation.
I did not know what he expected. His
grandfather had asked me to train him and I had
done so. He was now a knight and the only
alternative that I could see was for me to follow
him around like some mailed guard dog. His
future and mine were divergent and the older we
became the less we would have in common. I
was wrong but I did not know that for the fates
were conspiring.

The cubs and the lions came to visit with
me when they heard that I was leaving; some

were upset for they thought they had let me down while others were just upset. I was quick to put them right on the former and I told them that I would be returning and that I would train up the four new warriors. I was touched by the offers to find me employment with the retinues of their fathers. I had never been worried about the lack of employment. I was a sword for hire and I knew that I now had a name and could ask for a higher rate of pay than most men.

My servants and I left before dawn the next morning. It was partly to avoid fuss but mainly to be able to rest from the hot sun's rays. Officially we were travelling through the land of an enemy for the peace treaty and tribute arrangements were still to be finalised but the land through which we travelled was peaceful and the journey allowed me to get to know my two servants. Their stories were as different as could be. Abu had been a warrior, an archer and he had lost his arm during a fierce and bloody battle with fellow Muslims. He was open about the Christians that he had slain in battle and it was good that we could speak so frankly. He would be invaluable should I ever be called upon to fight Moorish horsemen for he knew how they fought. He was not bitter but he regretted the pointless battle which had seen him lose his arm. Had he been any other kind of warrior then he could have carried on but an archer needed two arms.

Geoffrey was from Anjou and had worked in the stable of his namesake, Geoffrey Martel, the Count of Anjou. As such he had enjoyed a good lifestyle for the stables in Angers were better than the homes of many men. He had been looking forward to a long and comfortable life until he fell out with the Steward of the estate. As with all such stories, it was over a woman. The woman preferred Geoffrey but Theobald the Steward, an older and more powerful man, wanted her for himself. While Geoffrey Martel was away campaigning, the Steward had a row with the woman whom he then murdered. The only witness was Geoffrey and when the steward blamed the stable hand, he had no choice but to flee for his life. He had stolen a horse and that compounded his crime and guaranteed that he could never return to his home. He travelled through Gascony working in inns and for minor lords but just when he found somewhere he liked, then his story followed him. He had had no choice but to seek work in the lands of Castile but a chance visit by an Angevin noble brought the story to light there forcing him to flee to Toledo. The Moors offered him work and he had lived amongst them for two years. He told me the story so that he would not have to flee.

"Geoffrey, King Ferdinand is a kind man and a clever man. Had you told him this story then you might have remained in Castile."

He laughed, "And how does a stable boy get to meet a King? Lord, you are a powerful man and an important one. I had heard of you before you came to the servant market. You might hold the attention of a King but not I. If this employment works out then I will be happy for you have good horses and, in my experience, those who are good judges of horses are fair men." He smiled, "Do dogs like you, lord?"

It was the strangest question I had ever been asked. I thought about it and remembered the dogs at Don Diego's, I had always had a way with them, "Aye, they like me and I treat them well."

"Then I am settled for dogs are the best judges of men and if a dog does not like you then you are a bad man!"

Abu rubbed his beard with the stump of his arm, "I do not like dogs!"

Geoffrey nodded, "That is because you are a Muslim. The rule does not apply to heathens!"

So began an argument, which, while not a serious one, lasted the whole time the two men worked for me and yet they became as close a pair of friends as I have ever seen. It was strange.

I had already decided that I would not go to the manor first. I was not sure that I would be welcome and I did not want to cause trouble for Maria or my former comrades. There was an inn in the town with rooms and a stable. The owner, Miguel, was a good man and it was where the men of the estate drank at night. I knew where the stables were and I assumed I could get rooms so I sent my two servants directly to the stables with our horses and I entered the familiar inn where I had drunk my first ale.

As I walked into the dimly lit and cool chamber, I saw that there were few people at the crude tables and barrels which served as seats.

Normally, at this time of night, it would be busy. However, that was not what shocked me, it was that Maria was serving customers. Her back was to me and she had not seen me but Old Miguel had and he roared out, "William, you are back but what have they done to your face?"

Maria whipped her head around and seeing my bruised and battered face, burst into tears, "Poor Will!"

She dropped the beakers to the floor, luckily they were made of wood, and she rushed to me. I held her in my arms as she sobbed on my chest. I spoke calmly to her as I would to Killer if I was trying to soothe him, "It is nothing and I am whole. I was sorry that Alfonso did not come back to you."

She pulled away and began to dry her eyes on her apron. "He died as he would have wanted for he was a warrior but I shall miss him more than you can know." She held me at arm's length, "What happened to you?"

I laughed, "I was hit in the face by a shield but the swelling and bruising will go down and the nose will just be slightly cock-eyed! There is no permanent hurt." I pulled her to me and hugged her, "I am glad to see you! Miguel, I need rooms for myself and my two servants. The horses are already in the stables."

"Of course. Anna, go and prepare the rooms!"

I looked down at Maria, "What are you doing here? Why have you left the estate?"

She linked my arm and led me to an empty table, "When he returned from Salamanca Don

251

Diego sent for me and said that as Alfonso was dead, I had no place at the hall. He told me to pack my things and leave. Lady Isabella tried to dissuade him but her words fell on deaf ears." I was stunned for whilst I knew that Don Diego was cold, I did not think him completely heartless. "Iago and the others asked him to reconsider and he said that they would be lucky to keep their places! He is a cruel man; it is as though my service to him and the family was as nothing."

Geoffrey and Abu entered and I waved them over, "These are my servants, Abu Mohammad and Geoffrey. This is my foster mother, Maria. Sit and speak with them while I go and talk to Miguel."

I was seething but I forced myself to remain calm. I think Miguel knew I was angry for he had a large beaker of ale waiting for me. "William, drink this and count to ten. I pray you are not hasty! Don Diego is a powerful man in these parts. He owns almost every building and every man, I would not lose my inn because you angered him. It is pointless and would avail you nothing for you are not a noble."

I nodded for I knew what he meant. I drank my ale, "I am not a fool, Miguel, and although I am more important than I was, here I am nothing. I may have my vengeance one day but it will not be soon." I drank half of the ale and nodded appreciatively, "Good ale. First, I must thank you for taking my mother in and offering her a job but she will need it no longer. I will pay for her food and lodging from now on. I intend to buy an estate but it will not be in Vivar. Maria will be the lady of my hall and she will have servants of her own."

His eyes widened, "You have made money with your sword?"

I nodded and told him of my adventures. I took a gold coin from my purse. "This will pay for our time here."

He shook his head, "For that, you could own this inn!"

"Nonetheless I will pay this and if there is coin left over then it will pay for the ale my shield brothers drink when I have gone."

"They will be in later."

"Good, now we will need food."

I joined Maria and my servants. She smiled, "You have chosen well, for these are good boys." I saw them both beam for Maria was an honest woman who wore her heart upon her sleeve. There was not the hint of duplicity about her; her eyes told all that she spoke the truth.

"You and Alfonso taught me well. Now I have much to say. You no longer work here; you live here so take off the apron and join us for food. "

"But Miguel needs me!"

I looked around at the half-empty inn, "I think that Miguel was being kind and I have repaid him for he is a good man."

"But where shall I go?"

"I have to go to visit with the King for he owes me a chest of money. Then I will buy an estate and you will run it for me. You will be the lady of the house. I shall have other servants eventually, but until we hire them then Geoffrey and Abu will have to do."

"What do I know about running an estate?"

I laughed, "More than me!"

Just then the door burst open and Iago, Pedro and Juan came in and their faces were as black as thunder. They did not look over to us but stormed towards the bar and Iago roared, "Miguel, a jug of your strongest wine! Tonight, I get drunk!"

I saw Miguel grin as I stood. The others were crowded around Iago and did not see me approach. Standing behind them I suddenly shouted, as though they were my young warriors, "Is this any way for warriors to behave?"

They whipped their heads around looking for a fight but when they saw me their faces lost their anger and they beamed. Iago grabbed me by the shoulders, "By God but you are a sight for sore eyes." Then he stepped back and laughed, "And that is a mark, not of a knight but a brawler! How did you come by it?"

I put my arm around him and said, "I will tell you all but first, Miguel, food for all and put this on my bill. Come, shield brothers, and meet my first servants!"

The mood had changed from one of anger to one of joy. After making the introductions I left nothing out as I told them of the siege and the subsequent night attack. By the time the tale ended the food had finished and time had passed so that the inn was emptying.

Maria stood, "I shall still be the servant this night. Come, Geoffrey and Abu Mohammed, I will take you to your room. These warriors will wish to talk and the talk may be too delicate for my ears and for a Muslim." She frowned at Geoffrey, "You are the first I have met from Anjou and I will reserve judgement on you but if you are aught like William's father then you are to be watched closely!"

We all laughed for the change in Maria since we had first entered was quite remarkable. Abu and Geoffrey seemed in awe of her already and she led them to the rooms at the back of the inn. I circled my arm and shouted, "Miguel, more wine and then join us!"

We had the inn to ourselves and we could speak freely. Miguel had ably demonstrated that he could be trusted and I intended to find out what had made Iago so angry. When Miguel brought over more wine, I was careful not to pour too much into my goblet. I needed my mind to function clearly.

"What happened, Iago?"

"Tonight, or when Don Rodrigo left?" I shrugged. "Don Diego changed after his son went with you to train with Prince Sancho. He became a bitter man. His wife and he have little in common now and he treats all of the servants badly. It was not so bad while Alfonso and Ramon lived for they took much of the abuse he hurled at us all. Maria, too, was also protected. When Rodrigo was knighted at Salamanca it drove him over the edge. He argued with his father and Don Diego left the King's army."

I suddenly realised that he had not been with us at Magerit but I had been so busy that I had not noticed.

"As soon as we came back, he rid himself of Maria and then this afternoon he summoned us and told us that he no longer needed warriors and from now on we were to be paid as watchmen and our tasks would include labouring on the estate. We will not stand for it for we are warriors and not watchmen!"

"And the others?"

"They either died at Salamanca or deserted on the way to Vivar. Perhaps they saw what we did not. Loyalty can be misplaced."

An idea began to form in my head but I had been drinking and I would not risk the words I wanted to say. "Iago, Pedro, Juan, you were my foster father's closest friends and my shield brothers. You have been badly treated and, while I am not a noble, I cannot sit idly by and watch this abuse. Endure it for a little while. I have to visit with the King and I cannot believe that he would sanction this treatment of such heroes being meted out by Don Diego. Maria will stay here and when I can find an estate, she will be the lady of the house. I need you to be close to her, here, until I can make the necessary arrangements. Endure the humiliation for it will not be for long. When I return, I will speak with Don Diego."

Iago nodded, "For you, and for Maria, we will do this. Had you not spoken then we would have left in the morning."

I clasped each of them by the hand, "I thank you."

Later, as I lay in bed, sleep did not come easily, it was not the bed it was that I had too much to think on. All the time I had spent with Rodrigo had had an effect and the plan which eventually came into my head seemed to me to be a good one.

The next morning, I left Geoffrey to watch over Maria and Abu and I headed to León and the King. I contemplated heading to Lion's Den first but I was not sure that Rodrigo and the Prince would have returned from Magerit. Instead, I presented myself at the palace. Although I was well known, respected even, I still had to wait. When I was finally admitted, King Ferdinand smiled for he was not only a good general but an intuitive man. After he died the title Ferdinand the Great was accorded to him with good reason. "Ah, Campi Doctor, you have come for your reward."

I suddenly felt a little mercenary and I offered an explanation, "King Ferdinand, I have discovered that my foster mother has lost her place in Don Diego de Vivar's home and I wish to make arrangements so that she can live in comfort. I will need the reward you promised me to buy a home."

He smiled, "And that speaks well of you that you care for the mother who raised you." Then he frowned, "Why has Don Diego done this?" Just then one of his senior officials leaned forward and whispered in the King's ear. He nodded and said, "Just so, just so."

The look on his face told me that the King condoned the action and I wondered what had been said in his ear to change his mind so rapidly. There would be little point in speaking of the injustice endured by Iago and the others.

"If you would go with my moneyer he will give you your chest. Have you brought men to guard it? Despite my rule, there are dangerous men out there."

I confess I had not thought of that. "I will be making arrangements, Your Majesty."

Raimundo had been the official who had whispered in the King's ear. Normally a moneyer was just responsible for minting the coins with the King's effigy upon them but I knew that Raimundo did more than that, he managed the finances of the vast Kingdom which King Ferdinand had created. As we headed to the treasury, he spoke with me confidentially, "What are these plans you make for your mother?"

"They are plans for me too, my lord, for I cannot see me being the Campi Doctor for Prince Sancho forever. I would buy a piece of land and use this treasure to help me make more money in the future."

He nodded, "If I might offer some advice?"

"Of course, my lord, for I am just a humble sword for hire."

"There is land available to the north of Burgos. When King Sancho of Navarre was killed at Atapuerca he had supporters who lived north of Burgos, Don Sebastian of Briviesca had the best estate and when he died at the battle without issue then the estate came into Crown hands. We hold the deeds to the land here for it is now the King's domain. If you would trust the word of Raimundo the Moneyer then I could arrange for you to buy it." He shrugged, "There is a motive behind my words, Hero of Salamanca, for we have been seeking a Steward to manage the land but finding someone trustworthy is difficult. You have proved your loyalty many times over and the Crown would have income generated from the estate."

What kind of fool would buy a piece of land unseen? The answer was simple, I would. I knew swords, horses, men and fighting. What I did not know was how to farm or how to choose a decent piece of land and I would trust this man whom King Ferdinand trusted with the finances of the Kingdom.

He must have sensed my indecision for he added, "My son was with the King at Salamanca and he told me how you saved the lives of many men by taking the gate. He was due to climb the wall next and I owe you his life. I will not cheat you, I swear on all that is holy."

"Then I thank you and accept your offer."

"Know that there will be no title with the land save that of Lord of Briviesca and that is just an honorific. You will not be knighted."

I laughed, "I think the fates have already decided that I will never wear spurs. It is good, Raimundo the Moneyer."

"It will take a couple of days for me to make the arrangements. Perhaps you could wait at Lion's Den and I can send your treasure there.

The King's guards will keep it secure but I do urge you to hire men to protect it. We are not a Taifa but there are still those who wish to take that which they have not earned."

"I will do as you suggest but I would see the coin anyway."

He smiled "And you would not be human if you did not wish to do so." He led me to the Treasury. "I confess that until my son spoke with me, I was surprised at the King's generosity. There were many men, Don Diego amongst them, who resented that they were not given more of the money they felt they had earned, but having heard more tales of you and met you then I understand."

Was there a warning in his voice? He was a clever man and I was a simple soldier but I noted the tone.

The two mailed sentries stood aside as Raimundo used his key to unlock the door to the treasury. One of the men handed him a burning brand for there were no windows in the chamber. He ducked his head beneath the door and he was lighting two brands in the sconces on either side of the door as I entered. I know not what I had expected but it was not this. There were no piles of coins cascading to the floor nor crowns and coronets. Instead, there were neatly stacked chests. Larger ones were at the bottom and smaller ones rose above them. Six chests were set before them. Four large ones and two which were half the size of the larger ones.

Raimundo went to one of the two smaller ones and opened it. I say it was smaller but it was still as long as my leg and as deep as my arm. He opened it and I saw, within, coins. The majority were silver but gold glinted in the light reflected from the sconces.

"This is yours and the one next to it is to be sent to the others who fought at Salamanca." He sighed, "It is a complicated system for I now have the tribute to allocate too." He smiled, "A happier task than worrying where the Kingdom will find its money. You are a rich man William Redbeard, Hero of Salamanca."

I reached in and took out a handful of coins. Turning, I smiled at the Moneyer, "Expenses!"

He laughed, "And you are a modest man for many would have filled their purse with coins. The estate will cost a fraction of the coins you have in here but as you will be receiving your share of the tribute then you will not notice the difference."

As I made my way back to Abu, I reflected that I could do worse than hire myself out to the royal family. Swords were rewarded for the risks they took in battle but once that was done it was the Kingdom that reaped the benefit. I realised that it would be too late to go to Lion's Den, for that lay some miles from the city and the palace. We stayed in an inn in the town. There was a servants' market there and I would hire more servants for Maria. She would need women about her. I would hire a few as well as a couple of labourers for the farm. I knew that I would also need a wagon. The chest was too heavy for horses. I was making more work for myself than I had anticipated.

The next morning, I left Abu and the newly hired servants in the inn. They all shared two rooms. I had found two young girls who looked keen and two burly men; none were older than twenty and that was what I wanted. Older servants would be used to their master's ways. I wanted them to be moulded by Maria. I rode alone to Lion's Den. The army of Prince Sancho had returned the previous day but Prince Sancho was not there. I presented myself to Don Raoul and asked permission to spend the night at Lion's Den.

He laughed, "You have not yet left Prince Sancho's service, this is only a leave but it is good that you ask."

I put my bags in the hall and was inundated with questions from my men. It was less than a week since I had seen them and yet they were full of curiosity. The conversation stopped when Rodrigo and Álvar strode in. My men left us and the three of us sat around a table.

"You have reconsidered, William?"

I smiled at Rodrigo, "I confess that I have not given one moment of thought to my future, Rodrigo." I told the two of them what I had learned at Vivar and of my plans to buy the estate.

Álvar looked angry but Rodrigo just nodded, "Then I know what my father has done. It is possible for a lord to excuse himself from fulfilling his feudal duties. There is little honour in it but some lords do this. They pay an amount to the King for the men that they are obliged to send to war. The King then hires mercenaries to

take their place. The Kingdom still has the army
it needs and men who do not wish to fight can
stay at home and make coin. My father does not
need warriors so why pay them as such? I know
it is wrong but my father likes money more than
anything and that is why the King will allow him
to do as he has done."

Álvar said, "Then nothing can be done
about Maria, Iago and the others?"

Rodrigo said, "You have come into your
inheritance now, Álvar. You, too, are a rich man
yet do you know what your steward does while
you are here? Do you care?"

"He is a good man! He would not abuse my
people." Álvar was very defensive.

"Yet even if he was a bad man you are the
only one who could do anything about this. The
King is above such things. He cannot look at
every injustice in this world and he relies upon
his lords and knights to administer the rule of
law and see that all are treated fairly. That is
why we must ensure that we, as lords, mete out
justice to all." He turned to me. "I will come
with you when you return to Vivar. It is time
that I spoke with my father and settled this issue.
There has been a gulf between us and now that I
am a knight we can speak as equals."

"Thank you, for I am no knight and the
Moneyer made it quite clear that my title, Lord
of Briviesca, brings little recognition outside of
the estate."

Rodrigo said, "Except that you are
committed to providing men for the King or did
not Raimundo mention that?"

He had not and I wondered at that.

The Prince did not return until the next day but once he heard that I had returned he sent for me and Rodrigo. The fact that he did not send for Álvar was a little worrying and I wondered if he still resented the fact that his brother had knighted him. It was a mistake for Álvar was loyal and if he thought himself slighted it would not take much to drive him into the clutches of Prince Alfonso.

I told the Prince of my tentative plans and of my new estate. He nodded, "It is good that you go to Vivar, Rodrigo, for you might talk some sense into your father, although I doubt it. William, I spy hope here. I have thought about your dilemma. If you are now a lord with land and an income them you could train your own men. How about this? When you have finished training my warriors, I will give you a stipend to train a body of horsemen at your new estate. When they are needed you will be paid the daily rate for mercenaries and fight for me."

I saw Rodrigo's eyes light up.

I also thought it sounded too good to be true and so I asked, "And what if there is no war?"

"Let me answer with a question. Is Spain ruled by one man yet?"

Before I could answer, Rodrigo shook his head and said, "No."

"Then there will be war. When every Taifa pays tribute to Castile and all the Christian Kingdoms are united under one Emperor of Spain then there will be no war."

"In that case, Prince Sancho, I accept."

Three days later my treasure and my papers and deeds arrived and I left for Vivar with Rodrigo and Álvar. I had made one journey and now I was about to start another. What I did not know was that this journey would be the start of the transformation of Rodrigo from a mere knight to become the hope of Castile.

Chapter 14

We left for Vivar two days later with a wagon laden not only with the treasure but also some mail, weapons and sundry items I thought we might need in the new hall. I had still to fully crystallize my plans but I talked of them with Rodrigo and Álvar as we rode back to our former home. I was older than Rodrigo but he was the cleverest man I knew and he was able to take my ideas and hone them. The result was that when we arrived in Vivar and we were reunited with Maria I knew what I needed to do. We left Maria at Miguel's inn to get to know the new servants and to look at what we had bought while we headed for the estate. We would leave for Briviesca on the morrow.

As we neared the estate, I saw Iago and my other two shield brothers, stripped to the waist and harvesting wheat with scythes. I shook my head and Rodrigo said, with an edge to his voice, "This is not the work for warriors. I have neglected my home, William, and people have suffered. I will not make the same mistake in the future."

We reined up in the courtyard and Rodrigo's mother rushed out to tearfully greet her son. It was touching. Other house servants also came to speak to the three of us. Don Diego remained, pointedly, within his hall.

"Is my father at home?"

266

She nodded, "He has changed, Rodrigo, and is not the man I married."

"Come, let us go and speak with him."

"I fear he will be angry if William enters the hall for he blames him and the oath he swore when William's father died as the cause of the dissension in his life."

Rodrigo had grown and he, too, had changed. He smiled, "Mother, I fear neither Moorish hordes nor the terror of a siege so I do not fear the wrath of a misguided father. I am one of Prince Sancho's oathsworn, Álvar is a knight and William is the Hero of Salamanca and a lord in his own right. Any other lord would be honoured to have us cross his threshold."

We entered. I had rarely been in the Great Hall and I was intimidated as I followed Rodrigo beneath the low lintel. Don Diego stood and jabbed an angry finger at me, "Get that street rat out of my home!"

Rodrigo's voice was as commanding as on any battlefield, "How dare you speak to the man whom the King calls, hero! He is Lord William of Briviesca and we are here at Prince Sancho's behest. Watch your words or I will have you arrested and taken to León in chains!"

"You would not dare! Do you know who I am?"

Rodrigo's voice became both quieter and more threatening, "Aye, you are the coward who sends other men to die and then hurls insults at real heroes. We three have both the King and the Prince's ear and believe me we have the power.

Now, will you sit and listen to our words or shall I make good on my promise?" I was not sure if Rodrigo was correct but his father believed him and that was all that mattered.

He recognised the threat and, in truth, Rodrigo had changed beyond all recognition since last he had left home and he sank back into his chair, already a defeated man.

"Maria, William's foster mother, was badly treated by you and should be recompensed for her loss of position!" He held up his hand as his father tried to speak, "Lord Briviesca is willing to forget that but you have also demeaned and diminished his shield brothers and reduced them to serfs and peasants. None of us can endure that. You will release Iago, Pedro and Juan to us so that they can regain both honour and the work for which they are fitted."

I had never noticed Don Diego's furtive eyes before then but I saw them flick between the three of us. His fingers drummed on the table and he said, finally, "I will accede to your demands for it saves me having three useless mouths to feed but know this, Rodrigo, that I disinherit you. When I die you will neither inherit this land nor this title. As of this day I have done with you!"

It was an empty gesture for there were neither brothers nor sisters and the King and his court would rule in favour of Rodrigo. More, I knew that Lord Lain thought more of his grandson than his son and it was likely that Don Diego would be disinherited by his father and

Rodrigo would be the beneficiary. The words were there to hurt but they did not.

Rodrigo nodded and turned to his mother, "If you wish to leave this man who lacks both honour and dignity then I have a place for you close to León." Rodrigo had also made enough coin to buy a small hall.

His mother smiled and kissed Rodrigo on the cheek, "A fine offer but I have my marriage vows, yet you should know this, Diego," and she turned to her husband, "unless you mend your ways then I will enter a nunnery and my inheritance shall go to our son now rather than when I die! Do not forget, Diego, that I have my father's treasure, kept for me by the Bishop of Burgos!"

Don Diego's shoulders slumped for he was defeated in his own hall and he nodded his acceptance. We left the hall and while Iago and the others were sent for, Rodrigo said to all that could hear his words, "If there are any who do not wish to endure the tyranny of Don Diego know that I, Rodrigo de Vivar, and William, Lord of Briviesca, seek loyal and hardworking servants who will be treated with respect."

There was hesitation until his mother said, "And any who leave go with my blessing."

Two women, close friends of Maria, raised their hands and two of the older house servants did so too. If we had made the offer in the fields then we would have had even more takers but time was pressing.

Rodrigo said, "Álvar, escort them to Vivar and the wagon when they have taken what they need from the servants' quarters."

It took time to fetch Iago and the others and Álvar had left by the time they returned. Rodrigo said, "William, these will be your men. It is only right and proper that you speak with them."

"Iago, Pedro, Juan, we have spoken with Don Diego and if you still wish to be warriors and ride behind my banner then I offer you a place at my table."

There was neither hesitation nor discussion and Iago simply said, "We will fetch our war gear!"

Don Diego would not allow them horses and so we carried their war gear on Berber and Babieca for the short walk to Vivar. As we walked, I told them of my plans and was more than pleased when they were as enthusiastic as I had been when Rodrigo and I had come up with the plan. Rodrigo and Álvar did not spend the night with us for he wished to visit with his grandfather. He left Vivar to travel the short distance to Lord Lain' estate. Rodrigo was no longer a naïve young man. He had an instinct that helped him to plan and to forestall his enemies. In later years, when he was El Cid, then men would wonder where his skill came from. I knew for I had seen it grow.

We loaded our war gear on the wagon. As we headed for our new hall, I rode Killer, Iago rode Berber and Pedro, Copper. Juan rode one of the new horses Geoffrey and I had purchased. The wagon was overloaded and I was grateful that we only had twenty miles to travel. The passengers dismounted as we climbed the incline to the hilltop town and hall to ease the burden of the horses. I say town but it was really a very large village. Its position had been chosen for defence and it was an ancient place. The stone wall around the hall was defensive. We had almost the whole afternoon to admire its position as we climbed the road to reach it.

There was a caretaker and two field labourers and they accepted, as I knew they would have to, the legal documents Raimundo had provided for me. They were happy, not to say relieved to be kept on as this was not the time of year to seek a new home. I entered a two-week whirlwind of work for I was due back at Lion's Den and I wished to leave Maria with a secure home. Iago and Geoffrey rode to Burgos to buy more horses while I rode the land with the caretaker, Pablo, so that I could see what I had bought as my first home. It was a farm of livestock and that suited me for I did not understand crops. There was a vegetable plot and it seemed to me that the estate would be self-sufficient but was at risk from cattle and sheep raiders. Those who lived in the village had a variety of trades but all kept animals and had their own plots of land which they tended. They were grateful to have a lord returned for the walls of Briviesca Hall were their sanctuary. I had brought many of the weapons I had taken on various battlefields and all of the villagers and my household were now armed and could protect Briviesca's walls in times of danger.

We left all too soon but I had given my word and I would keep it. The farewells were not tearful for Maria and the others were now their own masters and freed from Don Diego's tyranny. They could be happy again!

Iago and the others wore good mail hauberks which I had bought for them. Their older armour would serve as a reminder of their former life. Briviesca had a coat of arms and I adopted them. There was a red shield with three horizontal stripes. We painted the design on our four shields and Maria and her women were making us surcoats which they would send on to us when they were completed. Geoffrey and Abu accompanied us and they, too, were armed and would be similarly attired. I was silent for the one hundred and twenty miles ride to León. I would once again be Prince Sancho's man. The difference was that I would have three men to help me train my young warriors. Prince Sancho had promised that all but the four youngest would be knighted by the New Year and I wondered at that, for it suggested that he would need knights and that meant a war, but there appeared to be no enemies. My five companions were all happy as we rode for they all had a future which, until I had come along, had not been there. None of them cared that we might have to fight battles and that they might lose their lives for all of them had suffered despair and knew that this life, as hazardous as it might be, was preferable. I knew that once the four youngest warriors were knighted then I could return to my new hall and make it the training camp I had promised Prince Sancho. I was quite excited at the prospect for I would be my own master and the men I would shape would follow me.

Once we were back at Lion's Den, it was as though I had never been away and we spent the winter in the gyrus. The Prince kept his word and as each young warrior proved himself, he was knighted. It worked out to be almost two a week. The proof was simple. They had to last a bout with one of my three warriors; Iago, Pedro and Juan might not have been knights but they had been fighting for long enough to know how to do so. They proved to be hard opponents for they did not like to lose and fought well. When they were bested then we knew that the winner deserved their spurs.

I had long thought that Prince Sancho ought to take a wife. Rodrigo was of the same mind for we hoped that he would become King when his father died, but he needed a wife and legal heirs. Rodrigo came to give us the good news that Prince Sancho had a marriage arranged and he became engaged to a daughter, Stephanie, of the wife of King García Sánchez of Navarre. The daughter was from her first marriage. We all felt this was a good thing for a Prince needed children so that when he was king, he would have heirs to follow him. I do not think the Prince had ever met Lady Stephanie. The good news lasted less than six weeks and it seemed he was fated never to marry as his fiancée eloped, just after Christmas, with Sancho Garcés, an illegitimate son of King García Sánchez of

Navarre. It seemed bizarre to me that such a situation could have arisen. Whatever the cause it meant that Christmas was not the joyous time it should have been and Prince Sancho was eager for vengeance on the King of Aragon for the couple had fled there after they had eloped. It seemed we might have a war although I am not certain that King Ferdinand was quite ready to take on his half-brother!

By January most of my former cubs had been knighted leaving the four youngest warriors to be trained up. Prince Sancho had decided that my training school would end when they were trained, for now he had many knights and all were younger than he was. When he went to war, he would be able to lead just over three hundred well trained and disciplined warriors. To celebrate the last knighthood a tournament was held for all of Prince Sancho's knights. The prize would be that the winner would fight Don Raoul who had now fully recovered from his wound. It took a day and a half for the preliminary bouts to be completed and the last two knights standing were no surprise to me. It was Rodrigo and Álvar.

Both had the finest of armour and both had had their own swords made to their unique specifications. It was what good warriors did. A bespoke sword gave a warrior an edge. I could have had one made for me but there was something about holding my father's sword which more than compensated for the fact this it was not made for me. *Tizona* was the name of Rodrigo's sword and it had been made in

Córdoba by the finest Moorish weaponsmiths. Rodrigo and Álvar had travelled there and ordered it after Toledo had fallen. On the blade was etched **YO SOY LA TIZONA ~ FUE: FECHA AVE: MARIA GRATIA ~~ PLENA dOMINVSSMECVN**. It meant '*I am the Tizona, Hail Mary, full of grace; the Lord be with me*.' It was a beautiful sword with a fuller halfway along the length. It was longer than my leg and weighed more than two and a half pounds. It was so heavy that it took a strong man to wield it. It proved to be that rare thing, a weapon which had a power attached to it which none could explain. When Rodrigo used it he did not lose!

The last bout saw every single person from Lion's Den vying for the best position to watch such an eagerly anticipated fight. Iago and the rest of the men at Lion's Den watched the two warriors enter the gyrus with great interest, both professional and financial. I saw money changing hands. Iago was desperate for me to make a bet with him but I shook my head, "It would not be fair for I have trained them both and I know their strengths and their weaknesses."

He gave me a sly look, "And you know who will win?"

I smiled enigmatically, "For sure!" I would keep that to myself.

Rodrigo was too honourable to use Babieca for the combat as Álvar did not have as good a horse. He did, however, use *Tizona* for Álvar had also had a sword made, *Fortuna*, and so

Rodrigo was happy to use a sword he knew was better for Álvar could have had one made which was as good!

Prince Sancho had had a small stand made and he and his most senior of knights, including Don Raoul, sat there shaded from the sun. We were happy to sit on the fence which ran around the gyrus. As this was the penultimate bout, the last would take place in the afternoon, the two men knelt before the Prince and prayed. Then they rose and, after saluting each other began to prowl around looking for an opening. These were not practice swords that they were using, they were killing weapons. Neither had been given a fresh edge but a good blow to the helmet could still kill a man and a broken limb was highly likely.

Rodrigo was a cautious knight; by that I mean he liked to weigh up an opponent. He always felt that he could win but he wanted to win well. He knew Álvar and all of his moves but he reasoned, no doubt, that Álvar might change his style to upset him. He also knew that he, himself, was the fittest and strongest of all of Prince Sancho's knights. He was not as strong as I was but he was close and I would not have liked to be either man. It was Álvar who broke first in the bout. He launched a flurry of blows aimed at Rodrigo's shield, head and sword. Álvar had fast hands and the blows came in a blur of flashing steel. It was how he had won all of his bouts so quickly. I saw a smile crease across Rodrigo's face for neither man wore a ventail and they just had an arming cap, coif and

helmet upon their heads. Rodrigo knew how
Álvar would try to win and that he would not be
changing the style which had brought him thus
far. All of the blows were defended, deflected
and blocked. I saw Álvar flick his shield up in
anticipation of a strike that did not come. He
launched a second, even quicker attack. This
time Rodrigo took a step back as the onslaught
began so that the first blows were slightly
mistimed and lost some of their power; a clever
move on Rodrigo's part as it wasted Álvar's
energy. When Rodrigo still bided his time, Álvar
launched his third attack but he was tiring and I
saw his face reddening with the effort. This time
he did not go for the head or the shield but
attacked Rodrigo's legs. It was a subtle change
of direction and one I had taught them both. The
hauberk covered their legs but a two-and-a-half-
pound iron bar could break a leg if it was well
struck. This was a harder attack for Rodrigo to
defend as he was slightly taller than Álvar and
had to bend a little to block the blow with his
shield.

I thought, not for the first time, that a longer
shield, more like the Norman one, would be of
more use.

I saw Álvar's shield drop a little as did
Rodrigo and the warrior I had trained for the
longest time began his own, blisteringly fast
attack. He was using a longer and heavier sword
and so it should have been slower than Álvar's
but if anything, it was faster and the tiring Álvar
had no response. Rodrigo's fitness began to tell
and I knew it was a matter of time before it

would all be over. The final blow, when it came was one of pure genius. I knew all of Rodrigo's moves and strokes but I had not seen this one. He swung low and hard at Álvar's shield and made his cousin reel. He continued his swing and pirouetted on his left leg. Álvar's sword was held before him and Rodrigo's hit it with an upward motion and it flew from Álvar's hand. Everyone cheered and even Álvar clapped. It had been a spectacular victory. I knew that had either man been fighting any other knight the bout would have been over far earlier.

"What a fitting end to the morning's combats. We will eat and then see how Don Rodrigo does against my armiger!" Prince Sancho's delight was obvious.

Many of us felt that this was unfair. Rodrigo had fought three times in the morning while Don Raoul had just watched. Indeed, Don Raoul asked for a postponement to give Rodrigo the time to recover but Rodrigo was having none of it.

"I knew the rules before I began and I am content." Rodrigo sometimes had too much honour.

We all went to eat and Álvar and I flanked Rodrigo at the table which was set out with so much food that it groaned. My acolyte smiled and ate sparingly of bread and cheese. "It would not do to fight on a full stomach."

Álvar had no such qualms and he tucked in and ate as though he had not eaten for a week. Between mouthfuls, he spoke of the bout, "I thought I knew every trick you possessed, cousin, but that last one came as a complete surprise. I was mesmerized and knew not where to look! I thought my fast hands would win the day."

Rodrigo said nothing for he was modest. It was left to me to reply, "And against any other opponent, they would. If I was Don Raoul, I would fear that I was about to lose my title."

Álvar shook his head, "As good as my cousin is, Don Raoul is rested and he watched each one of Rodrigo's bouts. He will know his every move."

"You may be right, Minaya, but I am content to have won against my peers. Now a bout between William and Don Raoul might be interesting!"

I laughed, "You are dreaming now, Rodrigo, for I would not last but a few strokes."

Don Raoul was the biggest knight who followed Prince Sancho. I was the same size but I was not a knight. Don Raoul looked to be fresh as he strode to present himself to the Prince. His sword was the same length and size as Rodrigo's and the result of this bout would be down to skill and, perhaps, Rodrigo's exertions on the morning.

This time both men were cautious and when Rodrigo began the bout I wondered if he wished to end it early for he was tiring. Certainly, his movements seemed laboured. They both exchanged a few blows which were just testing the other out but Rodrigo was slower, each time, to bring up his shield or to block a blow with his sword. He also retreated more than he had in the other bouts. That there was a great deal of money bet on this bout became obvious for everyone was watching intently. Most men had bet on Rodrigo against Álvar but the odds were more even in this fight.

Don Raoul became more confident as Rodrigo apparently tired and he used blows which spread Rodrigo's arms and I knew he was going for a blow to Rodrigo's middle when his tired arms would be unable to react quickly enough and to block. His own counter-attacks were lessening but I knew that Rodrigo had a trick or two up his sleeve for I saw that he was not sweating, neither was he breathing hard and, as they came close to me, I saw not fear in Rodrigo's eyes but elation. The winning blow, when it came, was a variation on the one which had defeated Álvar. He pulled his arm back slowly and it was obvious that he intended to make a mighty blow to Don Raoul's shield. However, instead of swinging down, somehow, Rodrigo brought his sword down to point at the ground and then he spun on his right foot. He exposed his back to Don Raoul but the trick had worked and the Armiger's sword was already thrusting to where Rodrigo had been a moment before. I knew that Rodrigo had quick hands but as he turned, he managed to bring his sword to the horizontal and as he spun around, he brought the flat of the blade into Don Raoul's back. The armiger was already off-balance and striking at a man who was no longer there. Don Raoul fell to the floor and lay spread-eagled.

Rodrigo walked slowly up to him and, placing his sword's tip on the back of Don Raoul's neck, said, "Well fought, Don Raoul!"

The cheers for the previous bout were nothing compared with those which rang out around the gyrus. None of us had ever seen Don Raoul defeated but, equally, none had ever witnessed such a bout. Rodrigo sheathed *Tizona* and held his hand out for Don Raoul. Don Raoul sheathed his sword and embraced Rodrigo. The two walked arm in arm to the Prince who held the golden bejewelled dagger which was the prize. He handed it to Rodrigo and said, "A truly inspirational fight. You did well, as did you, Armiger."

Don Raoul shook his head, "I was armiger but that position should go to the best knight that you have. That was once me but is now Don Rodrigo de Vivar!"

It was a magnanimous gesture and Rodrigo could not quite believe it.

Prince Sancho said, "You are certain, Don Raoul?"

He nodded, "If you were to ask every man here, my closest friends included, they would confirm that there is only one man who could be Armiger to Prince Sancho and that is Rodrigo." He nodded to me, "The son of the armiger has trained him well!"

I laughed, "I taught him to lift a sword. What I witnessed this day came from God!"

Prince Sancho nodded, "So be it, Rodrigo de Vivar is my new armiger and God help our enemies with him to lead my knights in battle."

Castilian Knight

Chapter 15

Rodrigo took much persuasion for him to accept the position for he was sure that he still had much to learn. It was Don Raoul who persuaded him. "We have William Redbeard here and soon the last four knights will be trained. He can train you, although none of us thinks you need it and continue as your mentor after. This seems to me, something that has God's hand on it. He has brought the last of your father's oathsworn and when you go into battle there will be four warriors at your back who will keep you as safe as any man in Christendom. Prince Sancho is correct, with you leading our men then our enemies should be shaking in their boots."

Life changed that day for Castile; Rodrigo wanted more control than Don Raoul had enjoyed and he began to train Prince Sancho's knights in the same manner we had trained the cubs. I took it as a compliment that many of the training exercises had been created by myself and Rodrigo but he took them to a new level. Prince Sancho did not notice it but I did. The knights had as much allegiance to Rodrigo as they did to Prince Sancho; sometimes more. The Prince also took part in the mock battles and manoeuvres which Rodrigo and Álvar created. I used the gyrus too, with the four youngest warriors but, with such a small number of would-be knights to train, we often moved to the

smaller training arena and I was able to watch
the knights as they changed formation, shifted
lines, feigned retreat and, in short, became as
fine a fighting force as I have ever seen. The fact
that Don Raoul was such a keen supporter of
Rodrigo and all that he did helped, but the days
of idleness the knights had enjoyed ended the
day that Rodrigo took over.

Perhaps it was Rodrigo's new position or
the fact that we saw the household knights at
close quarters or that I was able to do my job
better, but whatever the reason the four young
men my three men and I were training improved
so much that by Easter they were ready to be
knighted and I could give Rodrigo my complete
attention. Before I could do so, however, a
summons came from King Ferdinand. His
vassal, the Emir of Zaragoza, was being attacked
by King Ferdinand's half-brother, King Ramiro
of Aragon, and had requested help. Prince
Sancho with his three hundred knights was to be
sent to the valley of the Cinca and the town of
Graus which was being attacked by Aragon. We
were going to war. Prince Sancho was eager for
war as he wished to avenge the dishonour of
having his fiancée elope with a king's bastard
and, I think, wished to show the world his newly
trained elite force of knights.

We might have just three hundred knights
but with servants, the guards for the baggage and
horse guards there were nearer five hundred of
us who headed east to Graus. Abu would be
invaluable to us on this campaign for we would
be fighting alongside a Moorish army! I would

need him not only as a translator but also as a military adviser. My Arabic had improved enough for me to converse with slightly more ease than hitherto but there were technical words that I did not know and Abu was able to translate those.

As we rode, Rodrigo questioned the Moor incessantly, Hassan ibn Hassan was a good translator but he was not a man of war while Abu was and he was happy to tell the new Armiger of the strengths of the Moors as well as the weaknesses. Don Raoul also rode with us for he knew the Aragonese army. King Ramiro of Aragon had a good army and its make-up was similar to ours. He had knights, foot soldiers, crossbows and bows. He had lightly armoured horsemen and he had siege weapons. It would be a battle like Atapuerca but without the fanatical knights of Count Bermundo who had not cared if they lived or died so long as they avenged their master.

Don Raoul had been Prince Sancho's armiger since Atapuerca but before that, he had been a sword for hire who had taken part in many tournaments and fought for other lords and princes. "King Ramiro of Aragon has a good champion, Pero de Garcés has never been beaten and he is younger than I am." There was a warning in his words for Don Raoul believed that Rodrigo's youth had helped him win the fight.

Rodrigo was not a fool and he asked, "Could you have beaten him?"

"In my prime, possibly, but not now. He is also a good horseman." He shook his head, "He is a most unpleasant man with whom you would not wish to speak, let alone dine, but he knows his business and he leads the men of Aragon. Do not underestimate him."

Álvar asked, "Do you think you might come up against him, cousin?"

Rodrigo nodded, "It is likely for I am young and, outside of Castile, largely unknown. When I am seen carrying the standard, he will seek me out."

Don Raoul nodded, "Champion defeating champion does not win a battle but it disheartens the men fighting. We are true knights and less likely to be disheartened." He turned and looked at me, "You and your three men will also be under pressure for you will be watching the armiger's back."

We were Rodrigo's bodyguard. Don Raoul had had three knights doing the same job but Rodrigo wanted the four of us. The thought had already occurred to me and, not for the first time, I was glad that my men and I had good mail, helmets, horses and weapons. We might need them.

Graus was well to the north of Zaragoza and was in a mountainous country. The King of Aragon, Ramiro, had tried to take the border fortress of Graus the year after Atapuerca but he had failed. I wondered why he chose now to make his attack for he must have known that King Ferdinand had to protect the Emir who was paying tribute to Castile! The emissaries who had come to King Ferdinand for help were with us now. Abu overheard their conversation as we rode and discovered that they were unhappy that King Ferdinand had sent so few troops.

The night before we reached Graus we camped at Barbastro which would become infamous the following year when Pope Alexander ordered a crusade against the men of Zaragoza. When we were there it was a stronghold and we were safe. I had told Rodrigo what Abu had heard and he told Prince Sancho. Of the three brothers, Prince Sancho was the boldest and the most forthright. As we ate, he asked the emissaries outright if they were unhappy at the numbers of men that the King of Castile had sent. When they tried to bluster, Prince Sancho showed his mettle and, through an interpreter, said the following, "The men I lead, my friend, are the finest in the whole of Christian Spain. They are the best trained and they are led by the greatest knight in Christendom. When we took Salamanca and Magerit it was these men who led the attack and it was their courage that won the day. When we have defeated our enemies then we will speak again and you can apologise to these knights whom you have insulted by your comments."

Seeing two of them actually cower and recoil before the onslaught, I felt a little guilty that I had spoken of what Abu had heard. In the event, it helped to give Prince Sancho the title, amongst our allies, of Sancho the Strong.

The Moors of Zaragoza were gathered to the south of the besieged town. Rodrigo and I spoke of this as we neared the huge encampment. "The Emir fears the Aragonese horsemen and that is valuable information for any future conflict. He is waiting for Prince Sancho to arrive. This way we only have one battle line to break. The men of Aragon will have to have their camps spread around the town."

I might have arrived at the same conclusion but it would have taken me much longer than the short time it took Rodrigo.

He continued, "I have no doubt that he will be of the same opinion as the emissaries but he will hide his feelings and his words."

He was right. As the bodyguards of the standard-bearer and the armiger, we were admitted to the meeting between al-Muqtadir and Prince Sancho. The Emir was an older man than I had expected. The Prince had met him when they had taken Zaragoza and they appeared to get on well despite the difference in their ages. He was a quiet man who did not look to be a warrior and yet he controlled one of the more powerful Taifa of al-Andalus, and as such he was an enigma. He must have had some skill to hang on to power and to defeat both the Emir of Toledo and the King of Aragon. He was not a man to take for granted and I watched him the whole time we were present at the meeting so that I might learn more about him. The Emir spoke Spanish and that helped for Abu was not permitted to be present. His lessons were helping me but I was not even close to Rodrigo who now barely needed Hassan.

The Emir appeared to defer to Prince Sancho and I could understand why. He had been defeated by our men and he knew that he needed our help to defeat men who were armed and led in a similar fashion to us. If he could have defeated the Aragonese then he would not have sent to us for help. Although his Spanish was accented, I could understand every word he said.

"The men of Aragon have the city surrounded. The men and defenders of Graus have a well and they have supplies of food laid in but the Aragonese have siege weapons and it is only a matter of time before the walls fall and then I fear that there will be terrible slaughter for these men are not the same as those led by your father. They are wild men with no control and they seem to enjoy butchery and rape. We sent for aid because we need men who can fight as they do. We needed heroes."

It was flattery and I knew Prince Sancho well enough to know that it would not fool him. I wondered if the Emir knew that Prince Sancho had an ulterior motive for fighting the men of Aragon. Did he know of the elopement and flight of Garcia and Stephanie? Abu had heard a rumour that the couple had fled to Zaragoza first.

Prince Sancho spoke, "You were right to ask for our help." He glared at the emissaries, "As I told those that you sent, we may not be a large number of men but we are the best that Castile can offer and my men are led by the great knight, Don Rodrigo de Vivar. It is he who will command our men for he is the general."

I smiled at the use of 'our men' for it implied that Rodrigo would lead the men of Zaragoza too. I suspect the Emir knew this but he merely nodded and waited for Rodrigo to speak.

"Emir, how many horsemen did you bring to this siege? By horsemen I mean your mounted archers and the men who are mailed, wear the jubbah and have horses protected by the tijfaf?" Rodrigo had garnered this information from Abu for Rodrigo was a perfectionist.

I was close enough to see that he had taken the Emir by surprise for he had pronounced the Arabic words perfectly. "You have great knowledge, I see. We have five hundred archers and the horsemen you describe are my guards and there are two hundred of them."

"And other horsemen?"

"There are five hundred but they wear no armour and are just armed with swords, shields and javelins. I would not have them face mounted knights such as you and your men."

Rodrigo smiled, "I have faced them and know that they are worthy foes." He turned to Prince Sancho, "Before I can devise a plan of battle, I will need to see the siege lines with the Campi Doctor and then I will need to meet with the men who lead the Zaragozan horse."

"Of course, and it will allow us to build a defensive camp. I am aware of the disaster which almost overtook my brother."

The Emir said, "I shall send an interpreter for you."

Rodrigo shook his head and replied in perfect Arabic, "There is no need, lord, for I can manage."

Once outside Rodrigo turned and said, "We will need Abu for this."

I waved over Iago, "We will need Don Rodrigo's guards and Abu."

As he hurried off Rodrigo said, "We just need Abu."

"No, we do not for we are going close to the enemy lines and they know Babieca and they know you. Let us be prepared, eh? I returned to Prince Sancho to protect you and I will do so."

He laughed, "If Álvar is my little brother then you are my elder." He gave a mock bow, "I will do as you say, Campi Doctor."

I had ridden northeast on the back of Copper but now I rode Berber. His nose had saved me once before and I did not want Killer to suddenly charge off towards the enemy warhorses! When my men arrived Rodrigo said, "Abu, we go to look at the siege lines. We will look at the enemy dispositions and the warriors we face but I need you to use your eyes to spy out the men of Zaragoza. They will be our allies and I need to know how they will fight if I am to defeat the men of Aragon."

He nodded, "Aye, my lord." He pointed straightaway at the men of the Emir's guard. "They are the best but they are also arrogant. They will think themselves superior to your knights."

I looked at the men who were lounging around the Emir's tent and I saw that Abu was right. There was contempt on their faces. I remembered that these had never fought against the knights of Castile for King Ferdinand's rapid march to take Toledo meant that they had not fought us. They would learn but Rodrigo had a hard job ahead of him as he knew exactly what our knights would do but not those of our allies. We rode through the Zaragozan camp. All of the horsemen were in the camp and it became obvious that those in the siege lines, behind the pavise and ditches, were foot soldiers. They had javelins, bows and arrows but no armour. They could not attack mailed men. As we rode from one river to the other which guarded our flanks, I began to wonder how Rodrigo would go about devising a plan to defeat the men of Aragon. This was not the country for bands of horse archers to draw knights onto our swords; we saw that the Aragonese had hired mercenaries. I saw Breton crossbowmen and Gascon archers. A crossbow bolt could pierce mail. I wondered if the Arab jubbah that many Moors wore in lieu of armour slowed down a bolt or, perhaps, prevented its penetration altogether.

Later, as we licked our wounds, I worked out what we had done wrong. Rodrigo had started in the centre of our line and, as we returned to our starting position, the men of Aragon knew that we would inspect the lines to the east too. It was a rare mistake from Rodrigo and from me. I had become complacent now that Rodrigo had shown so much skill. I had assumed that he was the finished product but he was not and he still needed guidance from me. I failed him on that day and it almost ended in disaster.

We had reached the eastern end of our line and spotted more mercenaries. We had also seen that King Ramiro had hired some Norman knights too. They were distinctively attired for they wore mail without surcoats and some had the longer kite shield. It was as we were heading back to the centre of our lines that ten of them who had been mirroring our perusal on the backs of their horses suddenly turned and charged at us. As we were looking ahead and they were slightly behind us they took us somewhat by surprise.

It was Abu who spotted them, "Lord, horsemen!"

I whirled around and saw that they had spears and were heading directly for us. They had soon got their horses up to speed. Even as I drew my sword, I noticed that their horses were smaller than ours but that small stature enabled them to get up to charging speed faster. They were spearing the surprised defenders who, like us, had not expected an attack as they galloped to take the prize that was Rodrigo, the Armiger of Prince Sancho. Rodrigo de Vivar became known for his ability to fight against the odds and that day was no exception. He knew that they would catch us and spear us in the back if we fled. He did the only thing he could, he turned and shouted, "Abu, behind us, the rest, shield wall!"

We had been fighting together since our time in Vivar. I think we took the Normans by surprise for we had turned and presented shields and swords so quickly that they must have thought we expected an attack. Iago and I flanked Rodrigo while Juan and Pedro flanked the two of us. My professional eye took in the fact that crossing the ditch and spearing Arabs had disrupted their line. They were not boot to boot and some had lost spears. The defenders had fled and there were none between us to slow them down. Behind us, I heard horns as Don Raoul reacted to the attack and he was sending knights to come to our aid. I worked out who would strike us first and saw the Norman that I would fight. He had a round red shield with what looked like four legs radiating from the metal boss. It was an old-fashioned shield such as my grandfather might have used and was larger than mine. He had a spear and his sword hung from his scabbard. Normans used their shields differently from us; they held them and their reins in the same hand. My smaller shield was strapped tightly to my arm and I had more flexibility. He would aim at my chest for I had a ventail which I had fastened as soon as I knew that we were under attack. He had no ventail and I saw that he was young and, like many Normans, was clean-shaven.

The fact that none of us appeared to be concerned must have worried some of the Normans for a couple slowed. Perhaps they had expected us to flee and that they would have speared us like pigs as we fled. The knight I would fight stood in his stirrups and pulled back his spear. Berber was not afraid but he snorted and stamped as though willing me to counter charge.

Rodrigo was a better judge of the moment than my horse for he shouted, "Charge!" at the perfect time. We all leapt forward when the Normans had their arms drawn back to strike. Had they thought we were mesmerized with fear? The young knight panicked and thrust his spear forward; it was a clumsy strike for he had not aimed it well and I deflected it into the air with ease. Worse for him was the fact that he had stood in the saddle and when I deflected the spear, he became unbalanced. With his reins in his left hand, he tried to regain his seat. I had a free swing at his back as he passed. He might have worn mail but I had a good sword which I had sharpened and his links broke. My sword bit through his gambeson and across his back. Blood spurted and then my sword grated across his spine. He threw his arms in the air as he died. I just had enough time to swing my shield back around and catch the sword of the next Norman on it and my backswing bit into his arm. Rodrigo had done even better. *Tizona* had taken the head of one knight and almost hacked a second in two such was the power of that almost mystical weapon. The survivors fled.

I glanced around and saw that my three men had each accounted for one Norman. The four survivors, including the one I had wounded galloped back to the Aragonese lines. I heard Álvar and Rodrigo's household knights gallop up as the Zaragozans all cheered our victory. In the scheme of things, it was minor but it changed the perception of both armies for they had seen that Rodrigo de Vivar was a force to be reckoned with.

Álvar shook his head, "Next time take us with you, Rodrigo!"

He laughed, "Why, I was in no danger. With these men around me, I can face any foe." He turned to Iago, "Take their mail, weapons and treasure; they are yours. I think Abu could do with more protection. When you have taken their heads and placed them atop their spears return to the camp with their horses."

We had begun the war!

The leaders of the men who would be following Don Rodrigo were gathered at the Emir's tent. I saw more respect than when we had passed the Emir's guards for they had seen what we could do. I confess that I understood less than half of what was said by Rodrigo for he spoke too quickly but Abu was at my ear and he was translating for me.

"I have seen the enemy and know how we can defeat them. This will not be the work of a moment like the instant a sword enters a man and ends his life. This will be a slower but more predictable event. It will be like the hewing of a tree where strokes are used to slowly destroy the mighty oak. We draw them onto our swords. I will use the horse archers to annoy the knights and pull them towards our knights and the guards. We will not fight until the end but, instead, we will withdraw and have them follow us to the arrows and javelins of those who guard the siege lines. Each day will see an escalation of our attacks. I do not want to lose a single warrior but I know that we shall so let us make them bleed. It will not be an early start. I want them to be ready for us as we make our preparations." He turned to Prince Sancho and the Emir and spoke in Spanish. "Tomorrow your banners will not be there. Prince Sancho, I will not fight as your armiger but as Rodrigo de Vivar. We save the royal banner for another day; we do not reveal our two leaders. It will be hard for you but I want them disheartened when you appear for the enemy will think that you bring greater reinforcements." He smiled and turned back to the leaders. "Are there any other questions?"

Muhammad ibn Hassan was the leader of the Emir's guards. His armour was the most magnificent I had ever seen and the helmet which he held in his left hand was topped by a bird and a red plume. At his waist hung a sword which was longer and more intricately decorated than Rodrigo's. "Where will you be, Rodrigo de Vivar?"

Smiling, he replied, "Why at the fore, of course, surrounded by my oathsworn, household knights and before the rest of Prince Sancho's retinue." I saw the respect in the warrior's eyes; it was the answer he had wished.

This was the first battle that all of those who had been trained by me followed Rodrigo into battle. They were Prince Sancho's men but, first, they were Rodrigo's and, I suppose, mine. It

meant we would be at the sharp end of the battle,
the tip. Once outside he summoned Álvar,
"Have my knights gather at my tent. I would
read with them and discuss what we will do."
Nodding, his lieutenant left. He turned to me,
"Will you be there?"

I smiled, "You know my reading skills and
besides, I think I know your mind now. I have
work to do with my men. I know your mind but
they do not and they do not read!"

He laughed, "You are right. When I fight it
is comforting to know that you are behind me
for I have confidence in you. My back is safe
and I can fight all the harder knowing that."

As I left, I realised that such a belief placed
an incredible pressure upon my shoulders. When
he had just been a knight of Castile it had not
been such a problem but now the fate of Prince
Sancho and the whole of Castile rested on Don
Rodrigo's shoulders. Iago, my men and my
servants were at our camp which was just behind
the tent of the armiger.

"You all did well today."

They were sorting through their loot and
Iago grinned, "And we were well paid! This is
good mail! These mercenaries do not trust their
shield brothers for all had full purses filled with
Aragonese gold!"

"Good, I am happy!" I turned to Abu, "And
you did well. I am sorry that you were in danger.
I should not have taken you so close to danger."

He looked offended, "Am I a woman, lord?
I lost an arm and not my, what do you call them,
bollocks?" Since Iago's arrival, his Spanish had

become somewhat more colourful! "I have learned to ride my horse, Fire. I will have a shield fitted to my left arm and tie the reins to my shield. I will be able to use a sword and protect myself. The mail Iago gave to me will protect me. I will ride with your other men lord or you can dismiss me."

Geoffrey nodded, "And I, too, would ride with you."

I shook my head, "Abu can ride with me for he is a warrior trained. You are a horseman."

"Then train me too, lord. I have the blood of warriors in my veins and Iago has told me that you are the best trainer of men he has ever seen. Surely you want as many good men behind you as you can have?"

I glared at Iago, "Then when you can best Iago you may have mail and ride behind me! God help you!"

To be truthful I was touched by the degree of loyalty my new men showed. I spent the next hour explaining what Rodrigo intended. We would divert attention from our allies. The horse archers would draw the Aragonese knights on to our spears so that they would not attack the Moors and they would go for us and Rodrigo. The young warriors needed to know that we would have to weather the storm.

"We will not be in the front rank, that will be the task of the knights. We will be behind Rodrigo and Álvar. Iago and Pedro will flank me and Abu and Juan will carry spare spears for us and be behind our three horses. Tomorrow you need your best horses. Geoffrey, I will ride Killer."

"Good, lord, for he becomes angry when he is left behind. He tries to take chunks out of Berber when he returns! Luckily, Copper can calm them both."

After we had eaten, we prepared our weapons and I felt excited for I was going into battle again but, for the first time, I would be led by a man in whom I had complete faith, Don Rodrigo de Vivar!

Chapter 16

This was the first time I had fought alongside non-Christians and I wondered how different it would be. They would not have a priest bless them before the battle and I doubted there would be the bawdy banter that always accompanied a Christian army. We lined up well behind the defensive ditches the Zaragozans had dug. There were wooden bridges which had been made and carried, during the night, so that we could gallop across them and steal a march upon the Aragonese. This first attack was to simply unnerve them. We were up before dawn and in position whilst it was still dark. The bridges were the places where we formed our lines. We could only cross them two abreast and then we would form up again on the other side. Rodrigo had practised this in the gyrus but this would be the first time we had used it in battle. We all had spears and lances for we would attack, first, those men who had ditches facing the Zaragozans. I knew that, if nothing else, the attack would take the Aragonese by surprise. This time I would have the privilege of watching Rodrigo go into battle. Hitherto I had been alongside him and whilst I had seen the results of his skill, I had not watched him actually fighting in a battle, I was too busy fighting myself. The main difference between Babieca and Killer was in their temperament before a battle. Babieca was calmness in horse form while Killer stamped, snorted and bit at any horse which was near him. I noticed the contrast even more as I waited, in the darkness behind the grey that was Babieca.

As the first hint of light appeared in the east, to our right, Rodrigo raised his spear and behind us, the horn sounded. It would alert the defenders but it would also tell those within Graus that an attack was under way. The horse archers before Rodrigo galloped across the bridges and the Moorish archers took advantage of the dim light to ride close to the Aragonese lines and then release their arrows. They were deadly and they were accurate for they were sending their arrows a relatively short distance. The Aragonese had archers too but a moving target is harder to hit, especially in the dim light of dawn. The Zaragozan arrows proved too much for those who were behind the ditches and pavise. The horses' height meant that the archers, releasing at relatively close range, could send their arrows down; the archers and crossbowmen were not knights and they fled. When their spearmen advanced then they were cut down too for there were no pavises to protect them. I heard an Aragonese horn and knew that the enemy knights were coming to rid themselves of the annoying fleas that were the archers.

The Moors had been given clear instructions and they obeyed. As soon as the knights charged them, they would turn and, sending arrows behind them as they retreated, gallop back towards us. Rodrigo raised his spear again and that meant the horn sounded the charge for us and the Emir's guards. All along our line mailed horsemen spurred their horses. The horse archers would find a way through us and Rodrigo would lead our knights to plough into the heart of the Aragonese line.

We quickly formed up and once Rodrigo saw that his men were in line, he spurred his horse. I watched Babieca leap forwards and heard his hooves as they clattered across the wooden bridge across the ditches. The second line awaited my command and I gave Rodrigo enough time to clear the ditch before kicking Killer in the flanks. He would leap further forward, eager to get into battle. The enemy might have been expecting us but that did not mean that they were ready for us. They had not known about the boards and had been preparing for a different sort of attack. To our right, I saw that the Emir's guards, good as they were had not as much discipline as we did and their lines were ragged compared with ours. The spearmen stood their ground but the sight of a line of knights with spears galloping towards them was unexpected. A few arrows were sent in our direction from some archers who had sheltered behind the spearmen, more in hope than expectation, and I thought that I would quite like a tijfaf for Killer, as the padded horse covering would protect my horse. Then the battle began.

Rodrigo's arm came back and lunged with the regularity of a weaponsmith beating out a sword as he skewered, first, the spearmen and then the archers who had escaped the Moorish

archers. Next to him, Álvar and Don Raoul did
the same although, by now there were few
targets. We were not boot to boot for we had had
bridges to cross and that, again, was part of
Rodrigo's genius. It allowed the Moors to ride
between us and, as soon as they cleared us our
knights would close up and we would become
tighter. I saw the looks of joy on the faces of our
Moorish allies as they galloped through us.
There were empty saddles but not many and
they would regard that as a victory. They would
form up behind us and allow their horses to
recover. If we had to fall back then we had cover
already in place. This was the genius of Rodrigo
for he used the best of our warriors and the best
of the Moorish warriors to create a new and
hitherto unseen combination.

The sun had finally cleared the hills to the
east and bathed the field ahead of us in sunlight.
I saw the Aragonese dead and they littered the
ground. Now that the line ahead was boot to
boot it was impossible for horses, no matter how
much they tried, to avoid stepping on them. The
bodies crunched and cracked as warhorses
carrying mailed men ensured, unwittingly, that
they were dead. Ahead of Rodrigo, I saw the
knights of Aragon. They were not arrayed as we
were and were not boot to boot. Worse, they had
just charged from their camp in no sort of order
so that there were clumps of knights ahead of
others. The eager ones and, perhaps, the younger
ones would be the first to die.

I watched Rodrigo as he pulled his arm
back. The first knot of knights had come directly

for him, Don Álvar and Don Raoul for they
sought the glory of taking out the leaders of our
knights and they sought the honour to be the first
to make a kill. When I had first trained the cubs
and we had fought our first battle I had heard
young knights boasting of what they had done.
Rodrigo was never like that. He rarely spoke of
his own deeds. I saw Rodrigo's arm come back
and although I could not see the knight he
fought, I knew that he would be defeated.
Rodrigo had a good eye and I had seen him
improve from that first day when he had been
upon my shoulders and I had run with him, at
the quintain. When he aimed his spear, he hit
what he wished to hit whether that was face, leg,
chest or horse. He had the ability to know the
perfect place to strike. I confess that I had tried
to train him to be that way but it is one thing to
teach and quite another for one to learn. He was
the only one who managed to strike the way I
had taught.

When the first Aragonese knights were
struck by Rodrigo and the others it was like a
crack of thunder. Spears splintered and
shattered, mail was rent asunder and men died. I
could hear their cries even though I was more
than twenty paces from them. They had attacked
our best knights and they had paid the price. The
eager young cavaliers lay dead, dying or
wounded and the surviving horses wandered
forlornly north and west as they tried to return to
their own lines. The knights who were wounded
would not last long for as I led the second line,
we struck them and the survivors who were

rising to their feet were slain, almost to a man. We thundered towards the main Aragonese camp and I could see the walls of Graus behind. If nothing else this attack by the elite of Castile would hearten the Zaragozan defenders.

Rodrigo had planned this attack meticulously and rather than accelerating, which the enemy would expect, he was slowing for that made us more cohesive and helped our horses. They would not be tired. A tired horse could kill a knight quicker than any weakness in his armour for a knight needed a horse that could move away from danger with a flick of the wrist. The main Aragonese line was approaching and it was led by King Ramiro and Pero de Garcés. They were not in the front rank but the banner of Aragon was there. I could see other banners too and knew that we would be outnumbered. The next part of Rodrigo's battle plan was the most crucial and also the one which could, potentially, lead to disaster.

The Aragonese horn sounded the charge and the two mailed masses of men were on a collision course. This was the first battle I had witnessed, on this scale, of knights fighting knights and it was terrible to behold. The two lines clashed and if the first coming together had sounded like thunder this sounded like Judgement Day! This time Rodrigo and our knights did not plough through them for they were halted by a solid wall of similarly armoured warriors. Spears were splintered and shattered. This time I saw some of our knights unhorsed. When I saw Rodrigo take out his sword then I knew that it was my time and I had to obey Rodrigo's orders.

I turned to Juan who held the horn, "Prepare to make the call!" Rodrigo had told every knight that he led what he expected of them. That was his style; everyone knew their part and they felt included in the general's plans. He was young but he was born with an old head. I counted in my head to fifty and then shouted, "Now! Make the call." As the last notes of the withdraw rang out, I shouted, "Open ranks and charge!"

That no one had ever done what we intended had occurred to me but we had such belief in Rodrigo that none had questioned his decision. I knew that Prince Sancho had been concerned that he might lose many of his best knights but he trusted Rodrigo enough to allow him the freedom to make the decision. The fact that this was his first battle in command still amazes me after all these years and more, that he trusted me, a sword for hire, to be a crucial part of the plan! Iago and Pedro moved away from me to allow our knights to pass through and I readied my spear. I saw our line of knights disengage and turn towards us. Rodrigo was grinning as he rode between Iago and me. We were not riding boot to boot but we were in a straight line and we would strike together. More, the enemy thought they had won and were charging recklessly, with no sort of order to end the battle and, hopefully, win the siege. They had broken spears and we had fresh ones. We were together and they were not.

We were upon them before we knew. I pulled back my arm and thrust at the chest of the knight with the raised sword. I am a strong man. Some say the strongest in our army and when I rammed the spear into the knight's chest, the head tore through his surcoat, mail and into his breastbone and chest. The spearhead was a large one and it drove through to his back. The ash shaft did not break and, as I rode his body was torn from the saddle and he hung, briefly in the air before I dropped the spear, drew my sword and shouted, "Fall back!"

I looked straight into the faces of the King of Aragon and his armiger, Pero de Garcés. They had stopped and his household knights had formed a protective barrier around him. In stopping they had lost momentum and it took time for a warhorse carrying a mailed warrior to get up to speed. Our horses could maintain their speed as they turned at the canter. Even as I was turning, I could not help but think that Rodrigo was a genius or some sort of fortune teller for he had predicted this. The sudden appearance of our mailed line had made the Aragonese halt. We galloped back towards the Emir's defences. I could see the line of knights led by Rodrigo as they approached our horse archers. The horse archers were spread out and Rodrigo led Prince Sancho's men back across the ditches. Our steady pace meant that our horses were not suffering and I kept a steady line. Behind me, I heard the sound of an Aragonese horn as their King realised that he had been tricked and they hurtled after us.

For a brief moment, I felt fear as I saw
Moorish horse archers draw on their bows and
then I remembered that these were allies. We
were just thirty paces from them when their
arrows flew over our heads and we passed
between their lines. I saw that Rodrigo had
halted and turned his knights on their lathered
horses on our side of the ditches which
surrounded our camp and we passed between
them to line up behind. By the time I had turned
a weary Killer to join the line, the Moorish horse
archers had halted the Aragonese charge and
they were already retreating leaving the field
littered with their dead and dying.

Rodrigo turned to Ahmad ibn Sulayman
who commanded the Zaragozan defences.
"Advance the line and clear the battlefield. We
will enlarge our defences and diminish the
enemy!" Again, it was pure genius for the
Aragonese had been beaten and would withdraw
to their own camp. They would be in no
condition to threaten our foot soldiers as they
moved our defences forward.

That day was the first time I heard Rodrigo
referred to as El Cid, the Arab said, "Aye, El
Sayyid, for I have seen, this day, that you are the
master of the battlefield! Can any stand against
you?"

He just smiled and then turned to me, "You
did well, William. Did you lose many?"

I had counted as we had galloped beneath
the hail of Moorish arrows, "I counted two
empty saddles."

He nodded, "We lost more in the initial attack but they, I think, had greater losses. Álvar go and arrange for the exchange of bodies!"

"Aye, lord."

This was normal for the Aragonese had withdrawn to their own lines realising the futility of attacking horse archers.

Rodrigo did not leave the field until the bodies had been exchanged and our losses became clear. We had lost eighteen knights. Amazingly none of them were the knights I had trained. Was that luck or had the training I had given, along with Rodrigo and Álvar, made a difference? As we rode back to the Prince and the Emir, Rodrigo commented on this. "The ones you and I trained were the ones who obeyed my orders, to the letter. My plan was a sound one and we could have eliminated any losses. I shall learn from this. I hope the knights of Prince Sancho do too." The losses had been the knights who had delayed their retreat or carried on for one more, apparently, easy victory.

The two leaders were delighted with the result. The horse archers and the Emir's guards had losses too but they were much lower than they had expected. I was with them as they discussed the next part of Rodrigo's plan. I was astounded that the two leaders so happily went along with the plans and ideas of such a young knight. I think, in Prince Sancho's case, it was because he had seen Rodrigo grow and develop before his eyes. In the Emir's case, I believe it was the charisma of Rodrigo for he was a gently

spoken knight and a courteous man. The fact
that he spoke to the Emir in his own language
obviously helped too.

"I think, my lords, that we allow a day or
two to elapse. It will help our mounts recover
and we can strengthen our defences for I would
not have a repetition of Magerit!"

"And then what? We cannot sit here
forever. The Emir's people will need to be
resupplied." Prince Sancho was anxious for a
swift victory.

"Then we have a night attack and we go on
foot."

"But we have brought knights!"

"And knights can fight just as easily on
foot. Do you not think, Prince Sancho, that King
Ramiro will also improve his defences? Those
defences will now be against horses."

The Emir smiled, "You have an eastern
mind, Rodrigo de Vivar. This slow and steady
approach is the opposite of the usual frenetic
attack favoured by your Christians. It shows a
subtle and clever mind." He had the Emir's
approval and so the Prince nodded his.

Although we had escaped relatively lightly,
men and horses had suffered wounds. Killer had
a cut along his rump. I did not know when he
had incurred the wound for there had been no
reaction during the battle but he was a warhorse.
Geoffrey and I tended to him. When the bodies
had been recovered, we had also reclaimed lost
spears and other weapons. I liked my spear
because I had had it made by a weaponsmith
specifically for me. The head was a little longer

than those used by other men but I had the strength to wield it and the larger size and narrower point enabled me to drive it deep within an enemy, its head widened mail almost instantly. I sharpened it, knowing that we would be called into action again soon. Our four newly knighted warriors had survived and as Rodrigo and Álvar were busy with Don Raoul and the Emir, planning the next phase of the battle they sought me out. They had ridden in the second line with me and they had seen our two knights killed.

"Campi Doctor, that we survived our first battle was down to you but better knights than we died. Is there luck on the battlefield?"

"The training helped you but it was Don Rodrigo's plan which ensured victory. As to your survival? Aye, you are probably right in that there is luck. When I went berserk at Salamanca, I was lucky and landed on the Moor I had slain. If I had not then I would be dead. Who decides luck I do not know. However, I do know that worrying if you will live or die in battle is the surest way to be killed. You have to trust to your weapon, your training and, most important of all, that your brother knights will stand by you."

They looked at each other and Phillip asked, somewhat nervously, "Yet you are not a knight."

I nodded and pointed to Iago and the others, "I am lucky. Before I became Lord of Briviesca these were my shield brothers. That makes us closer than brother knights. You four trained together and, if you are lucky, then you will have the same bond." I saw them nod and take in my words, "Do not worry about luck. Use the skills you have and improve upon them every day. That will help you survive. For my first few fights that was all that I did, survive. Knights fight few battles but each time they draw a sword and face an enemy it is part of their training and when they survive then they improve. We will fight again in the next few days so do not waste time talking with me, practise!"

The King of Aragon, or rather he and his armiger were responsible for making a liar of me. Before the plans of Don Rodrigo de Vivar could be set into motion a herald came to our line of defence. He rode to our lines and waited until the Emir, Prince Sancho and Don Rodrigo were present.

"I come from King Ramiro with a challenge. He would have his champion and yours fight a combat here, before our two armies. It will be to the death."

A collective gasp could be heard from all those who were assembled. This was not a rare occurrence but it was normally in a less public place. I looked at Rodrigo. He could refuse but if he did so then the heart would go from our army. Pero de Garcés was taking a risk or it may have been that King Ramiro was a gambler and counted on his champion defeating ours. It told me that we had hurt the Aragonese more than they had hurt us in the battle before the walls of Graus.

I saw the Emir look at Prince Sancho but before they could debate Rodrigo said, "I accept the challenge!"

Prince Sancho said, "Let us speak together first, Rodrigo!"

He shook his head, "If I do not fight then we might as well pack up and head for our home. This cannot be open for debate." He turned to the herald, "I choose horseback, spears and swords!"

As the one challenged it was Rodrigo's right to choose the weapons and the conditions under which they would fight. When the herald frowned then I knew that Pero de Garcés would not have chosen those. He nodded, "Very well, noon tomorrow!"

I joined the Emir, Prince Sancho and Don Raoul around Rodrigo, "You can beat him, Don Rodrigo, but he is a better warrior than I am and he does use cunning and sometimes underhand tricks."

We all looked at Don Raoul and Rodrigo nodded, "I thought as much and, unless I miss my guess, he prefers the lance and the axe."

Don Raoul nodded and laughed, "You are a seer! Aye, he likes the weight of the lance and the axe he wields has a sharpened hook which he uses to pull opponents from their horses."

Rodrigo nodded, "Emir, I would be grateful for a tijfaf for my horse. The last thing I need is for Babieca to be injured by the armiger's spear."

Prince Sancho said, "Attacking a horse is against the rules!"

"And this is not a tournament with your father presiding, Prince Sancho. This is a fight to the death and no one will stop because we cry foul. I would be killed and the King of Aragon would have won. A month from now no one would remember that he won by foul means. I, too, know of this man and that he has had a dubious path to the position of armiger. He has not played fair. I will not change when I fight him and I will have to trust to Babieca, *Tizona* and my mentor, William Redbeard. Come, William, I shall need your mind to prepare for this. You shall be my second."

It was rare but, in such combats, if one of the combatants was struck down with some malaise then they had to be replaced by another. The fact that I, who was not a knight, had been chosen, surprised not only me but the others too.

The Emir gave a wry smile and said, "You show wisdom, Don Rodrigo for this man looks like he knows how to fight and yet he is not a knight!"

I saw Prince Sancho colour. He could have knighted me, once, but the moment had passed and now he regretted it. I went with Don Rodrigo and Álvar to his tent. "I should have given you the chance to refuse, Will, for this could be dangerous."

I shook my head, "I am happy and besides I think that it is highly unlikely that you will be struck down with some pestilence overnight! However, I am intrigued as to why you chose me and not Don Raoul or Álvar."

Álvar shook his head, "I would not last five minutes with Pero, I know that. I have never beaten you, Will, and I am not sure that I ever will."

Rodrigo nodded, "And Don Raoul was broken when I defeated him. He had been unbeatable until then. If he went into battle with Don Pero then his mind would go back to the gyrus at Lion's Den. So, how do I defeat this Aragonese Armiger?"

I had seen many combats on horseback although I had only fought in training bouts. "If victory is attained on horseback that would be a rarity. It will probably end as combat on foot." Rodrigo nodded, "Which begs the question, why risk Babieca if you know that will not decide the battle?"

"Because I think I can gain an advantage on horseback. My opponent likes the lance and that means he uses his weapon to gain a quick victory. I will not aim for his chest, nor his shield. I will go for his leg. If I can wound him and unhorse him then he will be slower on foot and I will have the advantage."

It was another rule that if one knight was unhorsed then the other had to dismount too.

"He is older than I am which means he has more experience and, as Don Raoul told us, more tricks. I have my fitness and that is down to you, Will. What is the best way to wear him down for he will not be as reckless as Álvar was?"

Álvar had the good grace to nod his agreement.

I was on more comfortable ground, "If you manage to wound him then keep moving so that he has to turn to face you, that will increase the flow of blood; losing blood weakens a man. You have your spinning trick but do not do as you did before. You can only use it once for having seen it Pero de Garcés will remember it. The problem comes if you do not manage to wound him. If that happens then you will have to look for a weakness and I am not sure that he will have one." I suddenly laughed.

Álvar asked, "What is funny?"

"I have said that Pero may not have a weakness. Can you think of one flaw in this most perfect of knights with whom we have trained for so many years?"

Álvar laughed, "You are right."

Rodrigo shook his head, "You two are of little use!" He tossed *Tizona* to me, "Here, put a good edge on that and you, Minaya, can get out the chessboard. Let us sharpen my mind at the same time!"

How he slept that night I shall never know for Pero de Garcés had a fearsome reputation. While Álvar and Rodrigo played chess, and I put an edge to the sword I spoke with Don Raoul. "He is a nasty man with a cruel streak to him and I know that he will try to kill Rodrigo any way he can. He may even resort to poison." I looked shocked and he nodded, "I have heard of other knights who have used such a ploy. It is risky for the poison can hurt the killer. I will pray for Don Rodrigo this night for he is a good man. I was more than happy to step aside and let him be armiger. To be truthful, William, I seek a more peaceful life for I know that I am getting older but I would still like to have a wife and, who knows, children."

I nodded and spoke of Alfonso. "Alfonso and my foster mother, Maria, came together when he was older and they were happy. Sadly, they were never fated to have children but there are ladies out there who could bear children and you would be a fine catch for them."

He shook his head, "I have spent my life at war. What do I know about wooing a lady?"

I smiled, "Does it have to be a lady?" He gave me a quizzical look. "It seems to me that a knight marries a lady because he wishes advancement or connections to some great lord. He might wish a dowry. You seek none of those things. You want a woman to bear you children for you are rich." He nodded. "And you are as advanced as far as you wish to go. Seek a good woman. There are many out there."

He grinned and looked, suddenly, ten years younger, "It is a joy to speak with you, William, for you have an honesty about you which is refreshing. I can see, now, why Rodrigo has turned out as well as he has. His father is a failure but you have done more for him than any father could have done."

We were all up early the next morning. Rodrigo went to the priest Prince Sancho had brought with him and confessed. I had no idea what sins he could have committed for to me he seemed the perfect knight but it was what knights did before a combat that might result in their death.

A King, a Prince and an Emir would be watching and so there was a certain formality to the occasion. Chairs were brought out for the great and the good. The two armies were also there to watch despite the fact that the day before men had died and the day after would, no doubt see battle again but for this brief moment in time there was a truce. The knights and the lords had the best views while the rank and file peered where they could. Money exchanged hands and it crossed the lines. It was as though there was no siege and the two armies had gathered to watch this fight. Tomorrow we might be at each other's throats but on this one day, all belligerence was forgotten as men placed bets and made wagers. I saw little of this. Iago told me of it later. I was helping Rodrigo to prepare.

I had done this since he had been little more than a boy but this time, as I helped dress him, I examined each item as I fitted it. The stockings he wore beneath his chausses were smoothed so that they did not irritate his legs; such distractions could be fatal. The silk undershirt was of the finest quality for if the mail and gambeson were breached that was the last line of defence and it had to be pure and clean. We fitted his arming cap and coif but let his ventail hang. We donned his mail and I saw his shoulders sag as he took the weight. His surcoat topped it and then I placed his baldric around his waist and hung *Tizona* from it. His fingerless mittens hung from the hauberk and he was almost ready.

One of Prince Sancho's retainers would fetch us when the time was right. Álvar had his horse, Babieca, ready. I, too, was ready in case I had to fight; I wore my mail and my helmet was close to hand but I knew now that it was unlikely that I would be needed. "If I fall, William, know that I told Father Raimundo that all of my inheritance is to go to you. I have spoken with my grandfather and he intends to leave his money to me too. You shall have it all."

I was stunned, "Me? What about Álvar?"

He laughed, "He is richer than I am until I receive the inheritance from my grandfather and mother. No, I owe more to you than you can know. My father abandoned me but you have neither wavered nor faltered in all the time we have been together. You are as loyal as any and I shall repay that loyalty. When I have looked around since I was a boy, then you were there and that has helped me."

I nodded, "It is kind but as you shall win this day it is immaterial and when you marry you will have children to whom you can leave your riches. I am content. I have an estate and I have more money than I ever dreamed possible. Life is good, Rodrigo, for both of us."

Just then the herald came in and nodded, "It is time, lord!"

"Come, William, this is the day of Vivar!"

I led Babieca. My sword hung over my back, along with my shield so that I did not trip for I could feel the tension in the air. You could almost cut it with a knife. It seemed, to me, that the whole of Spain was holding its breath but, of course, none outside of the Cinca valley knew what was happening. Pero de Garcés also made his way to the centre where a herald and the Bishop of Huesca stood waiting. The two of us walked in step. It was easy for we were in tune with one another and it made me smile for then, I knew, that he would win! We reached the centre and the Bishop blessed both knights. He would act as adjudicator. He stepped to the side and the two knights faced each other.

That left the two of us and Pero along with his second. His second was an older man and I had no doubt that he was, like me, a token only. Pero would never have declined the fight. I was next to Rodrigo and I saw the eyes of his opponent and they were evil. They showed that he was a cruel and arrogant man and his words confirmed it, "Today I will kill you and take Babieca and *Tizona*! I will slay your horse and I will kill your sword and none will remember this nonentity of a boy from Vivar."

I would have drawn my sword and slain him there and then but Rodrigo held out his arm. "God will judge us this day and he will decide who has the right. May God be with you." Pero de Garcés declined the outstretched hand and I believe that regardless of Rodrigo's skill, God chose his champion that day!

They mounted their horses and I led Babieca to one end of the field. I said nothing to Rodrigo for what was there to say? My mind was like his and we knew each other's minds without words. I nodded and smiled as I handed him his spear. He turned and faced his foe. We waited until the Bishop lowered his crozier and then Rodrigo rode at Pero de Garcés. I had no doubt as to the outcome but, I confess that I gripped my crucifix and prayed to God. I had told my young knights of luck and that God gave luck on a whim. I prayed that he would give it to Rodrigo.

Chapter 17

I saw that Pero's horse was slightly larger . than Babieca but size was not always everything. How clever was Pero's mount? Both men were expert riders and I saw them using their knees as much as their left hands. Pero was riding faster than Rodrigo and I could not work out why he was doing so for the faster a horseman rode the less accurate was his weapon. If you were charging in a line then it might not make as much difference for a wavering lance or spear could still strike flesh. Here accuracy was all! Rodrigo, whilst still riding fast enough to give impetus and momentum to his strike, had Babieca and his right hand under perfect control. I saw their arms come back as they both prepared to strike. There was almost a hush across the two armies for until they clashed the battle had not yet begun. The two spears struck at the same time. The two men had ridden at each other spear to spear. Pero de Garcés had rammed his spear with all of his might at Rodrigo's chest, hoping to end the combat with one mighty blow and use his horse's speed allied to his weight to simply knock Rodrigo from his horse. Rodrigo's spear had ripped into Pero's leg above the knee. The crack and the splintering of Pero's spear as it smashed into Rodrigo's shield brought a cheer as the tension was released from the mass of men who watched. As they passed each other Rodrigo raised his spear and the head could be seen to be clearly bloodied.

Rodrigo was able to slow the quicker of the two and to turn his horse. When he saw that Pero's spear was shattered he threw his own spear to the ground and drew *Tizona*. I looked at Pero's second who gave me a wry smile. "Don Rodrigo is a cunning opponent but he has honour."

I nodded, "I know and he will win."

"Do you wish a wager?"

"A wager implies that there is some doubt and in this situation, there is none. I will not take your coin for God has already decided the outcome." We both made the sign of the cross.

Pero de Garcés had drawn his sword. I saw blood dripping from his wound. If Rodrigo dismounted to give himself an advantage then Pero would have to follow suit. He remained mounted despite the fact that Pero de Garcés' horse was bigger and the Aragonese champion would not be hampered by his wound whilst mounted. They rode at each other and, again, Pero de Garcés tried to use superior speed. Rodrigo realised the flaw in his opponent's character and, as they rode towards each other, sword to sword, Rodrigo jerked his reins to the right and the nimble Babieca took Rodrigo to the left of the knight of Aragon so that they were shield to shield and the slower speed of Babieca enabled Rodrigo to strike at the Aragonese knight. While Pero de Garcés struck air for Rodrigo was not where the blow was aimed, *Tizona* hit the champion on the back for he hit behind his shield. It was a mighty blow and the blow tore and ripped the surcoat revealing the mail beneath. Only Rodrigo would know if he had succeeded in tearing the mail links.

Both knights wheeled their horses around and faced each other. He could not repeat the same trick, firstly because Pero would be wise to it and secondly because both horses had slowed to a stop. Pero de Garcés now tried a trick of his own. He stood in his stirrups and made his horse rear and lurch towards Babieca. That he had trained him to do so was obvious and it looked likely that Babieca would have his head crushed but Rodrigo seemed to have anticipated the move and he jinked his horse away to safety. The Aragonese army jeered when Rodrigo showed his back to his opponent. Pero de Garcés spurred his horse and galloped at Rodrigo's back.

I heard Pero de Garcés' second chuckle, "Now he will die for Don Pero does not miss such inviting targets."

He did not know Rodrigo nor his clever horse. I saw that Rodrigo had invited the reckless charge and he pirouetted Babieca almost on the spot. He used his own shield to deflect the killing strike aimed at him hurriedly by Pero and then, as he carried on around, he smacked his sword into the back of Pero de Garcés. It was not a wild blow for it was aimed at the mail he had already weakened. It hurt the Aragonese knight for his arms came out to make a crucifix before he turned his horse again. Pero de Garcés had run out of cunning tricks and now he would have to fight Rodrigo from the back of a horse. That he was weakening was obvious and the trail of blood from his leg grew. I could not see the damage done to the mail of the Aragonese knight but if links were broken then the weight of the mail hauberk would shift and unbalance the already weakened warrior. Rodrigo knew his craft and I was certain that the second blow would have broken the integrity of the mail.

This time their swords rang together and I saw sparks fly. It was as though a bolt of lightning had struck the battlefield and a roar went up from both armies. Rodrigo had sparred with Álvar and his cousin had fast hands. Now Rodrigo showed that the training and preparation had paid off for he rained blow after blow on the shield, sword and helmet of Pero de Garcés. It would have weakened another man but both warriors were the best in their field. The two horses were also trying to aid their masters and they bit and stamped at each other. The tijfaf came into its own for Babieca was safe from the bites of the horse from Aragon and that battle was won by the horse called barbarian!

The battle of the horses meant that Rodrigo could not use the nimble feet of Babieca, and the spinning move which had defeated both Don Raoul and Álvar was not an option. That he was still thinking and planning was clear to those who knew him. The chess games with Álvar had helped him to think several moves ahead. The wounded leg and the cracked mail were part of that plan. Rodrigo could stand and use his height whereas Pero de Garcés could not stand due to his wounded leg and damaged mail and Rodrigo set up the winning strike well. They were shield to shield and both knights knew how to use the shield offensively. Rodrigo, however, was quicker and as he punched his shield at his opponent when Pero withdrew his shield, he then rammed the metal-rimmed edge of his own on to the left knee of Pero de Garcés, He hurt the knight for I saw his mouth open as he cried out. His words were lost for the two armies were baying and chanting the names of their own knight and champion. Pero de Garcés then, involuntarily, pulled his horse's head back and that allowed Rodrigo to pirouette Babieca to the sword side of his opponent and while Pero de Garcés tried to turn and face the new threat, Rodrigo stood in his saddle and raising *Tizona* brought it down towards Pero de Garcés' head. His weakened legs and the shifting, broken mail made his response slower than it would have been at the start. His sword merely slowed *Tizona's* progress but Rodrigo had so much power that the blow struck the top of Pero de Garcés' helmet. The noise of the strike could be heard above the baying of the crowd; it sounded like a cathedral bell being struck. When the sword hand of the champion fell to the side and his sword dropped to the ground, I knew it was over. The crowd did not and they expected Pero de Garcés to draw the second sword from his saddle scabbard.

I turned to the second of Pero de Garcés who shook his head, "He is now at your champion's mercy and this is a fight to the death!"

"Then you do not know Don Rodrigo de Vivar." I pointed as Rodrigo sheathed his sword and then picked up the trailing reins of his opponent's horse. He led him towards us. When he neared us, he said, "Your champion is dead or dying. It is his cantle only which keeps him upright. As if to prove the point, when they were just two paces from us, Pero de Garcés' horse skittered and the champion of Aragon fell from the saddle. When he hit the ground the strap on his helmet broke and fell from his head. His eyes were rolled back and blood seeped from a wound. He had blocked but not stopped the blow.

The army of Aragon wailed while the knights of Castile and the men of Zaragoza erupted into cheers. I said, simply, "You have won! Raise your helmet and your sword that all may see you!"

He nodded and he took off his helmet and threw it to me and then, raising his sword, made Babieca rear. He was given a new title that day for Prince Sancho stood and shouted, "El Campeador!" It means outstanding warrior. The name was chanted across the field of combat and from that day forth he was no longer simply the Castilian armiger, he was El Campeador.

The defeated and dead champion of Aragon lay on the ground. His second said while the cheers and chants rang out around us, "Don Rodrigo can claim both the horse and the sword of Don Pero, not to mention his other arms."

I shook my head for we had discussed this already and I knew Rodrigo's mind on the matter. "Take your champion and his horse for Don Rodrigo does not wish to take anything from this day other than the result." I looked into his eyes, "Castile has won and Aragon has lost. If your king has any sense then he will take his army home again." Rodrigo had accepted the challenge not out of any sense of glory but to save men's lives. He hoped that when he won the King of Aragon would take it as a sign from God. He was mistaken.

"I fear he will not do that. It was he who told Don Pero to make the challenge. He thought that one who had seen just over twenty summers would not be able to match the skill of the greatest champion in Spain."

That night we were back in our camp. Both armies had dispersed. The knights of Castile would drink and celebrate but we had Muslim allies who would watch and we did not fear a night-time attack for we had guards. Rodrigo and I dined with the Emir and Prince Sancho. I told them of the words of the second and Rodrigo nodded, "I agree. King Ramiro will take the fact that his half-brother, King Ferdinand, only sent three hundred knights to aid his ally as a sign of weakness. He will prosecute the siege for with Graus as his fortress he can threaten the heartland of Zaragoza."

The Emir nodded, "You are right, El Campeador, and you have shown us that you understand the strategy we should employ. If you were leading our army then what would you do?"

I knew Rodrigo had already thought this through for he had discussed it with Álvar and myself. "I would leave it for a couple of days. Send emissaries asking that they leave now that their champion is dead. They will not, of course, leave. When they do not then we make a nighttime attack on their camp."

Prince Sancho asked, "On horseback?"

Shaking his head Rodrigo said, "No, on foot. As William here told me, that strategy almost worked at Magerit. Emir, you have men who can move silently and use knives?" The Emir nodded. "Then we kill their sentries and use our knights and your guards to finish the task." He looked at Prince Sancho, "We go for the head of the snake and kill King Ramiro."

I saw Prince Sancho clutch his crucifix for kings and princes were not normally killed and they were certainly not targeted. Perhaps Atapuerca had changed everything. The Emir nodded, "So be it."

As Rodrigo had predicted the King of Aragon spurned all offers of peace and a safe withdrawal. We prepared for a night-time attack. Unlike most of the other knights, we would not fight in helmets but in a coif and arming cap. Fighting in the darkness, as I had discovered, was not something to be done in a helmet that restricted your view. Nor would I be using my shield. I would take a short sword as well as my father's blade. This would not be a formal battle with shield walls and spears. This would be a chaotic and bloody battle with no chance of quarter as men fought in a world of darkness and shadows. I was under no illusions, Don Rodrigo's plan had little honour involved. We were planning murder but as the alternative was a long and bloody siege which might result in the inhabitants of Graus suffering unnecessarily, then it was acceptable.

As we would be fighting in darkness and there was little to differentiate the knights of Castile from the knights of Aragon, we sewed white crosses on our surcoats so that our allies would not kill us by mistake. We also formed ourselves into smaller groups which would be easier to manage. I led one while Don Raoul, Don Rodrigo, Don Álvar, Don Juan of Burgos and Iago of Astorga led the others. We were each allocated a part of the enemy camp. The Emir's guards were similarly divided. The sentry killers would go in first and then we would follow. The Emir's horse archers would be standing by so that when dawn came if they were needed then they could hunt down any survivors who still wished to fight on. Both Rodrigo and I hoped that it would not come to that.

The next day the Aragonese showed that they were not finished for they made a costly assault on the walls of Graus. It was prosecuted with all that they had available to them as if King Ramiro wanted the town as weregeld for his dead champion. I had learned the word weregeld from Alfonso who had learned of it from my father and the idea of a blood debt seemed apposite. The men who climbed the ladders were brave but they were beaten back. That was the deciding moment for the Emir and the Prince. They ordered the attack for that night and in preparation, I gathered the knights who would follow me. They had all been specially chosen for I had trained each and every one. My three shield brothers would guard me but every knight would obey my commands. I was not a knight but I had earned their respect.

"We move together," I pointed to Iago, Pedro and Juan, "these three will watch my back. You will all do the same with each other. We attack in groups of four where one will fight and the others protect that one. With luck, the enemy will not have time to arm and don mail. I know that, for some of you, that shows a lack of honour and respect. Put those thoughts from your minds for they were offered the chance for peace and their lives. When their champion died, that was the moment when they should have realised that God had made his decision. We are absolved of any guilt but if any one of you feels that he cannot do this then stay here. There will be no stigma to such a decision." I allowed a pause and when no one spoke I continued. "We can take prisoners but they must tell you that they surrender and you will take their swords. If they do not surrender then they die!"

I knew that my words were brutal but the Prince and the Emir, not to mention Rodrigo, were keen to end this siege which had gone on longer than we had expected.

We waited in the dark knowing that killers were already creeping ever closer to the sentries and soon they would be dead. Each killer was accompanied by a second who would return to tell us when we could attack. This time the boards placed over the ditches would not warn an enemy of our approach for we would walk silently over them. I had no doubt that our attack would be seen at some point for men needed to make water while others would not be able to sleep. They had fought a battle and lost shield brothers. I knew myself that at such times sleep was elusive. Someone would be awake and see the figures ghosting through their camp.

The Mozarab who fetched us did not say a word but merely pointed. I nodded and led my men across the bridge. I had my sword and short sword already drawn and once we were across, I waited to allow the rest of my men to form their smaller sections. Iago and my other two guardian angels had their swords and daggers drawn. Once we were all in position, I led them across the five hundred paces of open ground to their camp. I found the other Mozarab killer close to the dead sentries. He nodded as we passed. He would then ghost into the camp to continue his grisly work. There were almost eight hundred of us and I knew that inevitably there would be a cry in the night which would rouse the rest but each step through the dark night brought us closer to their tents and increased the chances of success. In the distance, I heard a horse whinny. I knew that some knights liked to keep their horses close to their tents. It may have been such a horse which roused its owner for, as we approached the first tent, there was a scream and a shout of, "Alarm! We are under…!" The voice ended with a strangled croak as his life was ended.

I did not hesitate but rushed into the tent. The scream had woken the knight and his three companions. That they were good warriors became clear when they rose with weapons in their hands. I deflected one sword with my own and used my short sword to end the knight's life by slicing through his middle. I brought my sword down on a second and then there were none left for my shield brothers had ended all opposition. We left the tent and where the scene had been one of dark and silence when we had entered when we emerged it was like a scene from hell. Someone had knocked over a brazier and a tent had been set alight. The breeze was fanning the flames and soon other tents would be set on fire. Warriors, knights and men at arms had been roused and were ready with swords and shields. They were prepared to fight and it became obvious why when I saw, in the light of the fire, the standard of Aragon. The King's tent was close by and these would be his most loyal and fanatical knights. Fortune or fate had directed me and my young knights here.

There was little point in bemoaning the fact that we would have the harder task, we just had to get on with it. I waved my three men towards six warriors who were led by a knight. They all had shields and the knight had managed to don his helmet and gambeson. He swung his sword at my head. I blocked it with my own and then used my short sword. I was able to bring it into his side and it grated off his ribs. It was not a mortal wound and he punched me with his shield. He struck the side of my head and I became a little unbalanced. I swashed my father's sword before me and it made him step back and allowed me to regain my balance. The order with which I had led Iago and the others was now lost and they were busy fighting the men who followed the knight. That they would win was never in doubt for the three of them were as good, if not better, than most knights that I had trained. They were natural killers who might not have the finesse but knew how to get the job done!

The knight came at me again. I saw the blood freely flowing from his side. He would try to finish me quickly. He punched with his shield again as he brought his sword around in a wide sweep. It might have worked against someone armed with a short sword except that I was far stronger than most men and my well-made short sword blocked the blow with ease and, at the same time, I lunged with my sword. His swing had opened his wound and made the blood flow faster. He was slow to bring around his shield and my sword went through his gambeson, middle and emerged from his back. Life left his eyes. Withdrawing my sword, I turned and saw that the others had been despatched except for two who were on their knees and begging for their lives.

"We surrender! Mercy, lord!"

"Pedro watch these prisoners. Search the two tents we took for treasure for you, Iago and Juan." They were swords for hire and Roger of Bordeaux's experiences made me think of the future of my men.

I led the other two through the camp which was now a chaotic mess. The white crosses were largely unnecessary as the enemy were without mail but it helped me to see, a little more clearly, that we were winning. My knots of knights could be seen moving purposefully through this elite conclave of warriors.

I saw that many of the men who now stood protecting the King and his tent were mailed and ready to sell their lives dearly. "Iago and Juan, stay close."

I saw some of my young knights as they closed with the Aragonese. We were ready for the fight and they had been rudely awakened to one. It showed in the approach as the two groups collided. My men had heeded my words and one advanced, protected by three others. Against the experienced household knights of King Ramiro that was vital. I saw young Don Raimundo as he cautiously approached the grey-bearded knight. The knight held an axe and I realised that I had not given them much experience fighting against such a weapon. I hurried towards the fray and saw that I need not have worried for I had given them the basic shield skills and that was what Don Raimundo used. As the axe sliced towards him, he used his metal-rimmed shield to deflect the blow. Indeed, the head caught on some of the pieces of metal I had encouraged them to use to cover their shield. As the greybeard's hand was drawn down, so his middle was exposed and a quick dart with the sharpened tip of Don Raimundo's sword ended the loyal knight's life.

Then I had my own battle to worry about as we came upon four knights guarding the King's back. There were just three of us and perhaps we should have backed off but I saw that one knight was sporting a wound and none wore helmets, which told me that even though they were elite we might win. They had quickly donned their hauberks but were barefooted. Alfonso's philosophy had always been to attack if outnumbered and the three of us, in a small fighting wedge, hurtled into them. A sword came down to strike my shoulder even as I ripped my short sword up into the man's ribs and chest. I twisted, aware that his sword had cracked a bone in my shoulder. I would find it hard to raise my sword above me. I would be able to do it but it would hurt. Iago had slain the wounded knight and I used my sword to sweep up and across the back of the knight fighting Juan. I barely had time to lift my short sword to block the sword strike from another warrior who had appeared from nowhere. I had to resort to stamping on his bare foot with my boot. As he yelped and stepped back, I lunged with my sword. My collar bone still hurt but not as much as an overhead swing would have done and the tip tore through his hauberk and into his body.

There was a ring of dead men around the King and I shouted, "King Ramiro, surrender for you are surrounded!"

He laughed and shouted back, "Surrender to a peasant! You are no hero to me! You are the spawn of the devil!"

I knew that his words were intended to anger me but I did not react. In fact, I was flattered that he even knew who I was! However, before I could engage him a young knight rushed at me. As I could not raise my right arm above my head, I was somewhat hamstrung in my choice of strokes with my father's sword and had to use my short sword to block his blows. He had a shield and he punched me to the ground. It was as I was lying there that I saw Iago take on my mantle and engage the King. I had no opportunity to pay much attention to Iago for the knight who had knocked me from my feet now raised his sword to skewer me to the ground. I did the only thing I could; I swung my sword at knee height and, as his sword came down towards my prostrate body, my blade bit into the side of his leg and grated off his bone. He screamed and, dropping his own sword fell across me, blood pouring from the artery I had opened. The pain from the effort of the blow coursed through my body. I was handicapped by my wound and it took some moments to push the mailed, dead warrior, from my body.

As I scrambled to my feet, I watched Iago as he fought the King of Aragon. The King had a better sword and better armour. He should have been better trained and yet, as I watched and struggled to my feet, I saw that Iago had so much experience that nothing that the King did unnerved him. He took blows on his sword and his dagger. He stepped away from the swinging shield and sword and, most importantly, he kept his feet. He was also helped by the fact that the King was angry; he was fighting a common soldier who was not even a knight and as such he should have been easily defeated. In his eagerness to get at Iago he moved too quickly and tripped over the body of one of his own knights. As he tumbled forward, he fell onto Iago's dagger which drove up into his throat and then his head. Iago had not intended the blow, indeed, when I talked to him after the battle, he had said that he hoped to take the King prisoner. He knew there would be more profit in that! The King carried on falling and lay dead and I saw the shock on Iago's face. He had killed a King and that was unheard of.

"Iago, Juan, to me! This is not over yet!" We knew that the King was dead but most did not and until the realisation set in then they would fight to the end. With my two men flanking me we faced another handful of Aragonese warriors who ran to the aid of the dead King. That they did not know he was dead was obvious and they hurled themselves at us to try to protect what they saw as their wounded ruler. We were beleaguered and needed the help of one of the other groups of knights. They were fighting, largely, in the dark, although the fire in the tents had spread and there was a glow from the southern edge of the camp. The pain from the wound was growing for I had aggravated it by falling and then clambering to my feet. Soon I would not be able to hold my sword. The

King's knights had fought well and at least six of my own knights lay dead.

I fended off a spear which was thrust at my middle but I made the mistake of raising my hand and the pain made me, involuntarily, drop my sword. "Are you alright, Will!"

"It is nothing."

I was left with my short sword and I would have to fight left-handed. I saw the confusion on the face of the warrior with the spear and he hesitated. I could not lift my right arm but I could use it and I grabbed the spear behind the head with my right hand as he thrust it at me and pulled it towards me. Instead of letting go, he came with it and I rammed his body on to my short sword. Suddenly Juan dropped to one knee as he was stabbed in the leg. We needed Pedro and I had him watching prisoners! Things might have gone badly had not Rodrigo and Álvar suddenly rushed to our aid. El Campeador wore his helmet and he had a shield. He and Álvar were like a whirlwind in the King's camp. They hacked, slashed and punched the Aragonese that were trying to get at the survivors of my attack. I think I saw, that day, a different Rodrigo for he was fighting to save the lives of three of his comrades and, for him, this was personal. When he fought for kings and princes then he could be more detached but, and I guessed for he never told me, that he feared he was losing us. It was the only time I saw him approaching the berserk madness which I had suffered at Salamanca. Álvar was equally enraged and with Iago and myself joining them the last of the men

340

defending the body and tent of the King died for none would surrender.

A freak gust of wind from the south suddenly fanned the flames from the burning tents and what had been a threatening fire now became an inferno. Ahead of us, I heard men cry out as they realised that the King was dead and they fled.

Rodrigo nodded to the body of the King, "Álvar, Iago, we cannot allow the body of the King of Aragon to burn. Let us take him to safety." He looked at Juan.

I said, "I will see to Juan. You are right, El Campeador, and this will ensure that we have the victory your plan deserves."

The three of them raised up the dead King and I sheathed my two weapons. The flames were growing closer and as I took Juan's weight on my left shoulder, I looked for a safe passage. There was an open area, forty paces to the west of the tent. The flames were coming from the south and, it seemed to me, that was our only chance to escape. Already I heard the screams of men who had been caught by the rapidly advancing fire. It was not a death I relished and I forced myself to ignore the pain of the cracked bone as I laboured to take my shield brother to safety. The tents which were close to the King were all afire and the wind brought them closer to Juan and me.

"Leave me, Will, we cannot both make it!"

"Then we will both die for I will not lose another shield brother!"

The last tent before the open area suddenly burst into flames as we neared it. I had no choice and I ran through the flames. I felt my beard and hair begin to burn but we made it through. I think the pain in my collar bone took away the pain of the fire. Rodrigo and the others had laid down the King and when they saw us appear, covered in fire, they immediately covered our heads and bodies with their cloaks as they beat out the flames. I was choking with the smoke and could not speak. When the cloaks were removed, I saw that Juan had no eyebrows and his beard, hair and moustache were smoking.

Rodrigo began to laugh, "Well, William Redbeard we shall have to rename you for you are now William the Fiery Beard! But I am glad that you live for we have our great victory and now we can go home!"

Álvar nodded, "Aye, and with a hero whose name will ring out through all of Spain for you are El Campeador, the man who led, for the first time, Christian and Muslim! Our world will never be the same again!"

And he was right.

Epilogue

We did not leave Graus for a week. There were knights to be ransomed and war gear, mail and treasure to be collected. We also had our dead to be buried. Prince Sancho had lost fifty knights and that was too high a price to be paid. Rodrigo was already making plans to lessen the likelihood of such high losses in the future. He took me to one side the day we were to return home. "You and I need to look at how we train our men and how we fight. There were lessons to be learned here and we are the men who can implement changes." That was Rodrigo; he never stood still and was always striving for perfection. For my part, I was happy just to hang on to his surcoat and enjoy the ride.

We were on our way to speak with the Emir. He had sent for us. Prince Sancho was still busy dealing with the knights and their ransom. The Emir greeted us in the centre of Graus. He would improve the defences and only then would he return to Zaragoza. He had with him the leaders of his army and the Moor who had led the defence of Graus.

The Emir spoke to Rodrigo, "You are al-sayyid to my people, the Lord, and I have seen here in this most unlikely of places hope for our people. Know that I am happy for my men to follow your banner and for you to lead my armies. We are allies and I have told Prince Sancho that so long as you are part of his retinue there will never be a war between Zaragoza and Castile." He waved a servant forward and a chest was opened. It was filled with gold and jewels.

"I thank you, Emir, but I have reward enough from Prince Sancho."

"Take it for this was one of the chests offered to King Ramiro to stop him attacking the town. The fact that he ignored it and lost his life," he shrugged, "is Kismet." He turned to me, "And to you, Redbeard, know that we realise that you are a part of al-sayyid. We saw, when he fought the champion that it was you he chose to ride at his side and you never flinched. It was you and your men who ended this war by killing King Ramiro." He waved forward another servant who handed me a much smaller chest, "This is for you and your men. You too are a friend and always welcome in Zaragoza!"

And so we rode home, Rodrigo to the court of Prince Sancho and King Ferdinand while I went to the estate I had barely seen, Briviesca. The man the world now called El Campeador and I were still relatively young men but we both had a fame which neither of us could have envisaged before the battle of Atapuerca. We had lost friends and shield brothers but those losses had made us stronger. What we could not know was the direction our journey would take us. We had enjoyed the accolades and praise. It would not be long before we had to endure scorn, hatred and exile. But that was in the future and no man can know what lies around the corner. Perhaps, if he did, he would never leave his home!

The End

Glossary

Armiger- champion
Buskins- boots
Campi doctor -battlefield trainer
Jubbah- quilted garment worn over or beneath mail
Magerit – Madrid
Mozarab-one who fights for the Taifa states but is not necessarily a Muslim
Pel- a wooden stake embedded in the ground where men at arms would practice their strokes
Taifa –a faction or geographical area which followed a petty king or warlord in Iberia
Tijfaf- quilted armour for horses
Quintain- a target used by mounted men

Maps and Illustrations

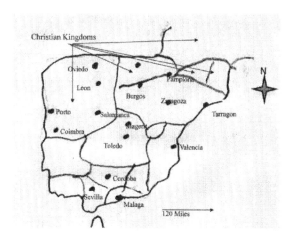

Historical Notes

Books used in the research:

- The Normans- David Nicolle
- Norman Knight AD 950-1204- Christopher Gravett
- The Knight in History- Francis Gies
- Knights- Constance Brittain Bouchard
- El Cid- The Making of a Legend, M.J. Trow
- El Cid and the Reconquista 1050-1492
- Armies of the Crusades- Wise and Embleton
- The Moors- Nicolle and McBride
- English Medieval Knight 1200-1400 Gravett and Turner

This story began to be written when I was about fourteen, more than fifty years ago and I watched Charlton Heston chew up the scenery in the great epic, El Cid. When I began to write the story, I did my research and found that the Charlton Heston El Cid was not the legend that I thought he was. I think that good as the film was the truth and reality showed an even greater Rodrigo de Vivar.

This is a story and while I have been at pains to write a historically accurate story, I have used the holes in history to make it fiction.

Most of what we know about El Cid comes from a poem, written a long time after the great Spanish knight died, "***Carmen Campidoctoris***". https://en.wikipedia.org/wiki/Carmen_Campidoc toris There is doubt about almost everything which happened to Rodrigo until he was already famous. Even the inscription on his sword, which I used is in doubt as the one in Valencia says that it was made in 1040 and that was three years before he was even born.

I have made his father a bad 'un as it suited my story but we know very little about him and his grandfather, the Lord Lain of my story, is better documented.

The only documented battles we have for this period are Atapuerca and Graus although King Ferdinand and Prince Sancho did manage to subjugate two taifa and make them vassals. The written records are a little vague and as most of the material we have comes from many years after Rodrigo's death, then it is hard to differentiate where the legend ends and reality kicks in. My philosophy is, if in doubt then make it up!

The kings, princes and emirs all existed and behaved, pretty much as I describe. King Ramiro was not killed by a knight but a Moor who could pass as a Christian! I gave Iago that honour. The story of Prince Sancho and his fiancée was also true and I had to read my research several times to work out that it was not, in fact, a brother and sister who married!

The term Taifa means a faction but the reality is that the Emirs who ran those states were, largely, warlords and the idea of Christian fighting Muslim is misleading. Christian and Moor would ally when it suited their purposes and they would act like sharks around a wounded shark when it suited, too. Briviesca was an ancient fortress but it was moved in the fourteenth century to its present position. Of the old settlement, there are few traces left and I have had to use my imagination.

I have used William as the narrator for I wish the story to continue after El Cid's death. (Sorry, spoiler alert!) I have, however, tried to use William to get into Rodrigo's mind.

I also discovered a good website http://orbis.stanford.edu/. This allows a reader to plot any two places in the Roman world and if you input the mode of transport you wish to use and the time of year it will calculate how long it would take you to travel the route. I have used it for all of my books up to the eighteenth century as the transportation system was roughly the same. The Romans would have been quicker!

Griff Hosker
October 2019

Other books by Griff

Hosker

If you enjoyed reading this book, then why not read another one by the author?
Ancient History

The Sword of Cartimandua Series
(Germania and Britannia 50 A.D. – 128 A.D.)
Ulpius Felix- Roman Warrior (prequel)
The Sword of Cartimandua
The Horse Warriors
Invasion Caledonia
Roman Retreat
Revolt of the Red Witch
Druid's Gold
Trajan's Hunters
The Last Frontier
Hero of Rome
Roman Hawk
Roman Treachery
Roman Wall
Roman Courage

The Wolf Warrior series
(Britain in the late 6th Century)
Saxon Dawn
Saxon Revenge

Saxon England
Saxon Blood
Saxon Slayer
Saxon Slaughter
Saxon Bane
Saxon Fall: Rise of the Warlord
Saxon Throne
Saxon Sword

Medieval History

The Dragon Heart Series
Viking Slave
Viking Warrior
Viking Jarl
Viking Kingdom
Viking Wolf
Viking War
Viking Sword
Viking Wrath
Viking Raid
Viking Legend
Viking Vengeance
Viking Dragon
Viking Treasure
Viking Enemy
Viking Witch
Viking Blood
Viking Weregeld
Viking Storm
Viking Warband
Viking Shadow
Viking Legacy

Castilian Knight

Viking Clan
Viking Bravery

The Norman Genesis Series
Hrolf the Viking
Horseman
The Battle for a Home
Revenge of the Franks
The Land of the Northmen
Ragnvald Hrolfsson
Brothers in Blood
Lord of Rouen
Drekar in the Seine
Duke of Normandy
The Duke and the King

Danelaw
(England and Denmark in the 11th Century)
Dragon Sword
Oathsword

New World Series
Blood on the Blade
Across the Seas
The Savage Wilderness
The Bear and the Wolf
Erik The Navigator

The Vengeance Trail

The Reconquista Chronicles
Castilian Knight
El Campeador
The Lord of Valencia

Castilian Knight

The Aelfraed Series
(Britain and Byzantium 1050 A.D. - 1085
A.D.)
Housecarl
Outlaw
Varangian

**The Anarchy Series England
1120-1180**
English Knight
Knight of the Empress
Northern Knight
Baron of the North
Earl
King Henry's Champion
The King is Dead
Warlord of the North
Enemy at the Gate
The Fallen Crown
Warlord's War
Kingmaker
Henry II
Crusader
The Welsh Marches
Irish War
Poisonous Plots
The Princes' Revolt
Earl Marshal
The Perfect Knight

**Border Knight
1182-1300**
Sword for Hire

Castilian Knight

Return of the Knight
Baron's War
Magna Carta
Welsh Wars
Henry III
The Bloody Border
Baron's Crusade
Sentinel of the North
War in the West
Debt of Honour
The Blood of the Warlord (Feb 2022)

Sir John Hawkwood Series
France and Italy 1339- 1387
Crécy: The Age of the Archer
Man At Arms
The White Company

Lord Edward's Archer
Lord Edward's Archer
King in Waiting
An Archer's Crusade
Targets of Treachery
The Great Cause (April 2022)

Struggle for a Crown
1360- 1485
Blood on the Crown
To Murder a King
The Throne
King Henry IV
The Road to Agincourt
St Crispin's Day
The Battle For France

Castilian Knight

The Last Knight

Tales from the Sword I
(Short stories from the Medieval period)

Tudor Warrior series
England and Scotland in the late 145th
and early 15th century
Tudor Warrior

Conquistador
England and America in the 16th Century
Conquistador

Modern History

The Napoleonic Horseman Series
Chasseur à Cheval
Napoleon's Guard
British Light Dragoon
Soldier Spy
1808: The Road to Coruña
Talavera
The Lines of Torres Vedras
Bloody Badajoz
The Road to France
Waterloo

The Lucky Jack American Civil War
series
Rebel Raiders
Confederate Rangers
The Road to Gettysburg

Castilian Knight

The British Ace Series
1914
1915 Fokker Scourge
1916 Angels over the Somme
1917 Eagles Fall
1918 We will remember them
From Arctic Snow to Desert Sand
Wings over Persia

Combined Operations series
1940-1945
Commando
Raider
Behind Enemy Lines
Dieppe
Toehold in Europe
Sword Beach
Breakout
The Battle for Antwerp
King Tiger
Beyond the Rhine
Korea
Korean Winter

Tales from the Sword II
(Short stories from the Modern period)

Other Books
Great Granny's Ghost (Aimed at 9-14-year-
old young people)

For more information on all of the books then
please visit the author's website at

www.griffhosker.com where there is a link to
contact him or visit his Facebook page:
GriffHosker at Sword Books

Made in United States
Troutdale, OR
02/25/2024